SLAVE TO
Love

Julie A. Richman

a

Julie A. Richman
Text copyright © 2015 Julie A. Richman

This book is a work of fiction. All names, characters, locations and incidents are products of the author's imagination. Any resemblance to actual persons, living or dead, locales or events is entirely coincidental.

Slave to Love
ISBN-10: 1-942215-32-0
ISBN-13: 978-1-942215-32-5

Cover Design: Jena Brignola
Print Layout & Design: Deena Rae E-BookBuilders

c

Contents

f

BOOKS
by Julie

Searching for Moore (Book 1)
Moore to Lose (Book 2)
Moore than Forever (Book 3)
Needing Moore Series Boxed Set
Bad Son Rising
Henry's End

Dedication

For Joy, Brenda, Lynne, Yvonne and Jill...

"Women who can run in heels should be feared."
~ Author Unknown

And to Brian and Liz
Rest in Peace

CHAPTER One

I am a slave. Seriously, I am. My shackles may not be what you're envisioning, as unfortunately, they are not crafted from leather with a hot, sexy dominant on the other end, flogger in hand. But they are trendy and cool and golden. Yes, my handcuffs are golden and they come with stock options, a 401(k), oodles of frequent flyer miles and hotel points and an Admiral's Club membership at the airport. I wear my handcuffs 24/7.

And I have no freaking idea where the key is.

＊＊＊＊＊＊＊＊＊＊＊＊＊＊＊＊＊＊＊＊＊＊＊

Eight-twenty A.M. and I already need an effing shower. Ugh. Running late for an eight-thirty meeting. I thought a cab ride would be the answer and certainly cooler and quicker than walking, or God forbid, taking the dreaded subway on a sweltering Manhattan morning. But no. I emerge from the cab, with my now translucent white silk blouse pretending it's a soggy second skin gearing up for our fabulous win in today's "Who's Got the Perkiest Nipples" contest. Shoot me. Just shoot me.

As I slide sideways into an elevator, the doors already half closed, I have the distinct honor of joining two techy nerd boys returning from their eight-fifteen A.M. smoke. Lucky me. The unkempt duo reek of cigarettes, yet I can't decide which is worse, that, or the stench of their general shoddy hygiene and filthy jeans. Nerd Boy #1 is enjoying my transparent, wet tank blouse and my not-shy nipples. I catch him and he pretends to look at my necklace, a gold mermaid, just grazing my cleavage.

The door opens on my floor. Eight twenty-six. I'm not late yet. On my way out of the elevator, I lean over and whisper to Nerd Boy #1, "Great necklace, isn't it. Would be better if it were pearl."

I hear him choke as I exit. Schwing.

Tanisha looks up at me from the receptionist's station and gives me *the* face. I have seen that face on many an occasion as her mood is more often surly than not. Wordlessly, she points one impossibly long coral clawed nail in the direction of the conference room, and in my head I can hear her saying, "Girl, you'd better get your ass in there, *now!*"

Fuck, I need coffee, is my last thought before I fling open the door to the lion's den.

The long conference table is full, with the exception of two seats. His and mine.

"Could your skirts get any shorter and your heels any higher? How do you walk in those things?" The whine of her voice is like nails on a chalkboard, and without my first cup of coffee, not going totally postal on her is a true attestation to my superior self-control.

"God didn't give me these legs to wear pants and ugly shoes," I retort, smiling sweetly at her. Bitch.

He enters behind me, "Nice to see everyone made it on time." Walking to the head of the table with the swagger of a former athlete, he sets down his iPad and coffee and unbuttons his rich navy suit jacket.

New York City men in suits. There is just nothing finer. And if he's handsome, smart and arrogant – I'm up the creek without a paddle. And I work for one. A very married one. But that doesn't make him any less attractive.

2

SLAVE TO LOVE

It's impossible not to smile when looking upon such a perfect specimen of a man. Kemp McCoy. C'mon, even the name. You just know the guy was bred to be the quarterback or team captain of something.

I laugh at my friends with all their fictional alpha-males in their books. I've been working for the ultimate alpha for years and I've watched him get more and more dominant, and domineering, as he's climbed the corporate ladder. He scares the crap out of most people. But I'm not most people. I'm one of the few in his inner circle, and I tell it to him just the way it is. Which is why I think he looks at me like I'm one of the boys. Great tits, fine legs and all.

We're all there in the conference room on this hot, sweaty morning in June, having arrived from different places throughout the country. All his direct reports. Me, the bitch who made the remark about my skirt, my counterpart/enemy, Cuntessa. Okay, she really does have a name. It's Susan. Susan Smith. Seriously, I kid you not. How boring is that? Right? Our marketing guy, Scott, finance dude, Tad, ops geek, Ray (Ray's cool and way fun to get trashed with), production king, Tony and Kemp's very hot and loyal admin, Angela.

"So, I'm sure you saw my memo on Friday." Kemp's demeanor is serious. The man is all about business, all the time, unless you are in the inner circle, then he might share tidbits from his personal life or cut-up over drinks. "Laura is no longer part of the team. It's no secret that if changes were not made, we were in jeopardy of losing our entire west coast sales force."

Laura was my other counterpart. She ran sales in the west. I've got the center of the country and Cuntessa runs the east. Three women going head-to-head in sales has its ups and downs. While it's very competitive and results and sales tend to be very strong, three alpha bitches in the pack means claws are sharp at all times and blood-letting is a regular occurrence. And Laura was a damn control-freak nut job. And I don't mean that in a good way.

"I received calls last week from our Top 5 performers in the west and it appears Laura insisting her staff stay out with her in bars until two to three in the morning when they were traveling together, has not been going over well with them. And it seems there was an incident last week where she kept pulling a waitress into her lap all night."

Cuntessa and I roll our eyes at one another. Laura's insanity is one of the few things over which we actually bond.

"Will we be hiring a new west coast sales director?" Cuntessa jumps right in.

Kemp makes a face, "I would if I didn't think you two bitches could handle it."

The man actually called us bitches. Which is probably an accurate assessment. Laughing, I lock eyes with him, "You're a fucking HR nightmare."

Yes, there I am in my short turquoise pencil skirt, and oh so hot, Christian Louboutin Pigalle Follies aquarium colored glitter pumps, and I drop the first F-bomb of the day, opening the window for a veritable shit storm which will undeniably follow.

"I think you got me beat, babe." Kemp is amused, his sexy smile making its morning debut.

Bitches. Fucking. Babe. Yeah, we're quite the crew. The funny part is, we're a highly profitable division of a Fortune 100 company. It doesn't get bigger than that. And we work our asses off. Work hard. Play hard. We are the definition of high risk, high reward.

"So, is that the answer," Cuntessa presses, "we get more work?"

"Pretty much." He smiles at her and I know her panties are wet. She's loved the man since the day he hired her whiney ass as a territory sales rep and climbed the ranks with him. His evil little protégé.

"Are we going to be compensated for this extra responsibility?"

4

I sit back, letting her do the dirty work.

"What do you think?" He gives her the "don't be stupid" look.

"I don't know, why don't you tell us." She's now somehow lapsed into something between a whine and baby talk and I want to slit my wrists. I have not had freaking caffeine yet, damn it, and I have to listen to baby talk. Kill me now. Please just kill me now.

"Yes, you'll both be nicely compensated. I'm taking her base pay and splitting it between you two bitches."

Cuntessa and I are now smiling at each other. Without even knowing exactly what crazy Laura's base pay was, it's safe to assume we each just got a six-figure raise or something close to it. Oh happy day!

Kemp looks around at the guys (the rest of his team are men), "The things I have to do to keep these two happy."

"So, how is this splitting up?" I ask, anxious to get every last detail.

"Well, since you're down in Texas and Susan is here in New York, I thought we'd do a north/south split. You'll take on Arizona, California, Nevada and Utah. Susan, you've got Washington and Oregon. We don't have much in the other states up there."

"She gets all of California? San Francisco should be considered the north. After all it is Northern California."

The greedy bitch is already trying to poach from my territory. "You picked up Washington State. You just got Microsoft and Boeing, so stop bitching." I know I'm sneering at her and I'm not even attempting to hide it.

California. I'm trying not to show how thrilled I am, but I am jazzed and want to get up on the conference table and do a happy dance in my sparkly shoes. I love the sales reps out there and our clients are to-die-for awesome. We provide outsourced services to all the major movie studios and a prestigious array of Silicon Valley companies and Napa/Sonoma wineries. I have just landed a big fat slice of heaven.

"You love Pinot Noir." I smile at Cuntessa as I reference the wine coming out of Oregon.

Her expression is less than friendly.

After three hours, Angela has lunch brought in for us as we continue to review accounts and quarterly projections. Cuntessa is still sulking over California and giving her best shot to wear down Kemp for at least San Francisco, as he attempts to eat a corned beef on rye. As I finish my sandwich, Angela places a steaming cup of hot dark roast coffee in front of me.

"I love you hard."

"Is this your first of the day?" she whispers discreetly.

She's surprised when I nod, then turns to Kemp, "Shall I make dinner reservations for all of us at the Old Homestead?" It's his favorite 'Old Boys' Club' steakhouse.

"I won't be joining you." Everyone turns toward him in surprise, he never blows off staff dinners when the whole crew is in town. "And I'll be needing these two for drinks," he points to me and Susan, "but they'll be back with the rest of you for dinner."

Generally, he does private sessions with me and Cuntessa that don't include the remainder of his directs. I assume we're going to get some dirt on his last conversation with the nut job, Laura, that he just canned, as well as some inside scoop on what's going on with top brass.

Kemp McCoy is on the fast-track for a top executive spot, and Susan Smith has made a near full-time job of trying to marginalize me and my team's success so that she becomes the heir apparent to his current position. One small problem for Susan and her minions — my team has taken the number one spot three years running, so she resorts to backstabbing, and commenting on my skirts and high heels, tits and nipples, to try and diminish me and my success.

SLAVE TO LOVE

My answer to her, go sell something, bitch. (Or "Did you and Hillary Clinton coordinate on pants suits and shoes again today?")

We wrap up at 5:30 and my brain is mush.

"Do I have time to go back to my hotel or are we going straight out?" I ask Kemp.

He looks at his watch. "You have time to go to the bathroom. Hurry."

Sitting in a cab in rush hour traffic, I watch the wilting people walk the stewing sidewalks of Madison Avenue and I'm profusely thanking the cab gods that the one we hailed actually has air conditioning, because there's way too much body heat being squished in the back of a cab with two other people on a June afternoon.

"Are we meeting someone?" I wonder if we are since he hasn't given us any prep information.

"You'll see," is the odd response I get.

Cuntessa finally asks, "Where are we going?"

"That I will tell you. The St. Regis."

"The St. Regis Hotel?" her voice rises an octave.

"The bar," Kemp clarifies.

I look at him, wondering who we are meeting at the King Cole Salon, the St. Regis' famed bar. I silently snicker thinking it's more of an infamous bar in my case, as my dating past includes the bar manager from when I was living in New York in my early twenties. Lesson learned from that relationship – if a guy tells you he has a history of commitment issues – believe him. No, you are not special. No, your relationship isn't different. He's got commitment problems. Believe him and run, if commitment is what you seek. Do not get attached to a man with commitment issues.

I'm smiling as the bellman escorts me out of the cab. The St. Regis is truly one of the grande dames of old New York. I am lost to visions of boyfriends past and hot, passionate kisses against walls, and champagne splashed on my body, while lying on the bar long after the last patron has gone for the evening.

Before we enter, Kemp stops us. "Okay, I don't want you two to go crazy, but drinks tonight are with Hale Lundström."

"Oh my God." Susan locks my upper arm in a death grip that I'm sure will leave nasty purple bruises.

I'm clueless, looking from Cuntessa to Kemp and down to what is surely going to be a bruised biceps. "Who's Hale Lundström?"

"You're not serious?" I can tell Kemp is already annoyed with me. He's worried that if I don't know who the guy is, how am I going to have any meaningful conversation about his business? "Have you looked at the Forbes fastest growing tech companies over the last three years? He's the founder and CEO of SpaceCloud."

"Oh, okay. I've heard of SpaceCloud, I'm just not familiar with him."

Cuntessa is staring at my tits and I look down. My nipples are flashing their high beams through the thin silk of my blouse. My memories of bar fucking must've gotten the twins excited.

"You need covers for those things," she comments and I can see Kemp is uncomfortable.

I look at her lack of anything sizable hidden under her Hillary Clinton blazer and shake my head, "Maybe I'm turned on by you."

"Very funny. But I bet you will be turned on by Hale Lundström. The man is drop dead gorgeous."

"Well, maybe he's a nipple man," I comment, as we follow Kemp into my old stomping grounds

As if seeing an old friend that I've missed for years, the Maxwell Parrish mural of Old King Cole adorning the back of the bar brings unexpected tears to my eyes. I was twenty-three. He was twenty-five. And I'd never before met someone who I clicked with, in every way, like that. We'd gotten into the habit of saying, "Hey twin," to each other because we were like mirror versions of one another.

Approaching the bar, I smile at the bartender, an older man with warm eyes and an inviting smile. He probably thinks I'm already drunk approaching the bar with such a huge grin. Either that or he's smiling back because he too is a fan of nipples and legs.

We're just feet away, when from the highly polished counter, a man in a navy blazer and worn jeans turns on his bar stool, immediately planting his sneakered feet on the floor as he stands, unfolding to his full height before us. His dark blue eyes are sharp and focused as he breaks into a movie star smile, taking Kemp's outstretched hand for a hearty shake. Loose wavy curls, slightly too long for a businessman, top a handsome face graced with a square jaw and slightly dimpled chin. The look is completed with a day's dark stubble. I'm thrown, the man looks like an Italian movie star. I was expecting a Viking with the last name Lundström, not Raoul Bova's younger brother.

"I'd like you to meet two of the best sales directors in the country," Kemp ushers us in. "Hale, this is Susan Smith, my east coast and now Pacific Northwest sales director and Sierra Stone, who manages the Midwest through California."

"Pleasure meeting you, Susan." Hale extends a hand to Cuntessa, gracing her with a smile that probably made her want to dance naked for him.

When he makes no move to greet me, I extend a hand, "Sierra," I reintroduce myself.

He looks at me, the affect in his eyes flat. "Yes, I got it the first time."

He doesn't shake my hand. *Douche.*

"What are you drinking?" Kemp turns around to us.

"Chardonnay." Cuntessa is so boring.

"I'll have a Red Snapper." The bartender's eyes are twinkling the minute he hears that come out of my mouth and I can't help but smile back at him. Kemp joins Hale with a Guinness.

Picking up my drink off the bar, Susan announces, "That's a Bloody Mary. What fancy name did you call that?"

I want to slap her, but just smile. "A Red Snapper." And I take it from her, immediately diving in for a much needed sip of the spicy treat.

"Why?"

"Because this is where the Bloody Mary was first created and the name they originally called it was the Red Snapper."

"You are a wealth of information," Kemp kids me.

"Well, long ago a friend of mine was the bar manager, so I've done my fair share of drinking here." I choose to omit the story that is dying to come out of my mouth. *See that spot on the bar right there? Yup, that one, right there. Well, one night, after four Red Snappers, I climbed up onto the bar and hiked up my skirt, (which was, yes, shorter than this one that I'm wearing tonight and I was, of course, going commando), and showed my boyfriend my brand new Brazilian wax, which he must've loved, because after he went down on me, he fucked me long and hard. And then he made me another Red Snapper. Obviously, on the house.*

"Legal issues were ironed out today and I gave it my blessing late this afternoon," Hale informs Kemp.

I watch Kemp's face take on a glorious smile as the two men engage in a vigorous handshake and backslapping apropos more for a locker room than a hotel bar.

Turning to me and Cuntessa, our boss announces, "Ladies, I would like you to meet our newest client."

Susan squeals and goes in for a hug with Hale, who bristles at her touch. The man is clearly not a hugger, although she didn't notice. SpaceCloud is headquartered out of New York, so the bitch just picked up a huge client that neither she nor her team invested any time in selling. This one was a gift, a huge fucking gift, which just fell into her lap. I want to puke. And the bitch was busting on me all day trying to poach San Francisco.

I smile, my poker face shining brightly, "Awesome news." And I signal to the bartender for another Red Snapper. With SpaceCloud now part of her portfolio, the balance of power may have just shifted, finally positioning Cuntessa's team to outsell mine. Hale Lundström doesn't acknowledge that I've spoken.

The ramifications of this news are horrendous, personally and professionally. If Kemp were to be promoted, and Susan had better sales numbers, there would be nothing stopping him from backfilling his position with his evil little protégé. I'm fucked. Totally and positively fucked. And it's this handsome man who has acted like I'm invisible that has caused my corporate demise.

I just want to kick him hard in one of his long jean's clad shins and then go off and cry, but I've got to take it like a pro, smile on my face. Which I do.

"When would it be convenient to schedule me, Susan and her team to come in and meet your team and get the ball rolling?"

Hale pulls his cell phone out of the inner pocket of his blazer and types out a message. "Let me get my admin on it."

Looking at my watch, I nudge Cuntessa. "We need to head downtown to the Old Homestead." I know from her look she wants to kill me. There's no way she wants to leave Hale and Kemp.

Hale stands and reaches into the back pocket of his jeans. As he moves his jacket to the side, I can see his slim hips and athletic ass. Damn he's a fine specimen, too bad he's a douche.

He pulls out his wallet and removes a business card and hands it to Susan. She digs through her purse and reciprocates.

"Well, nice meeting you." I can't get out of there fast enough. Between this too gorgeous for his own good, arrogant dude basically being rude to me, and Cuntessa getting the account gift of a lifetime, I've had enough. I need to get downtown to the Old Homestead and drown my sorrows in a very large, exceedingly rare and bloody ribeye. On the damn bone! Because it will be the only bone I'm thrown.

Hale turns to me and hands me a card.

"Oh, I'm not," I start to explain that my team won't be on his account, when I feel Kemp's hand on my back, pinching me. Shutting up, I dig out my card case and hand the man a card.

Glancing at it, there's a look of surprise on his face. "You're located in Austin?"

"Yes," I nod.

"Great tech town. Austin's our fastest growing division. We're adding 7,000 jobs to our facility there over the next eighteen months and more expansion planned over a thirty-six month period."

"Yes, I read that in the Austin Business Journal. Congratulations," hoping he doesn't pick up my bluff. *How the fuck did I miss that,* I wonder? That's huge news.

As I turn to leave, the elusive hand of Hale Lundström is extended for a handshake. I guess he doesn't have a germ phobia after all.

"Nice meeting you," I effortlessly lie. *Actually meeting you made me feel like shit. You're an asshole and you're gorgeous.*

He leans down and whispers, "You have perfect legs for Louboutins."

Making eye contact, to show him I'm not afraid of his inappropriate little games, I don't thank him for the compliment, but instead acknowledge with, "I know, don't I."

And with a quick smile, I'm off, and fighting very hard not to look back. I'm pissed. I'm excited. I'm confused. And I know, without a shadow of a doubt, whose face I'll be envisioning when I'm touching myself in my hotel room bed later in the evening. And there is no doubt in my mind that I will be touching myself.

CHAPTER

Two

It's impossible not to watch her toned calves as she walks away. Some women were meant to wear come-fuck-me shoes and short skirts and this is one of them. And that skirt, it's the color of the water at the Bitter End Yacht Club in Virgin Gorda. With a mermaid surfing the crest of her cleavage; damn, she killed me. I was a tongue tied ass. Louboutins, that skirt, that amazing rack and so little makeup, it actually looked like she was wearing no make-up at all. Girl next door gorgeous. Women like that were usually hiding behind a well applied mask, so expertly crafted that you never really knew what you were going to get in the morning. But this one – what you saw was exactly what you were going to get.

"They're quite a duo," I comment to Kemp.

Rolling his eyes, "Two of the best sales managers I have ever seen, but do not tangle with those bitches," he says affectionately. "They are without a doubt the most efficient and effective sales management execs in the company."

"They're so different." I need to know more about her. I know her team is not on my account and I'm disappointed. I'm also relieved.

"Night and day those two. And competitive as all hell."

"Different management styles?" I probe, as I drain my pint of Guinness.

"Understatement. Susan is very detail-oriented and manages with a firm hand. Sierra is a big picture person who looks for creative solutions and rolls up her sleeves to get into the trenches with her team."

"Sounds like you've got one manager and one leader," I offer my assessment of the two women.

Kemp thinks for a moment and nods.

"So who's your backfill?" I'm interested in seeing how he builds his organization for a successful future.

"Well, it's always been me and Susan from the start. I brought her into this division with the understanding that she would be my backfill when I moved into my next role. Promises have been made." He sips his beer. "Sierra joined us a while back from another team in the company."

"So the manager over the leader?" I press.

"It would be hard to go back on a promise, but Sierra is the better producer and as you picked up on, a leader. Her people would run through walls for her."

Leaning on the highly polished bar, "They appear pretty competitive. Would one work for the other?"

"What do you think?"

"I think whoever doesn't get the position will very quickly become a free agent." Picking up the fresh beer the bartender has delivered, it suddenly tastes sweeter.

Having recently received a lot of flak from the trade press, investors and my board on SpaceCloud's lack of females in top executive roles, Sierra Stone could be a natural solution to getting the heat off me. A proven performer from a Fortune 100 company with a solid track record, I wonder how I can get her up to speed on his dime for an easy transition when the time comes.

SLAVE TO LOVE

Sierra Stone could take care of a multitude of my needs. And looking at those legs and following that mermaid's tail on a daily basis would not suck.

No, not at all.

CHAPTER Three

"If I have to listen to her say Hale this and Hale that and we're interfacing with Hale's team on blah blah blah, I'm going to puke," I confide in two of my California staff. We've been friends from long before I moved into management and since I haven't been their manager, we've all remained close. Now they're working for me, which will have its challenges, but I know this inner circle will have my back and be my ears and eyes throughout the company. They will personally launch the SCUD missiles aimed at me from Cuntessa's team. The intel that works its way up through the sales force is crucial to survival in the cat and mouse corporate world. Without it, you're dead without knowing what even hit you. Yes, it's that harsh. Sometimes you're dead and don't even know you're dead. It's like living *The Sixth Sense*.

"Did you see who she put on the account?" Monica, my San Francisco rep comments, the sun glinting off her auburn highlights as we enjoy watching the hard bodied Malibu boys from our beachside table at Gladstone's.

Beverly, my girl in Los Angeles, rolls her eyes. "That Barbie doll who's having the affair with Bob Mannon," she laughs, "whom she refers to as her 'mentor'." And in a breathy voice, she does an imitation, "My mentor, Bob, gave me this book. It's positively brilliant. Have you read it? Bob is so brilliant."

We all laugh at the spot-on bimbo imitation.

"Who hasn't had an affair with Bob Mannon?" The question is rhetorical, but the three of us all raise our hands. "You know we are the only three in the company he hasn't nailed," observes Monica and for a moment I wonder what's wrong with me, but quickly shoo away that thought. Bob operates under the premise that the president title on his business card means all women in the organization are fair game to service his needs.

Barbie, who actually has a name, Robyn Stiles, is a tall statuesque blonde, who has no qualms about telling everyone she meets that her number one goal in life is to be the first woman president of the company. Fiercely loyal to Cuntessa, bringing in Barbie was a strategic move to engage Hale on multiple levels as a way to expand his billings. The woman is very attractive with a mane of long thick hair that is enviable. She has enough hair for three people and has totally perfected 'the fling'.

Just thinking about it pisses me off. Not that I should care who handles Hale Lundström, but the thought of him doing her and then having Cuntessa's team crush mine in the sales rankings as a result, really ticks me off.

"Is he as good looking in real life?" Beverly is looking at Google images on her phone.

I hate to admit it, but I nod. "He's handsome in that rich boy, and I know it, kind of way. But he's a man. He's very manly. He's not cute. He's handsome," I stumble.

"I think he grew up upper middle class, but not really in a wealthy family or anything like that," Monica has done some online stalking, aka client research, on the man. "What's so interesting about him is that he dropped out of MIT, so obviously the guy is really smart, then he joined the armed forces, and from what I read was a Special Ops guy, but there is not a lot of specific information about his time in the service."

"Special Ops, like covert missions?" Beverly's stalking begins in earnest, both thumbs racing over her phone's keyboard.

Monica nods. "All that makes him even hotter. Smart, rich, mysterious and can totally kick ass."

"Sounds great, and he's probably fucking Robyn." I hate that this bothers me. I really hate it.

But what I think I hate most is that I've worked my butt off to be the best that I can be, I've built a successful team and Cuntessa and crew waltz in, are handed an account they didn't sell – that they didn't earn on their own merit – and my promotion goes down the drain, while I listen to, "When we met with Hale and his people this week," "We had an amazing off-site teambuilding with Hale and his crew," "Hale is just so interesting to work with."

Hale, Hale, Hale. Fuck Hale Lundström and the techy cloud he flew in on.

***

Sun glinting off the ocean is the best way to start the day. Standing on the balcony of my hotel room the next morning, fresh orange juice in hand, this trip to work with my newly acquired California sales team is just what I needed to escape the 104 degree temperature in Austin, which is a great place to live, but summers are too long and too hot.

Even my cell phone ringing, and breaking the morning's peacefulness, can't wipe the smile from my face on this beautiful California morning. Walking back into my room to grab the phone, "Hold on a sec," I answer, "I need to pick the sand out of my butt."

"Slacker. Why aren't you working yet?" my boss asks.

"Why am I awake, is more the question?" We were out with the Universal Studios people pretty late last night and it's only 7 A.M. here. But my body thinks it is in central time.

"You didn't pull any waitresses into your lap last night, did you?"

"No, it was a slow night," I laugh. "I have really gotten an earful from the reps out here about that lunatic's antics. Thank God you canned her ass. So what's up?" I know he's not calling to check on the status of California.

"I need you to call Hale Lundström," he sounds a little nervous.

"Hale Lundström? Why?" Okay, now that one took me by surprise.

"Yeah, he's pulling together some very high level tech event in Austin and he's going to need some assistance."

"And you want me to talk to him?" I'm totally surprised. Number one, the man has staff there that I'm assuming he can work with to handle Austin events and number two, he and his team have Susan, Robyn and the rest of her crew to fulfill any of his needs from our company.

"It's not me suggesting he talk to you. He requested to speak to you directly about it."

I'm silent. Totally dumbfounded. "And Susan is okay with this?"

Kemp sighs and I can just picture his face, "I'll take care of that."

"She's not going to be happy." Susan and I are almost at a state of peaceful coexistence, which is rare — and actually pleasant. Our rivalry has been not so friendly at times and stepping on each other's toes on accounts has resulted in fierce and unpleasant battles.

"Honestly, I don't give a rat's ass if she's happy or not. Just make Lundström happy." And he hangs up on me.

I have no idea how I'm going to make this man happy. I'm totally clueless about his business.

My phone beeps again. This time a text from Kemp with Hale's cell number and the message, **Call him today**.

SLAVE TO LOVE

I text him back with the amazing news I would have shared had he not been so curt and hung up on my ass, **Oh btw, Universal Studios is comping us a table for ten people at a huge fundraiser they are doing for soldiers returning from overseas. Politicians (including several living Presidents!!, actors, performers, etc.). Totally "A" list Hollywood/DC kind of stuff. We should pick a select group of clients and make a client event out of it. I'll have Beverly and Monica put together a strategic list of their local clients to attend.**

Invite Lundström

I was thinking logistically it would be best as an event for local west coast clients, I respond.

Invite Lundström

I know better than to push any further or Kemp will blow.

Sitting on a chair on the balcony, I put my feet up on the wrought-iron railing. My hotel robe falls open and I laugh aloud. Yup, I'm going to call this man half naked. He won't have a clue, but I will.

"Lundström." He picks up on the first ring.

Even though I'm calling him, I'm startled, "Hale, hi, it's Sierra Stone, Kemp Mc…"

He cuts me off, "Hey Sierra, thanks for getting back to me. We're done here, close the door on your way out," he says to someone on his end. "How are you?"

How am I? The man wants something because he clearly doesn't give a shit how I am. This is the very same man who wouldn't shake my hand or acknowledge my presence upon meeting me.

"Great. What can I help you with?" I can't do small talk with this guy. He makes me nervous. And now that I have the Special Ops tidbit of information in my brain, I'm really intimidated.

"I'm pulling together an event that needs to stay under the radar."

"Okay. Can you tell me what kind of event?" *What the fuck does that have to do with me?*

"It's a very high level, very private tech think tank, C-Level execs of tech companies domestically and internationally and energy and technology foreign ministers."

"Okay." There's a silence. "I'm not sure what you're asking me. Do your marketing/events staff and PR people need the names of some folks on the ground in Austin to pull it together?"

"Because of the sensitivity of subject matter, the high profile of attendees, and the security necessary for the participants, this needs to be approached in a very different manner," he pauses. "Let's discuss it over dinner tonight."

"Are you in Austin?" I'm shocked. This whole thing is coming out of left field. Why is he talking to me about it? This is not my area of expertise and SpaceCloud is not my account.

"I flew in last night. How's 7 P.M. at Uchi?"

"Hale, I'm in Los Angeles working with my team out here this week and as much as everyone raves about Tyson Cole's cooking, I'm not a sushi person."

Silence.

"When do you get back?"

"Late Thursday night." I'm actually hoping he'll be gone by then.

"Okay, I'll see you then." And he hangs up on me.

What the hell is it with men hanging up on me today, I wonder? Ugh, now I have to reach out to him about the Universal Studios event.

Are you free on August 7th? I text him. **We have a table at an event honoring the armed forces and would love for you to be our guest. It's in Los Angeles.**

Will you be there?

Yes. Universal Studios (where the event takes place) is my client.

22

SLAVE TO LOVE

OK, it's in my calendar. See you Thursday night.

And here I am, lying on a chaise lounge on my hotel balcony overlooking the ocean, cool morning breezes licking my exposed hotel robe warmed skin, left totally high and dry by Hale Lundström and picturing him licking my nipples instead of the ocean borne breeze doing the job.

Yes, I admit it, I'm intrigued that he wants me on his special project, excited that I get to work with him, confounded by his sudden interest in me (which might not really be interest in me — that could all be in my head), and scared to death by how much real estate he's occupied in my head since first setting eyes on him at the St. Regis.

⋆⋆⋆⋆⋆⋆⋆⋆⋆⋆⋆⋆⋆⋆⋆⋆⋆⋆⋆⋆⋆⋆⋆⋆⋆

The text appears on my phone the minute I hit the runway in Austin and flick off airplane mode.

Welcome back. I'll meet you at the 24 Hour Diner on 6th and Lamar.

Driving downtown, I'm downright nervous. This man makes me so uncomfortable that I don't have butterflies in my stomach, I have actual cramps. Full blown freaking stomach cramps.

He's sitting in one of those curved booths along the wall, typing into his phone as I slide into the other side, keeping my distance.

"Hi." I'm trying to be so cool.

Looking up at me, I get a slow smile. A sexy, I'm going to eat you for dinner wolfish grin.

Keep it together, Sierra, I remind myself. *This is business, not a date with this guy.*

"Good flight?" he's succinct.

"Uneventful. So that's always good." A busboy puts down two waters in front of us and I pause before speaking again. "Are you in Austin often?"

"A lot more in the past few months as our presence expands here."

The waitress comes by and he orders two Bourbon Manhattans. I know I've got a "what the fuck" look on my face because he's smiling at me. He didn't even ask me what I wanted. I don't drink Bourbon. But for some reason I love that he didn't care and went ahead anyway. There's something so manly and hot in how authoritative he is.

"Don't like Manhattans?" He appears amused.

"I don't know. I've never had one."

The wolfish smile is back, "I figured maybe your bartender boyfriend made you a Manhattan in Manhattan."

My bartender boyfriend? How interesting that is the info about me that stuck with him. Very interesting.

The waitress is back, placing the dark amber liquid before us. Raising a martini glass, Hale toasts, "To winning," as he takes his first sip.

I'm sitting there, glass in hand, watching him, fumes of strong alcohol making my nose twitch.

"Try it," he demands.

Slowly I bring the martini glass to my mouth, peering over the rim. I immediately feel the burn as it hits my lips, leaving a scorched trail en route to my empty stomach. I can feel the rush as it enters my bloodstream and wonder if after the second or third I will feel comfortable with this way too handsome, for his own good and mine, man. My eyes have not left his as he watches me drink. There's nothing boyish about him. He's pure man, right down to the dark stubble on his defined jaw. I wonder what it would feel like trailing down my breasts to my nipples. The thought of the scratchiness makes me squirm.

"That's delicious," I smile at him, loving the warmth the alcohol is spreading right down to the far reaches of my fingertips. I nearly demolish the drink in the next two sips. Anything to relax around this guy.

Hale signals the waitress for two more Manhattans and I'll be damned if I'm going to protest.

Leaning in toward me, his gaze direct and searing, "I like a woman who can run with the boys."

Not breaking his eye contact, "I may have to pull off my Louboutins, but I can run with the best of 'em."

"That's what your boss says," he informs me.

"So why am I here and not Susan, Hale? She manages your business for us and has a much better understanding of your needs."

Pulling the martini glass from his mouth, he sputters the liquid and chokes slightly. By his smile I can tell he is amused. "Do you really think she has a much better understanding of my needs?"

Now I'm choking on my words, "Your business needs," I clarify.

"I wouldn't be so sure about that." He smiles and pauses for a moment before he continues. "Sierra, what I'm putting together is an unprecedented think tank event with very high profile participants that, in many cases, due to divergent politics, aren't usually seen on the same continent together, much less in the same room. From a logistics and security perspective, this event is going to provide significant challenges and honestly, the entire nature of it needs to be," he pauses, as if searching for a word, "rather clandestine, until we're finished and ready to announce what was accomplished."

I must still have a look of confusion on my face as he smiles. His dark blue eyes clearly display amusement for some reason.

"You're still saying, 'why me?'"

I nod as the waitress delivers two more Manhattans.

The corners of his mouth curve up as he reaches across to my nearly empty martini glass, plucking out my Maraschino cherry and depositing it on his outstretched tongue. He's taking obvious delight in seeing my jaw hang open as his tongue slowly draws the cherry into his mouth. I want to follow.

"Your cherry belonged to me."

Now he's just plain fucking with me.

"I turned you onto your first Manhattan," he clarifies. "Your cherry belonged to me." He's very matter-of-fact and serious, playing the innocent as he delivers his double entendre.

"You owe me," I mutter.

"Just name it," the man calls my bluff.

Picking up the second Manhattan, "I need food or I'm never going to be able to drive home."

A slight tic in his cheek tells me that might be his plan, so quickly flagging down the waitress takes on tantamount importance to me. I need to keep it professional and business-like with this guy, but that is so damn hard because I am seriously attracted to him. As I'm sure is every woman who crosses his path. And he's deliberately fucking with me.

"So let's get back to why me. You have staff here."

"I have techie staff here. I've got engineering management types. People who are great at staying focused on what they do, but don't throw them a curveball. What I don't have here is a single individual with the people, leadership and creative thinking skills to be my right hand in pulling this off. I don't have someone that I have the confidence will coordinate and execute all the details flawlessly. And that is where you come in."

"Thank you for those compliments, Hale," I'm trying to focus, but the Bourbon is having its way with me, "but you met me once for a few minutes, in a bar. Why would you entrust me with a project of this magnitude?"

26

"Based on multiple conversations with Kemp. You're a leader. You motivate people to run through walls for you. And that is a direct quote, by the way." He pauses and let's that settle in. "He's also described you as intensely loyal, able to hold important information in confidence, highly competent and easy to work with."

"And he's loaning me out?"

"At a steep price." He laughs.

"Well, this is highly unorthodox." I'm not sure whether to feel flattered or hurt, but I'm suddenly feeling like a rock star just sold me to another band for five grams of coke.

There is only one thing for me to do and that is take another healthy swig of my Manhattan.

With a gaze so mesmerizing that looking away is not even an option, "Everything I do is unorthodox. I play by my own rules, Sierra." Taking another sip of his Manhattan, he laughs. "And sometimes I don't. But I always make up the rules. Just go with it."

He hasn't released me from the unwavering eye contact, but as his finger shoots out towards me, I react, and my eyes follow it until it stops at the apex of my cleavage. He's touching me. A light, feathery touch. Looking up from his finger back to his eyes, the edges are now crinkled in amusement.

"Where's the mermaid?"

"Her chain broke," I choke out the words.

His finger is still there, searing into my skin, making the ache between my legs nearly unbearable.

"Well, maybe you need stronger chains."

And with a mere flick of his finger, I tumble down the rabbit hole.

27

CHAPTER Four

I'm really not quite sure what to do with her. She's not like the women I date. She's not like the women I fuck. Yeah, I have women in my company, just not in my inner circle. So, I'm not sure how to balance having a close work confidante that I want to bang. So damn bad.

Would it be a bad thing to keep her in the conference room after dismissing the rest of the team, lock the doors, pick her up and seat her on the edge of the conference room table. Feel her melt into my hand as I run my fingertips down the front of her silk tank top. When she shivers, twist her taunting nipples until they harden, then stop and listen to her moan. Would that lost animal sound be coming from what I was doing to her or because I stopped? I wouldn't wait to find out as I pushed her underwear aside, and harden even more, the moment I feel her wetness. Using her slick juices to moisten her clit, I'd finger her until she is gasping for air and reaching for me. I'd let just her nails and the tips of her finger graze my hard cock as I hang just out of reach. I would totally get off knowing that it is her need to grab me, making her wilder, and that crazed instinctual desire in her eyes would have me titanium hard. I need to be buried deep inside her.

I know my face is portraying a practiced and perfected look of deep concentration when my VP of Product Development asks for the second time, "Can we get the go-ahead on that, Hale?"

Shaking my head and drawing my brows together, "Give me your full brief in writing." I act as if there's something bothering me in what he presented, when in actuality I'm just buying time because I didn't hear a word he said.

Dismissing all my direct reports except my Security Chief, Anthony Palmer, and Sierra, this is the start of weekly status meetings on the think tank event, known as TFV1/ATX, which stands for Tech Future Vision #1/Austin, Texas and the three of us will be working very closely for the next three and a half months.

The text on my cell goes off.

Still on for kayaking? I'll swing by to get you. Let me know if you're running late.

One of the best things about being in Austin. Family.

In New York, I live my single entrepreneur CEO persona. In Austin, I'm the successful kid brother with the wild boy lifestyle and the cool uncle. My brother, Noel, a professor at the Red McCombs School of Business at the University of Texas, will always remind me that he can kick my ass in a kayak or on a basketball court no matter how much money I make. His wife, Carrie, is not beyond making me wear a pink apron with frills and handing me a cutting board, knife and a basket of vegetables, because I am her official "Salad Guy", and my three year old nephew, Oliver, the video game king, is already shaming me at Hedgehog's Adventure.

Nine years ago, when my brother took the position at UT he predicted the "Live Music Capital of the World" would become the next Silicon Valley. Based on not only the presence of Dell Computers, Freescale Semiconductor, National Instruments, IBM and a multitude of other tech giants, but because of the cultural embracing of technology entrepreneurs and the proliferation of technology incubators, both private and associated with the university. Austin, Texas had quickly grown into a town known for music, technology start-ups working right alongside the established giants and Formula One auto racing. In other words, a great town for entrepreneurs and people who like to have fun.

Eight years ago I started building a presence in the town, a small one at first. Doing so gave me access to the brightest techie minds and my family. What more could I need?

It's nearly 5:30 when we wrap up, "We cleared some office space for you for when you're here."

Sierra smiles at me. She's genuinely surprised. "Thank you."

"Follow me," I tell her as we walk out of the conference room.

Leading her down the hall toward her new office, I'm silent, still feeling the remnants of the fantasy I was having about her. It's so confusing.

She gasps as I open the door and moves quickly inside, standing by the floor to ceiling window that overlooks the architecturally distinct Frost Bank Tower with its segmented pyramid style apex. At night, the top of the building is lit white, a unique beacon on the Austin skyline. And here up on the thirty-fifth floor, we are the neighbor of the iconic Austin building top view.

Sierra turns to me, her smile unable to hide the awe. "If you want me slaving late into the night, this was a brilliant idea."

I laugh, but want to smack down my twitching cock. Just the mention of the word slave has me envisioning her as a slave to me. Legs spread far apart, tied to the bed post and taking every inch I selfishly ram into her.

It's in that moment that I realize the look in her eyes that I want to see when she looks at me. And I wonder, how do I make that happen?

There's a small box in the middle of the desk and I point to it. "That's for you."

Smiling, she walks to the desk and picks up the box. Looking at me, with her head cocked to the side, I can see she's confused by the box's mere presence.

"Open it," I urge.

Sierra looks as nervous as I feel, her hands fumbling with the wrap on the box. As she finally opens it, I wonder how she is going to take this.

Flipping over the lid, she takes in a deep breath and holds it.

I suddenly need to explain myself. "This should be strong enough to keep your mermaid safe."

"Thank you. I really don't know what to say. This is so thoughtful," she stammers.

Suddenly her office space feels too small for the two of us. I shouldn't have given her the gift. I'm usually so smooth and suave, and in control, and I'm just an idiot around this woman. What is that about?

Looking at my watch, I know Noel must already be waiting. Saved by the brother. "I'm running late."

"Yeah, I am too." She puts the necklace into her laptop bag.

As she steps toward the door, my hand naturally goes to her lower back to usher her out. And as if the most natural interaction in the world, my hand slips down the smooth fabric of her dusty pink skirt, with my palm settling on the rounded cheek of her delicious bottom.

Almost tripping over Sierra as she stops dead in her tracks, she looks up at me, the anger palpable, as her eyes lock in on mine.

"I don't shit where I eat," her angry snarl has me take a step backward.

Not waiting for my response, she speeds through the lobby, past my brother, and out through the front door toward the elevator banks.

What the hell was I thinking? The truth is, I wasn't thinking. My body just reacted to her. I'd been so deep in my head with the fantasy of her for weeks, that I just went over the line without thinking. I went over the line like she's mine.

Noel is just standing there, his back to me, looking at the door she just flew through. As I approach, I stand next to him silently, looking at the empty space.

"Who was that?" he sounds stunned.

"Her name is Sierra Stone," I explain. "We're working on a project together."

Finally, he turns to me. "She looks like Maggie."

"I hadn't noticed." And I hadn't. But now that he's said it, everything hurts. My head is throbbing, my heart aches.

"How could you not have noticed?" He doesn't even attempt to hide how ridiculous he thinks I sound.

"I really didn't." I'm now muttering.

"She looks like Maggie," he repeats.

And I know he's right.

She looks like Maggie.

CHAPTER
Five

"Men suck," I scream.

"What a douche." I'm talking to Monica on the Bluetooth in my car. I've been driving aimlessly around Austin for the past two hours, beating this current Hale Lundström incident to a dead horse. We call ourselves The Swale Club, for the dead race horse, because we can take any topic and beat it to a dead horse. And tonight, I am proudly holding the position of the club's honorary president.

"I can't believe he did that. First, he's pulled me away from my team's work, which is how I get compensated, then he gives me a gold chain and proceeds to think because he threw some jewelry at me that he can treat me like a fuck toy. I'm sure he'll now have Kemp pull me off his project and that's just fine."

"Don't be so sure," Monica generally has a very solid take on situations. "Did he look like he was sorry?"

"I don't know, after I blasted him, I just turned on my heel and walked out. I was seeing red. I don't even remember getting on the elevator."

I'm out on one of my favorite winding roads that skirts the shores of Lake Travis. Probably not a good idea to be driving here when I'm seething mad, but the feel of the road in the tight wheel of my BMW is total Zen for me. The stiff suspension hugs the curves and I feel powerful behind the wheel, as if I'm refueling the power that Hale tried to steal from me.

"I think if the guy was sorry, he would have reached out to apologize."

"Men are stupid, Sierra. He might be sorry that he offended you. He's probably sorrier though that you don't want to pay attention to his dick."

Laughing, "You know what, Monica, in another circumstance I'd love to pay attention to his dick. He's smart, he's sexy, he's charismatic. But this is work and I'm not going to throw it all away for some guy who thinks he 'bought' me from Kemp, and therefore, can do anything he wants to me."

"Are you going to tell Kemp?"

"I don't know." And I don't.

"He'd blow his stack," is Monica's assessment.

"I don't know. He really likes the guy." Kemp is having a bromance with Hale. It's like he wants to be Hale when he grows up. Would it be bros before hos? In any other case, I know Kemp would go ape shit over this, but with Hale, it's kind of like when you tell a friend their boyfriend is cheating, they always end up going back to the boyfriend and you end up without a friend.

"I do know. You are one of his people and he's very protective. His testosterone would go into overdrive. He would be pissed as shit and find a way to pull you off this project."

"And pull me out of my own event at Universal Studios so that I don't have to be there with him." The thought of not being able to attend my team's event with our hard-earned clients, and not see Hale again, feels painful.

Why do I want to see Hale again? I ask myself. And I know the answer. I want him to make it right.

But it's been over two hours and not a word, so it's unlikely that he even gives a shit.

Driving up the hill to my house in Travis Heights, just passing the small renovated Craftsman cottages on my street brings a feeling of solace that only home can do. With my WhatABurger orange and white striped bag in hand, ready for a serious pig-out, because comfort food is the only answer tonight, I get out of my car and head up the front walk to the little pale yellow, with white and cornflower blue trim, cottage that I call home. The serene colors always puts a smile on my face and I'm more than happy to see them tonight.

Lying across my welcome mat, which bears the message, "If you don't have wine, GO HOME," wrapped in pink and white tissue paper, with turquoise and white ribbon, are what looks like two dozen long stem pale pink roses. Opening the door, I bring my WhatABurger and laptop bag into the house, and kick off my shoes, before going back outside to retrieve the giant bundle of flowers.

Picking them up, I take a moment to bury my nose between the velvety petals and inhale their sweet perfume. A small white card is tucked in.

I'm an ass.

"Yes, you are," I agree aloud.

Looking at the handwriting, I recognize it is his. He personally filled out the card. Just after I stick my nose back in to steal the scent one more time, I also realize there is no florist delivery information on the card or envelope. *Did he drop them at my front door?*

Suddenly self-conscious. *He was here. He must've found out where I live.* Quickly pulling my face from the bouquet, I scamper into the house, closing the door and locking it behind me.

CHAPTER Six

*T*he text message **YES. YOU are.** in response to my note, "I'm an ass" is all that I've heard from Sierra. The next morning I am on a plane for New York. Part of me doesn't want to go, to be away from where I know she is. I want to try and continue to make amends, not let her out of my sight.

Yet the logical part of me, which has always been the most dominant, knows it is the best thing in the world to get on that plane; distance myself from the tangled cross wires binding us together. If I don't get on the plane, I will ruin everything. Just as I always do.

And when I need to get away, there's no place better to get lost, and lose myself, than the streets of New York City. I thought running the SkyTrack at my health club, Level 9/NYC, would give me the answers I needed. Approaching mile six, I'm still struggling as to why I hadn't seen Sierra's resemblance to Maggie before Noel pointed it out. Is that the source of my attraction to her? Or am I not even really attracted to her and just using her to fill a corporate need, succumbing to board pressure? Whatever is motivating me, I am making a mess of it all. Or am I out of my mind crazy attracted to her with her slightly wild, dirty blonde hair, fresh scrubbed face and Louboutin-perfection legs.

The only thing I know for sure by the time I've completed mile eight, is that I am running through scenarios in my head that will give me reason to contact her. I want to hear her voice. I need to apologize, more significantly than by just leaving flowers at her front door, and I haven't done that, I have not offered a real apology. With every day that has passed, I know I am making it worse, but have convinced myself that she doesn't want to hear from me and that I need space from her to examine my motivation.

Coming out of the locker room after a hot shower, I am surprised to see the owner of Level 9, Schooner Moore, on the premises. He and I have gotten to know each other a bit through a private NYC entrepreneurs group, and I know he is spending less and less time overseeing his vast health and entertainment club empire, and more time on a charitable foundation he's building for physical therapy rehabilitation in developing nations.

Across the facility, Schooner is handing something off to a guy in dark glasses and a baseball cap, who looks a lot like Jesse Winslow, lead singer of the band, Winslow. The guy then heads across the complex's rotunda with a redhead. The beachy waves in the redhead's hair reminds me of Sierra's golden waves. Laughing to myself, everything reminds me of Sierra.

As the guy and the redhead walk away, Schooner turns and I catch his eye, "Hale, good to see you." Schooner Moore's hand is outstretched, as he crosses the facility toward me with long-legged strides. "You should have let me know you were coming in."

"Last minute decision. No meetings scheduled and I thought a run would do my head some good."

"I know that feeling. The track has always been my place to work through things. Either that, or my boat," he laughs. "Well, let me know if there's anything my staff or I can get you. Good to see you again." And with a clap on my back, one of the master entrepreneurs of our time is off.

SLAVE TO LOVE

Entering my office the next morning, I am immediately accosted by Susan Smith who appears to be lurking in the hallway. She follows me into my office, a terrier traipsing at my heels and takes a seat.

"From our perspective things seem to be going well working with your team. How would you rate it?" She pressures me for an answer.

"Feedback from my staff has been good. I haven't heard anything negative from my directs, but I haven't been involved in the day-to-day. You should check in with them."

"Yes, I'll do that." And with less than a breath of air, she launches into, "If you are pleased with my team's performance, it might add more continuity to handle the project you are running out of Texas with my group at the helm."

"Susan, that project is not a staff level project. There's a reason why management is so intimately involved. Does it really make sense to bring you into Austin when Sierra is based there?"

Just saying her name brings with it a sense of longing that I'm not expecting.

"Hale, I'm personally interfacing with many of your departments and personnel, including your direct reports. I clearly have a better working knowledge of your organization. So yes, I think my familiarity with multiple aspects of your organization will bring a more tangible benefit than mere logistics."

I sit back and regard Susan. She is cut-throat all right. Cut-throat and competitive. A man in a black microfiber Hillary Clinton suit. Usually I like people who will do anything to get the job done. But backstabbers are not a favorite.

"Except that Sierra is doing an exquisite job. Honestly, I don't know what I'd do without her. She is so talented." I'm saying this partly because it's true and partly for Susan's benefit, to really piss her off and shut her down.

I look down at my Breitling watch, "If you'll excuse me now I need to get on a call. If you wouldn't mind shutting my door on your way out."

Susan smiles, attempting to be professional, but she's ready to blow a gasket. I have visions of her chopping off kittens' heads.

Sierra's going to have a tough time with that one going for her coveted promotion. Susan played her hand. She will do anything it takes to swipe that job right from under Sierra, including sticking a knife in her back and twisting it while she is smiling in her face.

I often admire some of those qualities, a drive to conquer, but I'm not digging it in Susan. *Is that sexist of me,* I wonder. Or am I just protective of Sierra, who seems to be going about doing it the right way, even if the right way doesn't always produce winners.

And maybe I should want Susan to be the victor in this battle. Sierra will never work for her. She'll try to micromanage her right out of the company, because she's threatened by Sierra's creativity and leadership skills.

And that would make Sierra Stone a free agent. One already with ties to the management team in my company.

It's nearly 6 P.M. when I shut my laptop down. Stretching my legs out in front of me as I turn to look out the window, the city seems so quiet and tame from up here, its fuel line of energy a trickle instead of its normally steady flow. Staring at the rooftops, I take on that sense of calm and quiet, relishing it for a moment at the end of my work day, because I know the minute I step out of the front door of the building, I will be immediately swept up into that energy flow and feel the frenzied current coursing steadily through my veins.

My sixth sense, well-honed through intensive military training, tells me that I'm no longer alone in my personal sanctuary and as I spin my chair back to my desk, I'm not at all surprised to see Robyn Stiles, even with her stealth approach, posed in my doorway, as if testing positions for a boudoir photo shoot.

"You look like a man who could use a drink." She dips her head, looking up at me through lashes that appear to have been recently purchased.

This is a woman who is used to getting her way with men, her poses have been perfected, her lines well crafted. She gets what she wants and I'm betting her close record is excessively high. She truly is the perfect sales person and her product, I'm sure, coveted by many.

With her legs long and toned, her walk practiced, as if she were prowling a catwalk, she glides across my office, uninvited, to a chair across the desk from me and slowly crosses her legs. She knows I'm watching and is enjoying giving me a show. It's impossible not to imagine them wrapped around me and I've got the feeling she knows exactly what I'm thinking and figures she's halfway home.

"I am really enjoying my work with your company, Hale." Her pupils are dilated. "I really respect what you've built. At some point, I'd love the opportunity to really sit down and get your opinion on what you think would be the best career path for me. I would love to be with an organization as progressive as this."

I laugh, "It would be bad form for me to be poaching employees from my vendor." Although that is exactly what I'd love to do with Sierra.

"That's not what I meant at all," she back-peddles. "I would just really love to have someone as a mentor who understands the technology marketplace and how to successfully position for the future.

Mentor? Position? Yeah, I know what position she'd like to be in. Flat on her back on my desk.

This woman is trouble. Camera in purse, blackmailing kind of trouble. Granted, she would make great arm-candy at industry functions, charming the boys' club left and right as she worked the room. She wouldn't be dazzling anyone with her superior intelligence, but no one would get past her store-bought rack to notice or care. She is the perfect sales person/account executive until she finds just the right executive to marry her and produce perfect looking children.

"So, what about that drink?" she presses.

I'm transfixed on her body language and how aggressive it is. With the slightest of signals or encouragement on my part, she would gracefully end up on my side of the desk or on my desk or against the floor to ceiling windows. And that is *exactly* what she wants me to be thinking.

I watch her full fuchsia painted lips move, but all I can hear is Sierra in my head, "I don't shit where I eat." And I know that not only is that good advice, it's the perfect advice for me in this circumstance, because this one is a deceitful master that might be difficult to get rid of. Thanks, Sierra.

I look down at my Breitling, "Oh wow, I didn't realize it was so late. Excuse me." I stand as I slip my laptop into its case. "I don't want to keep my girlfriend waiting."

Grabbing my phone as I get in bed, I do my nightly last email check of the evening. Disconnecting from work doesn't happen when everyone's paycheck depends on you. I'm just not the type of personality to be able to flip a switch and turn it off.

And there it is, an email from Sierra Stone. I can feel my heart beat faster just seeing her name. The subject is 'Information Needed for Universal Event'. Okay, a business email, that's safe and a place to start. An entre to rebuilding some sort of rapport. Trust.

Scanning through the body of the message. It's very professional. They need my social security number for Secret Service clearance because U.S. Presidents, past and present, will be in attendance. Chuckling as I think, *she should only know the level of security clearance I have with the government. She'd be shocked.* I'm as equipped to protect a President as the staff that will be guarding them. I just wish she felt safe with me.

Sierra should wear that turquoise skirt and the Louboutins she was wearing on the night we met, I muse. It would get Bill Clinton's testosterone revved up, for sure.

Reaching the end of the message, I realize that although totally professional and appropriate, there is nothing personal about it. Quickly scrolling to the top, I immediately check the distribution.

Ugh, I groan aloud.

A bcc: to the entire group of invitees. She lumped me in with all of their other clients. The ultimate in pulling away and letting me know that I was just a client. Keep it professional and impersonal.

Perturbed, I get out of bed and stand by my windows, overlooking the lights of lower Manhattan and beyond, down the Hudson River to the Narrows.

I have fucked this up on every level possible. I am so drawn to this girl, and not because she looks like Maggie, as Noel would have me believe, but because she's smart, and smart-mouthed and fun. She has this girl next door charm with a dash of daring and adventure thrown in. I can see us together. I really can. I know the magazines profiling me as one of the Top 25 Hottest Entrepreneur Bachelors or whatever the hell the title of the month is, would have me paired with a model, a glamour girl, or at the very least, a Robyn Stiles type. But that's not who I see myself with. I see myself with a woman who can give me a run for my money in the boardroom and wake up next to me in the bedroom and not give a rat's ass that she has no make-up on and her hair looks like I've fucked the crap out of her. And she's still gorgeous. I see myself with a woman who tells me, 'I don't shit where I eat', and I damn well had better respect that.

I see myself with Sierra Stone.

And I know it's time to get my ass back to Austin and make this right. Somehow.

CHAPTER
Seven

He's really handsome, his pale hazel eyes are incredibly striking and I like the way he holds my eye contact when we speak. His full, beautiful lips expand into what is a breathtaking, captivating smile. And he's got this sun-bleached hair that is thick and full, and he keeps brushing it out of his eyes. By any definition of the word, this guy is hot. Tall, well-educated, eloquent, interesting, career-oriented. And nice. Check. Check. Check. Check. Check. Check.

And I'm sitting here at the Salty Sow, an ultra-hip gastropub in East Austin that he chose, trying my hardest to stay engaged in the conversation and keep my mind from wandering, from wondering. Is he back in Austin? Has he even thought about me? What does he think of me?

But the bigger question is – *what is wrong with me?*

He's a narcissistic creep who treats women like shit and I just need to get through the California event at Universal, his Austin event and the planning meetings around them. Get through that and then I'm done with him. His business totally reverts back to Cuntessa's team. And then hopefully, this totally OCD obsession I have with him will evaporate.

I haven't heard a word my date has said to me in the last minute. His name is Tyler and I need to join him at this dinner and come back from wherever la-la Hale Lundström fantasy land I've been hiding in. He deserves it and even more so, I deserve it.

Excusing myself, I go to the ladies room, where my obsessive behavior continues. No phone calls. No texts. No emails. The mirror isn't confessing any great secrets. I look the same. So why do I feel so damn different? I feel like I've lost myself. Sierra is gone. I see her, but she's gone. And I want her back. Not this pathetic shell who is so obsessed with this douche who doesn't give a crap about her.

The Sierra I know would never pine over a man who disrespected her. She'd kick him in the balls and tell him to fuck himself. Not fantasize about him and keep checking her phone every two minutes like a silly teen waiting to be asked out to prom. Who is this pathetic girl? It certainly can't be Sierra Stone.

Rejoining Tyler, I've brought with me from the ladies room a brand new resolve. Live in the present. The here and now. In my head I'm hearing an old song about loving the one you're with and wonder if I should make that my theme song.

He's actually the nicest date I've had in a long time. He embodies the quintessential Austin ethos, laid back and friendly. And I need to give him a chance. I really need to give him a chance.

Don't fuck this up, Sierra.

Flying back first thing in the morning. Need to meet.

A text from Hale. Our first contact in ten days. I'm elated. I'm angry. My heart hurts and I don't know if it's happiness or despair. Need to meet could mean anything. I'm trying not to read too much into it.

Sure. When? My fingers are shaking.

SLAVE TO LOVE

Dinner This is so Hale, no question mark after it asking me if I'm available.

Where? Oh Sierra, you are so easy. You didn't even make him work for it.

I'll pick you up at 7:30

Pick me up where? I need him to clarify it.

At your house, Sierra. I can hear the exasperation in his text and I'm amusing myself.

That's really not necessary. I'll meet you somewhere. You haven't contacted me in 10 days, douche, so now I'm going to fuck with you a little.

I will pick you up at 7:30

Seriously, it's not like it's a date or something.

Just promise me you won't shit in the restaurant. Ha-ha, amusing. Throw my own words back at me.

I'm very professional on business dinners, Hale. I'm shaking my head. I can't date him. This is business. Anything else will end badly for me. Very, very badly.

Yeah well, we have a dinner date tomorrow night. Goodnight, Sierra. I really don't like being dismissed.

Hale I've let five minutes pass.

Yes, Sierra

My ass is off-limits The guy needs ground rules.

So are you saying your ass is not on the table?

Yes

I can still work with that. Goodnight, Sierra. Dog.

Girls will be girls. It doesn't matter if we are sixteen, thirty-three (my age) or sixty-three. Girls will be girls. And based on that irrefutable fact of the universe, I am forced to call an emergency meeting of The Swale Club.

Three-way call initiated. Text shared with all parties. Monica and Beverly up to speed, it's time to beat this topic to a dead horse.

"You have to call Cuntessa about something tomorrow and dig around. Find out if she saw him in the last few days." Beverly is all about gathering facts and then putting together a strategy.

"I'm reading this," Monica cuts in, "you really have to look at the sub-text. It's like he's totally over this exile and just wants to come back and go for it. He's really very funny, Sierra. I like his sense of humor."

Why am I the only one not laughing? I really need to lighten up.

"The ass comment," Beverly laments, "I'd kill for my darling husband," her voice drips with sarcasm, "to say something like that to me."

"He wants your ass against a wall, Sierra. Or maybe on your kitchen counter."

"Well, that's not happening. I have to work with the guy. We have two very major events to get through. When I no longer am in his 'quasi-employ', then maybe we can explore having something. This might not mean anything. This could just be his normal pig self." I keep reading his words. Just reading his double entendres is killing me. I want to know what his mouth tastes like and what it feels like to be nestled against his muscular frame. I want to know if my kisses can get him hard. And I want to feel their power pressed up against me.

"You'd better call us immediately after he leaves," Beverly demands.

"If he leaves," Monica loves to torment me.

CHAPTER Eight

*T*ravis Heights is quintessential Austin. The location, bordering the Colorado River, makes it prime and expensive real estate and like many other older Austin neighborhoods, homes are being bought strictly for the choice location of the lot and then knocked down, giving way to large new homes next door to 1940's Craftsman cottages.

As I pull up to Sierra's house, I think how much it looks like her. Sunshine and comfort, amid change. And I wonder if what is changing is actually me. A year ago, I would have been banging Robyn Stiles in my office and last night she just grossed me out.

Taking a deep breath before I knock, I have no idea how to play this. The last time we saw one another I was completely inappropriate. She has to be nice to me because basically she works for me. But what would she be feeling if work were out of the equation? Would she even return my texts?

Lifting my hand to knock feels like an uncovering of my fate and I'm immediately grabbed by that uncomfortable clench in my belly, something that I learned to quell overseas and does not happen often to me. I am not yet ready for this answer.

Her smile is automatic as she opens the door.

"Hale." She seems genuinely happy to see me. "Come on in."

Relief is instantaneous, fears dispelled by just a smile. Refreshing is the word that comes to mind, especially after the likes of Robyn Stiles, as I take in the girl that mirrors her neighborhood. Quintessentially Austin. In a short white linen sundress and well-worn cowboy boots, Sierra is clad in Austin's version of "dressed up". With loose tousled hair and not a lot of make-up that I can detect, she looks even more beautiful standing here than the dream that's haunted me for ten days.

"Great place," I look around as I peer over her shoulder, so that I don't stare at her too long. It reminds me of a beach cottage. The walls are a sky blue that gives the place the feel of a perfect sunny day.

"Your garage is probably larger than my whole house," she laughs nervously.

"This is really nice. Did you do the decorating?"

She nods and I continue, "I'm always amazed by people who can put things together and create a great space." I pick up a photo of Sierra with two other women, they are clearly laughing hysterically.

"Would you like something to drink?"

I can tell that I am making her uncomfortable as I stalk around her living room, picking things up and learning about her by her choices in the finely crafted surroundings. It's the coffee table that catches my eye.

Pointing to it, "Sticks?"

"Yes." She looks amazed that I know who created the beautiful hand painted table depicting the four seasons.

"Surprised I know that, huh?" I raise my brows, feeling very proud of myself.

"You must have a girlfriend that enjoys dragging you to high priced craft furniture stores."

She's astute and has totally nailed me here.

"Ex-girlfriend who loved New Hope, Pennsylvania." I can almost see her mind spinning and I answer the question, "But we never bought any."

"Okay."

It's evident that she's not sure how to answer me. I am really making her uncomfortable. The opposite of what I want to happen.

"Here's the shocking part. I'm the one that liked it. She didn't," I confess.

"That in itself is reason enough to make her an ex." Sierra smiles for the first time.

Laughing, "Damn right." And I get my second smile from her.

I look at my watch, "Hey, we need to head out."

"Where are we going?" She grabs a big oversized soft leather bag.

"The Carillon."

"On the UT Campus?"

I nod. "Have you been?"

"No, and I've always wanted to go there."

Sierra stops dead in her tracks when she sees my car. "What is that?"

Laughing, "It's a Lotus." I'll never tire of saying that.

"I probably should not have worn a dress." Sierra is looking at the car, clearly trying to figure out how to negotiate her way into it.

"You look very nice tonight." She knows I'm messing with her by the amused look on my face, and I am silently praying she's commando under that dress and really sweating it out. "Do you need help getting in?"

Smiling through gritted teeth, "I think I'm capable of getting into a car."

"Okay."

Smiling, I fold my long frame into the low seat of the Lotus. It takes practice to get in and out of a low street racing car. And I've never done it in a dress.

"Ready," I ask mockingly, eyebrows raised, when she's finally in and tugging at her hiked up hemline.

With a dirty look, she whacks me in the arm. "Ass."

Laughing, "We've previously established that." And down her street I tear, loving the guttural sound of the engine and feeling like a teen showing off to my girlfriend.

Just a few minutes later as we're pulling up to the building housing the restaurant, Sierra concedes, "I'll bet this is a great car to take out into Hill Country."

"Totally, we should drive out to Bandera some weekend." I did it again, just overstepped it with her, because I'm not thinking, and it just seems so natural.

Parking the Lotus, I quickly head to her side to help her out. She gives me a look and I laugh, "I'm only trying to be a gentleman." I feign innocence.

"Mmm-hmm." Even her mmm-hmm is dripping sarcasm.

Not commando. White lace. Oh God, she's destroying me. I want to rip them off and lower her onto my lap. Impale her and discover what kissing does to her with my cock inside her.

Damn it. Will I be able to keep the promises I want to make?

Our waiter comes by and I order two Manhattans, smiling at Sierra.

"Craving cherries?" Her eyebrows are raised.

Oh man, she really is going to kill me tonight.

"Only if they are yours."

"You want mine?" she asks and I can see she feels it. She feels our energy.

"More than you can imagine."

"I would hate to deny you."

"Good girl. Then don't."

The waiter places the Martini glasses in front of us and I lift mine, "Good to see you again." And I hope she can see how sincere I am.

"Good to see you." She takes a sip and her nose scrunches up. "This tastes different."

"They make theirs with rye whiskey instead of bourbon."

Another two sips and the cherry is no longer submerged. Sierra reaches into the glass and plucks it out. About ready to pop it into her mouth, she catches my eye and smiles. She's just messing with me. Reaching out, I grasp her slender wrist and slowly pull it to me. Taking the tips of her thumb and forefinger into my mouth, I suck the cherry out from between her fingers and show it to her on my tongue before slowly chewing it, a smile firmly planted on my face.

I'm still holding her wrist and with my free hand, I signal to the waiter for two more.

"We need to talk, Hale."

I can see she is struggling. We are in such dangerous territory and we escalate there quickly and too easily. She is clearly unnerved and I'm not sure if it's by her own behavior, mine or what happens when we're together. Her eyes search mine as if she is hoping to find some truth. I loosen my hold on her wrist and pick up my drink.

"Let me start by first saying something I have yet to say to you. I'm sorry, Sierra. I'm sorry I disrespected you."

"You treated me like a bimbo, Hale. That is just not acceptable." She stops and picks up her drink. "As a woman in the corporate world, I have to work twice as hard to get to the same place as my male counterparts. So I work three times as hard. And I'm good at what I do, really good. So for you to treat me that way, is just not excusable."

"I don't even know how to explain myself. I know what I did was inappropriate and wrong. I was touching you and then I was *touching* you."

"I have never crossed the line in business. Men can do it. Women can't. When men do it, they get an "atta boy". Women get labeled as sluts and never taken seriously again from a business perspective. I've worked really hard to get where I am."

The sincerity in her eyes is eating at my gut. How do I even explain this to her? How do I tell her?

"It wasn't my intent to offend you or disrespect you and I totally understand why you feel the way you do. I had no right to be touching you. You didn't give me that permission and I way overstepped my bounds by taking something you didn't give me."

When she remains silent, I cave. I'm crumbling. This girl has no clue that I would do anything for her.

"It's just," I pause, knowing if I continue to speak, I'm going to sound like a lunatic, "it's just, I wasn't thinking and it felt so natural and right to be touching you. Unfortunately, it was inappropriate and offensive to you."

"Would you grab a male colleague's ass?"

"No. But if I'm going to be totally honest with you, I would never be fantasizing about a male colleague's ass."

The shock that registers on her face is almost comical. But not quite.

"You fantasize about my ass?"

"Your ass is gorgeous, Sierra. I'd have to be dead not to notice it." I kill the last sip of my second Manhattan.

With the timing of a Swiss clockmaker, the waiter approaches the table, handing Sierra her menu first and then one to me. I make eye contact with the man and he beats a hasty retreat.

Looking down at my menu to put a halt to the conversation for now, I pretend I'm reading the chef's specialties, until I hear her small gasp. Looking up, our eyes meet. The surprise conveyed in hers are the reaction I was hoping for as I raise my brows, silently asking her to answer.

Across the top of her menu, the restaurant has printed the message:

Let's start over again, Sierra.

CHAPTER Nine

y heart is melting. I want to stay mad at him, but I can't. What he did was wrong. No doubt about that. But I think I understand now that we are both fighting something we're really not quite sure how to handle. And probably not doing a good job of it.

I can't believe he had the restaurant print a personal message to me on the menu.

"Yeah," is all I say as I meet his deep blue eyes, eliciting a smile that makes the edges of his eyes crinkle. The man is so damn handsome and I fear I'm going to break every rule I live by and become the ultimate hypocrite after all the shit I've given him.

"Here's the thing, Hale," I need to lay it out there for him so that there is no confusion. "While we're working on your project, we really need to keep it a work relationship."

"I understand." He nods and I'm having problems concentrating on anything but the dark stubble on his jaw that makes him look so damn masculine. Hale Lundström is a man, he is not a little boy. And he's the man that I want. "What I'm struggling with," he goes on, "is how do we stop our rapport, our banter? The cherries, for instance. And do we even want to stop that? It's our way of getting to know one another, Sierra."

"I don't know," I'm shaking my head. "This is really confusing."

Hale flags down the waiter and orders yet another round of Manhattans. He responds to my wide-eyed look with a laugh, "Don't worry, we'll eat plenty of food to sober up before I make you get back in the Lotus; but one more drink will decimate both our walls so that we can be really honest with one another."

He's right, his words resonate and make the little hairs on the back of my neck stand up. Admitting that I think about him obsessively, wondering what it would feel like to be pinned underneath him as he uses his muscular thighs to nudge mine open is probably more honest than I want or need to be.

When the waiter delivers our drinks, I'm almost afraid to take the first sip.

"To crashing through walls without decimating all boundaries," he pauses and I take a sip. "Yet." He finishes his sentence and I choke.

"Are you sure you're okay to drive?" We're waiting for the valet to bring the car around. A typical summer's night in Austin. The setting of the sun has yet to cool the still evening air, even as it approaches 11:30 P.M.

"Sierra, if I were not okay, we'd be in the back seat of a cab right now."

"We'd?" I'm surprised.

Laughing, "Yes, we'd. Because first we'd be dropping you off in Travis Heights and I'd be walking you safely to your door. And then the cab would be taking me home."

"Wow, you've almost got me believing you're a gentleman."

"I do have manners. I just don't always display them. As you've already witnessed."

"Where do you live?" I'm dying to know.

"In The Austonian," he's somehow surprised that I don't know he has a residence in the skyscraper where he's got the executive office space, where my office is when I'm working on SpaceCloud business. "The other half of the floor is my apartment."

Wow. I'm suddenly uncomfortable at how close I've unknowingly been to his bed. And now that I know, well, that adds another level of distraction. I'm going to have to keep myself from fantasizing about nooners.

The valet pulls up with the Lotus. "Sweet ride," the kid excitedly says to Hale.

"Need help getting in?" The smirk on his face shows how much fun he is having fucking with me.

"Maybe that should be my question to you," I shoot back without missing a beat.

His laugh is hearty, "Baby, I never have problems getting in." And he folds his long, muscular frame into the car with the ease of a mountain lion.

Me and my smart ass mouth. I am never going to make it to TFV1 without 'shitting where I eat', if this keeps up. I can't let that happen. There's so much on the line. Kemp's promotion is imminent. I cannot throw it all away now. No matter how overwhelmingly attracted I am to this man.

The physical space in the cockpit of this tiny car is my enemy right now. We are so close together, that with every turn my knee brushes his hand on the stick shift and there's nowhere for me to move away. I hate that part of me wants to throw caution to the wind and turn my back on everything I know to be true. I hate it. And what I really loathe is my fear that I'm going to lose this battle at the most critical juncture of my career.

We cross the Colorado River and turn left on Riverside Drive. It'll only be five more minutes in this car with him until we are pulling up in front of my house. Conflicted? That's a freaking understatement. I want my personal space back, but I fear the emptiness when he retreats. The last twenty-four hours have been overwhelming and confusing. *Is there a right or a wrong?* I ask myself. *And is he worth the risk or will he be the biggest colossal mistake of my life?*

I don't know that I can risk that.

Pulling into my driveway behind my car, Hale cuts the roaring engine. Immediately, he opens his door and I'm relieved as he vacates my space. He's around the tiny car in a nanosecond, opening my side and offering me a hand to help me out. Biting my tongue, I hold back making a smart ass comment.

Instead of letting my hand go, he threads his fingers through mine as he sees me to my door, as promised. We are so fucked. Or maybe it's just me that's so fucked as my hand remains nestled and lost in his.

Letting go, he raises his finger to the top of my cleavage, touching it. "No mermaid. I like the mermaid. Why aren't you wearing my chain?"

"Because I fear I'll get tangled up in your chains." And with that simple admission, Hale Lundström finally got the truth he was hoping the third Manhattan would bring.

CHAPTER
Ten

The scent of eucalyptus and the fragrance of brightly colored perennials, mingled with hibiscus and bougainvillea crowd my senses, pushing forth memories of past stays here at the Beverly Hills Hotel. I didn't even realize I had these memory imprints, but the perfumed onslaught has deposited them at the forefront of my brain. I wonder if the memory imprint will change after this trip. Will smelling this medley of scents now forever be associated with Sierra Stone?

The schedule doesn't begin until tomorrow morning with breakfast in their President's bungalow. It appears that I am the only out-of-town client and therefore, the only one spending the night at the iconic *Pink Palace*. Kemp had extended the invitation to meet them in the Polo Lounge when I arrived, and I head there directly, after checking into my bungalow.

Strolling in, I scan the vast room in search of Kemp and Sierra and amongst a sea of California blondes, I spy her loose waves immediately and head in their direction. Kemp sees me approaching and stands to greet me. Sierra and the other man at the table look up. I catch her eye, hoping she can read my non-verbal body language telling her how happy I am to see her again.

"Bob Mannon," a fifty-something grey haired man of medium build stands, extending a hand.

I gently lay a hand on Sierra's shoulder to let her know that she doesn't need to get up to greet me and don't miss the opportunity to deliver a slight, yet imperceptible squeeze. It's been over a week since our last TFV1 meeting and I would kill to whisk her out of this lounge and ply her with Manhattans.

"We just ordered drinks," Bob informs me. "Let's get the waiter over here for you."

Facing Bob, I take a seat between Sierra and Kemp. When the waiter arrives and places a Manhattan in front of Sierra, I press my thigh against hers and inform the waiter, "I'll have what she's having," hoping she'll pick up the iconic line from *When Harry Met Sally.*"

When my drink comes, we toast.

"How's your Manhattan?" I ask, my voice low.

"Orgasmic," her reply is a little more than a whisper, accompanied by a smile, which elicits the same from me. She got the movie reference. The girl got my joke. It doesn't get better than that.

Immediately Bob takes center stage, first thanking me for my business, and then asking appropriate questions to better understand SpaceCloud past a basic understanding he's gleaned off the website and from a debriefing by his staff. Kemp can talk about my business nearly as well as I can and launches into a long term partnering conversation. By the time the waiter serves our third round of drinks, we've nearly inked a deal on some long term projects.

With just pretzels and nuts on the table, I'm wondering if Bob is going to move this little shindig into one of the on-site restaurants, but when he orders another round and turns his sights on Sierra, I know that is not in his plans for the evening. The only thing he wants to make a meal out of is her.

"You're really too pretty to be hanging around with this motley crew." He's expecting her to say something complimentary, which is a typical response to a line like this.

"I've been telling myself the exact same thing all night," she quips.

Although Sierra meant to deflect his oncoming advances with humor, she inadvertently took the hunt to a more challenging level. Like a big game hunter, Bob Mannon has every intention of dragging out the prize at the end of the evening.

Turning to me, Sierra looks apologetic, "Hale, I'm so sorry, but I'm going to bore you here with a little shoptalk."

"Not a problem." I know what she's doing. She's taking control of something uncomfortable and masterfully maneuvers it back to an appropriate and comfortable place.

"Bob, let me run you through the details for tomorrow that didn't end up on the itinerary." She smiles at him, "We have limos picking up each of the clients and bringing them here for breakfast at your bungalow. For that portion of the itinerary, you're going to get to see two of your favorite ladies, Monica Green and Beverly Binns. They are going to be here for the breakfast, as all the clients attending, with the exception of Hale, are all theirs."

"Oh Monica and Beverly, they're always a delight. They won't be joining us for the rest of the day?"

"No, we only have a table for ten, so it will be the three of us and seven clients. They are bummed, so expect to get an earful."

"Do we have a good table?"

This guy is shallow. What's important to him is bizarre. Sierra is trying to give him vital information, which if he'd only listen, would make him look very good to the clients he's about to meet.

"The best," Sierra placates him. "All the Presidents, dignitaries and movie stars have to pass our table as they make their way to where they will be seated and to the stage." She pauses and smiles, "Don't worry, I took good care of you."

I watch as she does a skillful job with this tool, but he has his sights set on one thing for the night. Getting between her legs. *Fucking douche.*

"We really need to take a close look at your future." Here it comes, he's starting to dangle the bait.

"Oh, and why is that? You want me to take out this guy here?" She smiles at Kemp, putting a hand on his arm.

Kemp laughs, but I can see he is uptight. He's letting Sierra handle it, as he should, but he's ready to leap if Bob bests her.

"We're a team," she tells Bob.

As the outsider, I feel as if I am watching a carefully orchestrated ballet and if the lead ballerina goes down, disaster will ensue.

Pulling a keycard from his pocket, he slides it across the table to her. "Bungalow 4."

Sierra laughs and slides the room key back. "If we're going to talk about my future it's going to be in your office when we're all sober."

"The best deals are made outside of the office," he informs her.

What a jackass.

"Great. Then the details of my next promotion can be hammered out at Peter Luger's over big steaks the next time I'm up at headquarters."

"Oh, so you like meat," the jerk replies.

I can see the muscles twitching in Kemp's jaw. Sierra is one of his people and his instinct is to protect, like a lion protecting one of the females in his pride from a dangerous interloper. I totally get that, but both his and Sierra's futures can quickly come to a broken halt in the next few minutes if he goes after this guy in the way I know he wants.

"I do," Sierra pauses, as she intently continues to stare into his snake-like eyes. "Except I'll be the one doing the stabbing."

Zing.

Slowly, it washes over Bob and when it finally permeates his brain, he breaks out into raucous laughter.

"Sierra, you are such a delight. So bright." And he reaches across the table to squeeze her hand and palm her his keycard.

"You are relentless," Sierra shakes her head, still trying to deal with this in a joking matter.

She slides the keycard back to her boss' boss.

"Relentless." She's still shaking her head.

I feel like such a douche watching this and knowing what a jerk I've been and what I've put her through. This scenario I'm witnessing is making me sick, and I realize that to be handling it with the dexterity and finesse that she is, comes from practice. And I'm angry and like Kemp, want to reach out and protect her. Which is ironic, because not all that long ago, the protection she needed was from me.

Being a business owner, I make the rules and don't have to live by anyone else's. Being part of a bigger structure, as Kemp and Sierra are, they have a game to play, to master, learning a set of skills that will insure their survival or demise, including landmines to be dodged.

I feel like I've just taken a masterclass in corporate battlegrounds and how to come out unscathed. Sierra is a warrior and I've just learned more in the past few hours on how to treat/not treat valued employees.

I am humbled and I am sickened and I want to get her out of here. Now. I can't watch another moment of this, nor can I let her endure it and not do anything. I can't do what I'd really like to do, because that would jeopardize her and Kemp.

I want to save her.

Pushing my jacket sleeve back, I look at the Breitling. "Wow, I didn't realize we'd been here for so many hours." Looking at Sierra, "What time do we start again in the morning?"

"7:30."

"Time changes always kill me," I lie and push my chair back to get up. Sierra and Kemp rise with me and both see the escape route illuminated in front of them, as they agree they're feeling the time change and that we've got a long day in front of us.

Bob falls into step with me, right behind Sierra and Kemp, as we exit the Polo Lounge. He doesn't even attempt to hide raping her ass with his eyes and I just want to smash him like the insect he is. We stop at the elevator and he brazenly slips the key into an outer compartment of her purse before bidding us goodnight and heading toward the path to his bungalow.

Sierra just sighs and shakes her head. Silently, the three of us enter the elevator. Staying near the door, I ask the others what floors they are on. Kemp is on two, Sierra three.

At two, Kemp bids us goodnight and I ride with Sierra to three. She turns right out of the elevator and I fall in step beside her.

"You're down this way, too." It's more of a statement than a question.

"No." I laugh.

"You're not?" She seems momentarily confused.

"You know I like to see you to your door safely."

She nods, smiling and then takes me totally by surprise, slipping her small hand into mine and threading our fingers together. It is an excellent déjà vu.

Digging out her key, she smiles up at me as she inserts it in the slot, "Thanks for walking me to my room."

I just nod. There's so much I need to say, especially after this evening, but the words are escaping me. Finally, "I like to know you're safe." It's my former military training and I want her behind that locked door, with the safety latch on.

Her smile is making me feel things that are so foreign to my M.O. and I want more than anything to go into the room with her.

Instead, I put my hand on her cheek and smile because her face actually fits into my palm. Leaning down, I press a kiss to the middle of her forehead. "7:30. I'll see you then."

And I wonder how I'm going to wait that long as I start my way down the long hall toward the elevator.

CHAPTER Eleven

y face fit into his big hand. Swoon. Just freaking swoon. Touching my cheek, I close my eyes, trying desperately to recreate what that just felt like. Falling back onto my bed, I actually laugh aloud. I'm thirty-three, not fifteen. Yet, I'm still holding my cheek.

"It's been too long since I've been laid," I mumble as I laugh alone.

"What a fucking night," I begin my monologue and yes, I am talking to myself aloud, like a crazy person. "Bob Mannon is a huge whore. What a fucking sleaze bucket. Kemp needs that man's job yesterday and that slimebucket needs to be put out to pasture with all the other useless old corporate whores. Robyn can keep him. Ewww. How the hell does she fuck him? God, I need a shower."

I think of poor Kemp. He looked like he was about explode a few times tonight. At one point, I actually saw Hale touch his arm to warn him down from blowing. I know he wanted to be protective, but it wouldn't have done either of us any good. Catch-22. So, I used humor to deflect it and made a joke out of it, but seriously, does he think I'd throw it all away for a ride on his nasty old dick? What a moron.

And the joke is, I was sitting between Kemp McCoy and Hale Lundström, two big handsome dark-haired, blue-eyed men who make women drool. And he really thought I was going to stroke his ego and his dick and lose all credibility with my boss and my client because of the title on his business card. *Asshole.*

Getting up off the bed, I grab my purse from the desk and fish out the keycard to Bob's bungalow. Ick. I'm getting the willies just touching it and spastically, as if it is singeing my hand, I toss it into my empty metal garbage pail. It lands with a ping.

"Score," I declare to no one and then laugh. "That's the only score you're getting tonight, mister."

Heading into the bathroom, I look at my eyes in the mirror and decide, I look really tired. It's 12:30 A.M., but my body thinks it's 2:30 A.M. Still feeling a little drunk and very hungry, I roam back out in search of the mini-bar and find it hidden in the armoire under the television. I always hate taking anything out of a mini-bar because the prices are so ridiculously inflated. But with no dinner in my belly and too much alcohol, I grab the large bottle of Fuji water and a package of chocolate covered blueberries, convincing myself they are significantly healthier than the Pringles, which I'm sure, like cockroaches, will survive the destruction of mankind.

Fishing around in my suitcase, I find my white tank top, aka pajamas, and pull off the clothes that I have been in for way too many hours. There is no better feeling in the world than ditching a bra at the end of a long day. My sigh of relief is loud and long.

Wandering back into the bathroom with my water, I check out the Natura products, opening the little shampoo bottle to take in the wild chamomile fragrance.

Should I shower now or in the morning?

Morning wins out as I peel my contact lenses from my very dry eyes and start to wash my face. The sound of the phone ringing literally makes me jump. It's so loud, reverberating off the bathroom tiles. I'm confused. It's then that I notice there is a wall phone mounted next to the toilet.

It's nearly 1 A.M. Who the heck is calling?

"Hello."

"Atta girl." It's Kemp.

I laugh. "Atta girl? Atta girl what?"

"Atta girl," he repeats and I remember he's half tanked. "You did good tonight. You really impressed the boss."

"Well, I don't know about that." I wonder if Kemp has spoken to him.

"Trust me, he's very impressed with you."

"Okay, well, that's good I guess." I really have no idea what to say about it and it's probably best if I keep my opinions to myself this evening. "I'm glad it ended up well and happy to see that Hale committed to additional business."

"Yeah, that was sweet. Susan and her team are obviously keeping him very happy."

"So it seems." I want to puke. Susan and her team? Seriously? Umm, Kemp, maybe me working with him on his special project has something to do with it. Geesh.

"Alright, well get some sleep," he mumbles and I picture that he has just rolled over in bed and will be passed out cold in a nanosecond.

Shaking my head, I look at the phone in my hand after he hangs up. He was checking up on me. Fucker. What he really wanted to know was if I were still in my room or had I gone to Bungalow 4. I know he was happy to find me in my room, but damn, he should have known I would never compromise my integrity and my career – and certainly not so openly. If I were going to do something stupid, I'd be smarter about it.

I finish up in the bathroom and consider searching the room for the room service menu to check out what they serve all-night, but decide it's probably best just to turn the air conditioning down really cold and get horizontal under the big, fluffy comforter.

Pulling back the blanket, I eye the bed adoringly. I need to curl up and catch a few hours sleep before tomorrow's gala event. Getting into the bed, I smush my body around on the crisp, cool sheets. My stomach growls at me and I tell it to shut up as I turn on my side and find the perfect position.

Knock. Knock. Knock.

"Hold on a second," I call out, startled. Jumping out of bed, a look through the peephole reveals Hale.

I'm in a white tank top and undies.

"One sec, okay?"

Shit. Flicking on the desk light, I head to my suitcase in search of my favorite travel sweats, a pair of loose gray sweatpants that have been a part of many hotel nights.

With a deep breath, I open the door, fully aware that I have no make-up on and I'm wearing a white ribbed tank with no bra (so he's not going to even notice the no make-up part).

"Hi," I greet him with a smile.

"Hi." Returning my smile, his eyes travel from my face to my breasts, where he gets an immediate hello from my damn too friendly nipples, who are showing off for him. *Look at me. No, look at me.* Realizing what he's doing, he looks back up, his face a portrait in guilt. Holding out a bag, "Nobody fed you tonight, so I brought you an Original Tommy Burger. It's meat you don't have to stab. You can just use your hands." His smile is so damn sexy and I know my nipples are now straining to be released from their tank top prison. *Let us go, bitch.*

Accosted by the luscious smell of greasy beef, I snatch the leaking bag from Hale's hand. I didn't realize quite how hungry I was until that very moment.

"I didn't know what you put on it, so there's ketchup, mustard and mayo in the bag."

My hand is already covered in grease as I begin to dig into the sack, "Ketchup and pickles," I mutter and then look up at him, "Would you like to come in?" I've got the burger in my hand now and I'm poised to go all cavewoman on it.

Laughing, "Thanks, but I think I'll let you enjoy your meat in peace. Night." He smiles and with a wave he is off down the hall.

Scarfing the burger down as the door closes behind me, I'm wondering if my ravenous attack on the greasy meal has grossed him out, causing his hasty departure or if my slutty little nipples did the trick with their aggressive behavior. Either way, I never said thank you or good night to him.

With hands cleaned and teeth rebrushed, I crawl back into bed and grab my phone to text him. *So, was he checking on me, too?* I wonder. A burger at this hour? Is he just taking care of me? Or was he concerned he wouldn't find me?

I didn't thank you for the burger or say goodnight.

Did you enjoy it? You gave me meat. Of course I enjoyed it.

Understatement! I didn't realize how hungry I was.

If I'd known we weren't eating dinner tonight, I would have taken you out for a proper meal. Hmm, sounds like a slam against Bob.

LOL. If I'd known we weren't eating tonight, I'd have been ditching out with you a lot earlier for a delicious burger.

Well, big day tomorrow, so get some sleep.

You, too. And thanks, Hale.

My pleasure. Good night, Sierra.

The sound of my cell phone ringing hurts my eyelids. And maybe my hair follicles, too. Everything hurts. Fumbling on the night stand, I grab the shrill devil and see it's Monica calling. But it's only 6:15 A. M. What the heck?

"Hello." Ugh, I sound so rough.

"We're here. What room are you in? We're coming up."

Swinging my door open a few minutes later, the harsh hallway light is too much to bear and I hide back under the covers the minute they are in the room.

"Rough night, Princess? You smell like a distillery." Monica is very amused by my appearance.

"Very nice," is Beverly's assessment as she stalks the room. "You management types get treated very nicely while us peons get to come for breakfast and aren't even invited to the main event." She references the fact that only Kemp, Bob and I will be representing the company at Universal Studios today.

"Give Bob shit about it when you see him later." I then proceed to tell them the story about the night before.

Jumping off the bed, Monica grabs the garbage pail. Pushing the Tommy Burger bag aside, she finds the key and screeches, "Noooooo."

Holding the sides of my pounding head. "He's gross."

"And Robyn fucks him." Beverly is shaking her head and then goes into her spot-on Robyn imitation. "He's my," pausing and in a breathy voice, "MEN-tor."

Even laughing hurts, but when the three of us are together I'm usually crying I'm laughing so hard, and this morning is no exception.

"When did you get the Tommy Burger?" Monica tosses Bob's key back into the garbage, its rightful place.

"Hale brought it to me last night."

"When?" Beverly needs facts.

"I don't know. It was late. I was already in bed."

"Oh my God, he was checking on you to see if you were with Bob." Monica gives Beverly a look.

"You think? I was wondering that last night. Do you think that's what he was doing?"

"Absolutely," Beverly concurs with Monica. "After you told him you don't shit where you eat, he had to make sure you didn't take off with the president when you wouldn't go with him. Male egos are so fragile."

"I can't wait to meet him. Go dry your hair and get dressed so we can get down to Bungalow 4, the Sex Palace." Monica shimmies.

Emerging from the bathroom, I'm dressed and ready to start this day that's been in the planning for months now. Dressed in a white silk tank, turquoise pencil skirt, Louboutins and for the first time in months, my mermaid necklace, with its new chain that drops the mermaid to the top of my cleavage. I know a certain someone will enjoy this outfit. Déjà vu.

"You look gorgeous," Monica gives me the once over.

"I can't wait to meet this Hale." Beverly is already at the door.

Grabbing my turquoise suit jacket, I sling it over my arm as we head out of the main building and down the path toward the now infamous Bungalow 4.

CHAPTER *Twelve*

Entering the bungalow, which is smaller than mine, I immediately search for Kemp and Sierra. Laid out on the dining room table is a breakfast spread of croissants and pastries, fresh fruit and two warming trays containing Eggs Benedict and breakfast potatoes. A sidebar holds coffee, tea and juices.

Heading straight toward the woman serving coffee, I grab a cup and make my way to the patio where Kemp is talking with an attractive short-haired woman.

He extends his hand and we shake. "I'm feeling last night," he admits.

Laughing, "I'm right there with you, bro."

"Catherine Wilpont, Hale Lundström." Kemp takes care of the introductions. "Catherine is VP of Marketing for Barrington Pharmaceuticals and Hale is…"

She cuts him off, smiling at me, "Yes, I know who Hale is. I've been following your company for quite a while now. I like to keep track of New England natives."

"Where are you from?"

"I grew up in Connecticut, but went to school in Boston. You're an MIT guy, right?"

Clearly she's read up on me. "For a short while, and then I joined the armed services."

"What an interesting path. I was boring. Four straight years at Harvard and then on to Penn for my MBA."

She just had to namedrop the schools as if I'm going to be impressed or find her more attractive.

Hearing a ruckus, I turn around and there is Sierra with two women, two very loud women. I recognize them from the picture in Sierra's house. These are the two she is laughing with in the photo.

Kemp lets out a chuckle, "Two of the quieter members of my staff have arrived. Excuse me."

Left with Catherine on the patio is not where I want to be. She's a space invader, standing closer to me than I'd like.

"I think I need a refill," I gesture with my coffee cup.

Sierra's back is to me as I walk through the French doors. The turquoise skirt and the Louboutins. She is killing me and it's not even 8 A.M. yet. Coming up close behind her, I lean down and whisper, "Sleep well?"

Turning, she smiles up at me, "Yes, my bed was very comfortable." She emphasizes the words, my bed, and I wonder if she's giving me a message about checking up on her. "I could, however, use about another six hours sleep."

She's wearing the necklace, and without thinking, I reach down and let the chain slip through my fingers. "I love the outfit," I say, loud enough for only her to hear.

"Me too," she smiles.

"Catherine," Sierra's friend calls out to the pharmaceutical lady and I'm brought back to Bungalow 4 from wherever I momentarily just went with Sierra. "Catherine, let me introduce you to my boss, Sierra Stone," the beautiful mocha-skinned woman announces.

"So nice to meet you. Beverly has told me so much about you and the innovative programs you've been running." Sierra touches my arm, "Have you met Hale Lundström yet?"

"Yes, we met a few minutes ago out on the patio." Catherine starts to move close to me again, but Beverly seems to have her own agenda.

"How come you are not my client? Don't you have a Los Angeles office? Everyone has a Los Angeles office." Taking my arm, she steers me away from Catherine to an auburn-haired cutie who is holding court. I recognize this woman as the third person in the photo in Sierra's house.

"Monica, look who I found," Beverly announces to the other woman.

Gasping, "You really are gorgeous." And she latches onto my other arm. "You know, you really should not be with that New York team. We are so much more qualified and creative. You should be working with us. And wouldn't you rather be working with Sierra than Susan? She dresses like a man." Monica finally takes a breath. "Let's get Kemp over here and do the deal. Kemp, why isn't he our client? Who do you even have him stuck with, that Robyn girl?"

And out of the blue, Bob Mannon appears, "Who mentioned Robyn? Now, she's a favorite of mine. So talented."

"He's her mentor," Monica whispers to me, choking.

"Talented at what?" Beverly has the skills of a ventriloquist. I swear her mouth didn't move.

Choking on a sip of coffee, the two of them look at me like we're sharing a secret. "So, aren't you enjoying working with Sierra?" Monica asks, but doesn't wait for an answer. "She's so brilliant. You're really lucky to have her."

"Yes, I am lucky," I concur and the look on Monica's face is saying, "Don't fuck with her, buddy."

By 8:30 A.M. the bungalow is filled with clients and staff as we finish off our breakfast and they break us up into groups of five and usher us off into two limousines.

Catherine has successfully taken on the role of my shadow and settles into the seat next to me in the back of the limo. Kemp is with us, but Bob and Sierra are in the other car and the thought of him anywhere near that turquoise skirt has my blood boiling. The only saving grace is that there is another female client in there with them and I'm sure he is turning on the charm for her.

Upon our arrival at Universal, Sierra immediately begins working with the event staff to get us credentials, check clearance and procure our itineraries for photos with the Presidents. Bob is signed up with Bush 1, Kemp with Bush 2, and Catherine with Clinton. I chose to forego the photo op.

"You're not going to have your picture taken with one of the Presidents?" Catherine is surprised.

I shake my head and grab a glass of champagne off a passing tray. "Would you like one?" I'm being polite, but I really need to ditch the shadow. Handing Catherine my champagne glass, "Let me go flag a waiter down for another." And I make my escape.

Wandering toward the secure area, I'm not surprised to see how tight security is with three former Presidents and the current seated President in attendance. In the secured area, I see the Joint Chief of Staff as well as the Secretary of Defense. They've really gone all out for this event. Even members of Hollywood's "A" list are in queue for a photo op.

"Lundström," a voice bellows from my left.

As I make my way over, that feeling of love and brotherhood floods through me.

"Dawg, look at you in your suit." A bear hug follows.

"I'm a guest today," I laugh.

"I'm just a working stiff. POTUS is mine today." Jeff Garber will always be a brother no matter how many miles or years separate us. Two missions together, one to Afghanistan, the other to Syria and there was never a better wingman. "Smitty's here too. He's got

Clinton. We'll get you back there to say hello. Damn, it's good to see you, bro."

Jeff's focus shifts to my left, "Well hello, Ariel." Garber is a big, good looking guy and when he sets his sights on a pretty lady, he's known to close the deal.

"Ariel?" she laughs.

I look down and he's talking to Sierra.

"Yeah, the Little Mermaid." He points to Sierra's necklace.

Laughing, "Ah okay." She finally gets it.

"Sierra, this big lug here is Jeff Garber." He needs to know she's with me and I softly touch her shoulder.

"Okay, I see you've already got a bodyguard, so I can't offer my services."

Sierra looks from Jeff to me, clearly confused by the conversation.

"Jeff and I did two tours overseas together," I explain.

"You've got the best guy here in the world to protect you," he informs her.

"Oh really." Sierra looks surprised.

"He'll keep you safe," he reassures her.

Sierra looks at me questioningly. I just smile and shrug my shoulders. I know she hasn't always felt very safe around me, so this really is ironic. With what I've been feeling for her being so far out of the safety zone, she probably does need a bodyguard to protect her from what I'd like to do to her.

Looking down at the thin white silk tank, I can't get the image out of my mind from just a few hours ago of what she looked like in that white ribbed tank and sweats. I wanted to pick her up and walk her back into that room, throw her onto her back on the bed and start sucking and biting those gorgeous nipples right through her tank top before lifting the wet shirt and feasting on them.

I am obsessed with her nipples. I'm an ass man. But I am totally obsessed with Sierra Stones' nipples and the need to suck them and hear her moan underneath me and to find out how wet that makes her.

"Hey, let's get you back there to say hello to Smitty." Garber pulls me from the abyss, which is good, because I've already got a semi from that little interlude.

"I haven't seen him in at least three years," I comment, trying hard to bring myself fully back from that visual.

Speaking into his right cuff, "Need coverage at four." A moment later a non-descript man in a dark suit falls in next to Jeff and we're on the move. Putting a hand lightly on Sierra's shoulder, I guide her to walk with us. Her look is silently asking me what is going on and I just smile and raise my brows.

"I can't wait to see the look on his face." Jeff claps me on the back. We're approaching the section cordoned off for President Clinton.

As we walk past the line toward the front, the woman behind the table begins to protest, her voice alerting the closest Secret Service agent, who takes one look at us and breaks into a huge smile, "No way." The shock on his face is priceless. "They'll let anyone into these things and I thought it was a classy event."

Smitty and I hug with an affection rarely seen among men. "Dude, what are you doing here?"

"I'm a guest," I explain.

Smitty nods at Sierra, "Ma'am."

"Ma'am? Now I feel old. I'm Sierra." She extends her hand.

"So you're with this guy?" he inquires, shaking her hand.

"Well, I don't know that I'm with…" she begins.

Smitty turns to me, "I'm glad. You deserve to be happy."

A raspy voice interrupts, "You weren't going to come say hello?"

I catch Sierra's face and her wide-eyed surprise as President Clinton approaches and I'm enveloped in yet another bear hug.

"Boys, you didn't tell me we'd be seeing Lundström today."

"We didn't know."

"Mr. President, this is Sierra Stone." It's a rush to be able to introduce her to a two-term President who knows me personally.

"Pleasure meeting you, Sierra." He shakes her hand. "I love that mermaid."

"Sir, we're falling behind schedule," the woman from behind the desk apprises President Clinton.

He actually looks afraid of this woman, "I need to get back to work here. Great to see you again, Hale. I've been following that company of yours." He claps me on the back. "Sierra, nice meeting you." He's giving her the full Bill Clinton charm and then looks back at me, "Take good care of her," he commands.

As we walk out, they make an announcement that the program will soon be starting and to please find our tables. Sierra is quiet as we walk back to the pavilion. Finally, as we're about to enter, she stops and puts a hand on my arm. "Hale, who are you?"

Shrugging my shoulders, I just smile. I would love to tell her who I am and everything about me. I'd love to confide what's shaped me, what drives me, what's happened in my life. I want her to know. And I've never wanted anyone to know.

"Seriously, Hale. What was that?"

"You know I'm former military."

"I know. But what did you do? Most former military do not get that kind of greeting from the Secret Service and former Presidents."

"I defended this country, Sierra."

She doesn't slip her hand in mine, just entwines our pinkie fingers. Smiling at the surprise move, I tighten my pinkie, giving hers a hug.

Leaning down, I whisper in her ear, "Now can I grab your ass?"

She elbows me laughing as we walk through the pavilion toward our table. I know I look like a loon with a huge smile on my face. So far this has been a good day. But all good things must come to an end. As we approach our table, I note there are only two seats left and they are on either side of Catherine.

I give Sierra's pinkie a final squeeze before disengaging and taking my seat on the other side of Catherine for the remainder of the afternoon and a very fitting and heartfelt salute to the men and women of our armed forces.

CHAPTER
Thirteen

*A*rriving back at the Beverly Hills Hotel, everyone is milling about in the lobby, still charged from the high of today's event. A new set of limos are waiting to take each of our clients back home, with the exception of Hale, who is staying at the hotel. I take the opportunity to speak one last time with each of them and thank them for being our guest.

Monica and Beverly have come back to the hotel to see their clients off and I'm still riding on an adrenaline high from the day. The entertainment portion of the program was beyond expectation; the perfect blend of comedians, politicians, singers and actors, but more than anything, being able to participate in giving thanks to our troops has elevated my spirits beyond belief.

After the last guest has left, we retire back into the Polo Lounge, where I vow tonight I will eat.

"Oh my God, I need to talk to you two," I tell the girls. "I have so much to tell you when we get to my room later." I can't wait to tell them all about Hale and the Secret Service and President Clinton. *What the heck did Hale do when he was in the armed services,* I wonder. The greetings he received were mind blowing, like he was some mega-hero.

Settling in at the bar, I order a Manhattan. Desperately, I want to go up to my room and change clothes. I've been in the Louboutins since early in the morning and my feet are numb, but

I'm going to stay in this outfit as long as I need to, because I know a certain someone loves it. Ugh. I'm pathetic, I know.

"Where is he?" Beverly whispers and I shake my head. "Probably in his room catching up on a whole day's worth of email." We're already on our second drinks and I can feel the effects of the Manhattan. The cherry looks lonely floating in the long stemmed glass.

"Invite him to dinner with us. He's so cute. Let's just make a reservation for four. We'll ditch these other losers." Monica is looking down the bar at Bob as she speaks.

"Let's just give him some time to work. The man has a business to run," I insist.

"Okay fine, but I'm getting something off the bar menu now because I'm not going to let them starve me the way they starved you last night." Monica scans the menu.

After the third drink, still no sign of Hale. "Okay, I'll text him." I acquiesce. "I'm starving."

Would you like to join a few of us for dinner? We're down in the Polo Lounge, but we're going to get out of here.

Twenty minutes later there's still no response.

"Do you think he fell asleep in his room?"

"I don't know," Beverly is getting cranky. "Let's just get out of here and get dinner."

I shoot another text to Hale, **Let me know if I can bring you anything.**

"I'm a little worried," I confess when we're already halfway through dinner and he hasn't responded. Then I wonder if maybe he got a call from Jeff and Smitty and went out drinking with them. They were all so happy to see one another.

Still, I can't get him off my mind. Wondering what happened and will I see him tonight. I want to see him tonight. When we walked through that pavilion today with our pinkies entwined, it just felt so intimate, like we were together and that it was our secret.

SLAVE TO LOVE

It isn't until I'm already in bed that my cell phone buzzes with a text message. Reaching for the phone, I have to read it twice. It was the last thing I expected.

Had to go back to New York. Great event today. Thanks for having me.

And what surprises me even more is my reaction when I begin to sob uncontrollably.

★★★★★★★★★★★★★★★★★★★★★★★★★

"He just left? That is so weird." I'm at breakfast with Monica and Beverly on the terrace of my room before leaving for LAX.

"He just left. 'Great event. Thanks for having me.' Totally cold." I'm obsessing over this. This is going to turn into a full blown, formal meeting of The Swale Club.

"Don't read into it. He could've been shooting off a note quickly as the flight attendants were closing the cabin door." Beverly is trying to be the voice of reason.

"Call Cuntessa," Monica suggests. "If she's over at his office today he would've totally talked to her about the event. It's already lunch time there."

"Okay, what should I call her about?" My mind has gone blank. "Oh, I know, I'll congratulate her on the new business Hale is giving her team."

Calling her cell, I put my phone on speaker so the girls can hear the conversation.

"Hey," she squeaks.

"Hey, so what is this shit? Now I have to do all your selling for you so that you can kick my ass in the rankings."

She laughs, "Kemp called me yesterday morning to tell me. We are already all over that one. Robyn and I are meeting with some of the new people this afternoon to start working on a preliminary scope of work document. I heard that was some event yesterday."

"Yes, it was amazing. Did Hale tell you about it?"

"No, Kemp did. I haven't seen Hale. I thought he was still in California with you guys."

"No, he left yesterday." I'm trying to act nonchalant, as if that were always the plan.

"And he came back to New York?" Susan is surprised.

"I was under the impression that was where he was going."

"Robyn, have you seen Hale this morning?" she asks. Robyn must be right next to her.

"No. And I just passed by his office and it's dark. He's not here today."

"Sierra said he came back to New York," Susan informs her.

"Well, he's not in the office today. Maybe he's with that pushy girlfriend of his."

I look at Monica and Beverly, my mouth hanging open, but make a quick recovery.

Laughing, a laugh I know is forced, but sounds authentic. "Oh no, he's got a pushy girlfriend?" My tone is saying, give me the scoop, let's dish on this man.

Susan is telling Robyn, "Sierra is laughing about the pushy girlfriend."

And in the background we hear Robyn say, "Oh God, yes. He is always running out of here to be with her. She's got him on a very short leash."

"Hey, I've got another call coming through, I'll call you guys back." And I disconnect the call.

"What a fucking douche dog." I'm so angry and hurt. "So, he thinks he's allowed to run around without his leash on when he's in Austin and pee all over my yard. Oh my God, that's gross." I sit back in my chair and close my eyes.

"He's a player," Monica surmises, "just another fucking player."

Tears are starting to roll down my cheeks. "I don't know why I'm so disappointed. It's just all about the chase for him."

"For most men," Beverly hands me a tissue.

"I am so glad I haven't slept with him. I don't even want to do that event of his with him. I wish I could just give him back to Susan and Robyn and let them deal with him." I know I'm sounding like an unprofessional brat, but my heart is bruised, feeling like someone punctured it and let all the hope run out.

"This doesn't make sense," Monica is shaking her head. "We watched the way he looks at you, Sierra. Beverly and I were talking about it after you guys left for Universal yesterday. He is totally into you."

"He wants to fuck me, Monica, that's all. I'm just a conquest, nothing more and then he goes home to his girlfriend." Dabbing my tears away, "I hate him."

Without even ever having slept with him, I feel more betrayed by this man than I ever have by any other with whom I've been involved. It felt like we were taking the time to get to know one another, personally and professionally. We were working together on projects like partners. We were building trust and rapport. It felt like we could be something really special.

But it was all a lie. The man I met who grabbed my ass in a boardroom was the real Hale Lundström.

And his friends told me that he would keep me safe. Ha. What they should have warned me was beware the traitor. Beware the cheater.

***

It's a really weird thing for me but when I am hurting, depressed, feeling out of sorts, Central Market, an upscale grocery story with the best, and sometimes weirdest, produce in the world, is a place I can go that instantly makes me feel better. I don't know if it's the bright, happy colors of the fruits and vegetables, the wonderful scent of organic herbs, the smell of fresh baked breads or perusing the cheese shop by country, but walking around in Central Market, it feels like the aisles absorb my pain, leeching the hurt from my veins and heart and leaving me numb, but in less misery.

I'm in the white wines of Southern France, a long, thin green glass bottle of Pinet de Picpoul in hand. I've been home a little over a week and trying my hardest not to think about him. We emailed one another twice during the week. Strictly business, there was no hint in any of the correspondence that we even knew one another.

He's over in the reds of Italy. Turned part way toward me, I can see his profile as he studies the bottle.

Son of a bitch is back, I think, after the stabbing pain in my chest subsides. An adrenaline rocket has just been launched into my bloodstream giving my heart a hard knock.

I'm on the move without thinking, it's just a gut reaction as I work my way toward his aisle.

"Guess you're back from New York, huh?" it's out of my mouth the minute I step up to him.

I'm not prepared for what registers on his face as he looks up from the bottle. His initial expression is filled with unabashed love and in a nanosecond I feel it deep in my heart. But just as quickly as it appeared, it evaporates into shock.

"Maggie?" He looks as if he's going to pass out, but recovers when he sees my reaction.

Maggie? Who the hell is Maggie? And this is not Hale. His features are rounder than Hale's. They look almost exactly alike, but I'd describe the man standing before me as really cute, while I'd use the term really handsome on Hale.

"You're Sierra."

Now I almost pass out. *Who is he and how does he know who I am?*

"I'm Noel. Hale's brother. I saw you leaving the office one day and asked who you were."

"Because I look like Maggie?"

He nods.

"I see." Looking down at the floor I'm filled with another wave of pain. Did Hale seek me out to work on the project with him because I look like someone named Maggie?

"Is he back in town?"

Noel shakes his head. "No, he's still up in New England."

"New England? Shows how much I know. I thought he was in New York."

Noel looks incredibly uncomfortable and I'm not sure why, but I need to get away.

"Well, nice meeting you. Say hi to your brother." I practically knock over a woman with a small child as I rush away.

Looking back, I see she and the little boy are now beside Noel and they are all looking at me.

CHAPTER
Fourteen

*S*tanding outside the Nantucket Angler's Club, I'm glad this weekend is almost over, although being on the island always fills me with an odd combination of dread and solace. As I walk the narrow cobblestone streets of the historic district, the old weathered-shingled homes and businesses provide a distinct comfort that harkens my earliest childhood memories, and the smells and feels of summer. There is no place I feel more at home than on the island, and especially, those ancient streets.

The Angler's Club is another story, with the exception of the dining room where, with just one taste of their fried clams and lobster salad rolls, I can be transported right back to the perfect moment in time, the time before the shrieking of gulls circling in the sky could be felt deep in my chest. Beyond a once a year feast on the lobster and clams, I never want to be here, for reasons obvious. Yet, I never want to leave as if somehow just my mere presence can rewrite history. I, who have become the master of creating something from nothing, am impotent in recreating the one thing that I long to create.

Changing one moment. One single moment.

And I hate the fact that I am a mere mortal who will never possess the power I most want.

"Nice ceremony today," Jim Shannon, the club's director of tournaments and awards, comes to stand next to me, as I look at the docked boats moored just the other side of New Whale Street.

I nod in acknowledgement.

"She would have been thirty-nine this summer."

Again, I nod in acknowledgement.

"Do you think Noel will ever join you?" Jim's known us since elementary school.

"With his teaching schedule and Oliver it makes it harder. It always falls smack in the middle of first semester for him," I wonder if I'm explaining or just making excuses for my brother.

"I think it would be good for him. He loved her." Always the sensitive one, his calling to be a pastor is probably something we could have correctly guessed at by the time he was eight.

"We all loved her." I keep staring at the boats in the harbor, because if I look at him, he might see the truth. And I can't let that happen.

"Yes. Yes, we did. We all loved her."

And so concludes my annual early fall sojourn to Nantucket to award the trophies in the Nantucket Angler's Club Margaret Myers Annual Memorial Shark Tournament.

On the road to Providence, not five minutes outside of Hyannis and Noel texts. I expect, "How did it go?"

I met Sierra. Is not what I expected.

Where? I feel the rush immediately in my blood stream.

Central Market. She was buying white. I was buying red.

How is she? Is she OK?

I don't know her. How can I answer that?

What did she say?

She asked if you were still in NY.

Was she wearing the mermaid?

What?

Necklace. Mermaid necklace.

I didn't notice it if she was.

You would've noticed it, brother.

Hale, what are you doing?

Driving. Thank goodness for voice to text.

No, what are you doing with Sierra?

Presently nothing. But maybe there is no time like the present.

She's not Maggie. Is this some passive/aggressive thing to get at me or work through your shit?

Geez, Noel. Sometimes a cigar is just a cigar. Let it go.

I called her Maggie by mistake. I was surprised and taken aback when she approached. Gut reaction.

You did what? Talk about passive/aggressive, bro.

Turning my phone off, I toss it across the passenger seat of the rental. That conversation is done. Totally done. I don't even want to see his next response.

He called Sierra, Maggie. Great. Just great. Lord knows what this girl thinks. No woman wants to be called by the name of another woman. And how the hell did Sierra meet Noel?

Fifteen minutes later, I reach for the phone and turn it back on, ignoring Noel's six subsequent texts, I hit send to a number programmed into my cell.

"Hi, I'm booked on a flight from Providence to New York City later this afternoon and I'd like to cancel that and rebook myself on a flight to Austin, Texas.

It's time to set things straight.

It's dark as I pull the Lotus into her driveway, but there are lights on in her house, so I assume I won't be waking her when I ring her bell.

"One sec," I hear from inside and see the sheer curtains move.

"Hale?" Opening the door, she stands there with her head cocked questioningly.

And I react. I react to the loose, wild hair, the tight, short jean cut-offs, the blue plaid cotton shirt over a white ribbed tank. I react to no make-up, no bra, no shoes. I react to Sierra Stone standing before me, caught totally off-guard.

Taking her face in both hands and backing her up against the door frame, I use my whole body to pin her in place. My mouth is on hers the minute she opens hers to speak, my tongue seizing that very moment to thrust in and claim what I have wanted for so long. What I have waited for.

There is nothing soft, sweet or sensitive about this kiss. This kiss was born out of a desire so deep that I can't shake it, as it bombards my every waking thought, and has distracted me for months to the point where I am living and breathing to take her hard and possess her. This has now gone well beyond want and need. Tasting her mouth has haunted me since she walked into the bar in The St. Regis rendering me practically speechless, this total anomaly with her sparkly Louboutins and fresh, clean face. This girl next door gone wild.

As the tension recedes from her body, her arms come up to wrap around my neck and she begins to kiss me back with the same fervor and intensity that I'm kissing her. I drop one hand from her face to the curve of her delectable ass. The ass that got me in so much trouble to start with. Wrapping my palm around the cheek, I squeeze it hard as I pull her against me, eliciting a moan that gets me even more excited. I let my fingers stray into her crack as my other hand drops to the other ass cheek. Rubbing her against me, her noises become more prominent, creating the beginning of our story. I need her more than she can imagine. More than she's ready to hear me tell her, as I simultaneously pull her against me and press her against the unyielding door frame, my tongue deep in her mouth, exploring and claiming. Finally.

I feel her legs part slightly and grind myself into the seam of her short shorts. The sound she makes is like telling a race car driver to start his engines. For all intents and purposes, I am fucking her, with all our clothes on, in the open doorway of her home. I press her to me tighter, my hard cock pointing up and making my jeans excessively tight. I need to feel her rubbing against it. So totally out of control as I start stabbing her with my hips, our kiss still not broken.

"I want you," I breathe into her mouth.

She answers with a moan that is more like a whimper. I swear she's close. And so am I. Like two fully dressed teens. And I feel like a teenager around her. I have to have this girl. I've somehow managed to get the crotch of her jean shorts moved to the side and my jeans are now pressing into her sticky lace underwear. I apply as much pressure as I can knowing she's about to start quaking.

Pulling her mouth from mine, Sierra buries her face in my shoulder. I feel her shuddering as we stand very still and quiet. Moving my hands off her ass, I wrap my arms around her tightly, holding her. Safe in my arms.

"That was for me," I whisper in her ear.

Pulling her face from my shoulder, she's searching mine, but I'm not quite sure for what. She looks sad. Her eyes look dispirited and my chest hurts at the thought that it's probably me that has made her feel that way. What we've got is convoluted and inconsistent. That's not the way to start a relationship.

Finally she speaks, "But was it for me?" She pauses and the pain is palpable. I don't understand what she's asking. "Or was it for Maggie?" And then it is clear. Crystal clear.

Caught off guard, my mind stumbles and reels. My first inclination is to hold her tighter, for fear of loss. I can't let her get away. Shaking my head, I stare steadfastly into her eyes. "For you, Sierra. That was for you."

I can tell she wants to believe me. *What the hell did Noel say to her?*

Leaning down, with one hand now on her cheek, I kiss her very softly on the lips, the polar opposite of the kiss we just shared. "I know we can't be anything until after TFV1. I understand that and I respect it and I will respect you." With my fingers gently trailing down her neck to the collarbone, I move to one finger as I trail down to her cleavage. "But until then, I want you wearing my chain, mermaid."

And with a pressing of my lips to her forehead, I am off, down the driveway and revving the engine of the Lotus as I head down the street.

CHAPTER
Fifteen

*M*y legs are shaking as I watch the tail lights of his car recede down my street. *What the hell just happened?* I think I just got 'taken'.

Closing the door, I walk back to my bedroom and pick up the necklace off my dresser. After fastening it around my neck, I sit down in the middle of my bed and grab my cell phone where I attempt to compose the perfect selfie of just cleavage, hair and the necklace. I want to show enough, but not too much. Sorry nipples, you don't get featured in this shoot.

The shot is perfect. Just enough to kill him. Not enough to end up on the internet.

I send the text without any message. Just the picture.

Don't take it off.

You're very demanding of me for someone who has a girlfriend. Are you this way with her, too?

I'm not sure I know what you're talking about.

Oh really?

Really.

Your girlfriend in New York. How would she feel about our kiss tonight?

That wasn't just a kiss, Sierra. We inked a deal. And I don't have a girlfriend in New York.

That's not what I've been hearing.

Well, you're hearing wrong.

Oh really?

Really.

There is silence for a while because I don't respond. Sitting in the middle of my bed, just staring at the phone, rereading his texts. Who is lying to me? Someone is lying to me.

Sierra

Yes

I don't have a girlfriend. I haven't had anyone in my life for a year and a half.

What happened to her?

She wanted to get married.

Is that a bad thing in his estimation? I wonder. Women who want to get married should be avoided at all costs?

You're not the marrying kind.

She had bad taste in furniture ;). And I don't know that I'm not the marrying kind, I just didn't want to be married to her. Ah, Miss New Hope. The Sticks hater.

Was that Maggie?

No.

That *wasn't Maggie? It was another one? How many are there?*

So, Maggie is another one?

No. It's not like that.

Then what IS it like, Hale?

Sierra, it's not a text conversation.

Oh God, that sounds serious.

A face-to-face?

Yes.

I have a feeling this is going to upset me.

It might. But not for the reasons you are thinking.

You really have me off balance, Hale.

That's why I had to push you against a doorframe.

He's funny.

Mmmmm

:-) That was hot.

It was.

Sierra, I don't want you to worry about anything. I'm not going to mess with you. Not personally or professionally. We never got to talk about Universal and the Polo Club. That first night was a huge eye-opener for me and I feel like shit for having put you through the things I've put you through. But I'm not like Bob.

I have so much to lose, Hale.

Your dignity is not something I'm looking to compromise. Tonight was the real thing, Sierra. Please believe that.

I want to.

I was out on Nantucket this weekend. Which I will tell you about when we're together. I was heading back to New York, I have meetings there this week, but I diverted to Austin.

To kiss me?

Yes. To kiss you. I'm flying back to New York first thing in the morning, but I'll come back to Austin next weekend.

He flew to Austin to kiss me. Holy cow, he's got my heart racing.

OK

Sierra

Yes

Are you OK?

No. Yes. I don't know.

Am I okay? Seriously, dude? You've got me so that I don't know whether I'm coming or going.

I'll be in Austin all next week.

I'm in Chicago next week.

Drats!

Can you get out of it?

No.

I understand. OK, well we have the weekend. And then again when you get back. We need to coordinate schedules.

Coordinate schedules. Did he just say that?

Hale

Yes

I'm going to miss you.

Ugh, I can't believe I admitted that. I am such a loser. Why did I give him that power? He who talks first loses. Basic rule of sales.

I miss you already, mermaid.

Oh wow. Serious sigh. It wasn't a power thing for him.

Mermaid. He's nicknamed me mermaid.

Touching the gold chain around my neck, I'm giddy with love, lust, whatever it is that has me feeling fifteen years younger than I am. Laughing aloud, I get this idea to send him a picture every day that we're apart showing the chain still around my neck ... still chained.

Oh Hale Lundström, I have a feeling resisting falling in love with you is a senseless waste of my energy.

If only we can hold out until after his event when our direct business relationship ends. Even though he's a client of my company, I'll have more latitude to explore this thing, this wonderful, confusing crazy thing between us, after his event is over.

CHAPTER
Sixteen

*I*t's a little before lunch on Wednesday when Susan and Robyn knock on my door.

"We heard the Universal event was pretty spectacular," Susan uses that as an opener as they both migrate into my office, uninvited, and take seats.

"It was definitely filled with Hollywood and political royalty." I know I'm smiling thinking back on the day and all its unexpected surprises.

"Was the entertainment good?" Robyn has her long, thick hair draped over one shoulder.

"It was. The combination of people they brought together to honor the troops was outstanding. The whole program was very moving."

"Did you meet Monica and Beverly?" There's snark in Susan's tone and I can feel the competitiveness creeping into the conversation.

"Yes, I did. They are a lot of fun, those two." I see a look pass between Susan and Robyn in response to my comment, which makes it the perfect time to fuck with them. "I'm wondering if we should just move over everything to the Los Angeles office."

Robyn's fair complexion turns a whiter shade of pale and she begins to stutter. "But aren't you..."

"I really hope you haven't spent your commission check yet." I take it a step further, looking at her, my demeanor totally serious.

Susan stiffens and is about to launch into a heavy duty sales pitch, which I'm not up to stomaching, so I smile and say, "Ha-ha. Gotcha."

Grabbing her chest dramatically, "Oh Hale, you practically gave me a heart attack." Robyn stands and comes around to my side of the desk. Latching onto one of my hands, she places it on her chest. "Feel that. Feel what you've done to me."

Taking my hand away, "Why don't you grab a cold water out of the refrigerator. It might help."

"I think I just might." Walking slowly so that I don't miss her ass which is packed into a short, tight, shiny red dress, she bends over to grab a bottle from the fridge's lowest shelf. From Susan's vantage point, she can't see anything; from mine, however, Robyn is treating me to more than a glimpse of her ass, as I've now got a full view of her commando recent Brazilian wax. Sitting back across the desk from me, she makes direct eye contact and smiles as she crosses her long legs.

And I'm very glad with my military training that I've got great basic instincts. There's not a chance in hell I'm going to fall for her game.

It's impossible not to see the irony in this. Here Robyn sits here across from me using every sexual weapon in her arsenal to try and ingratiate herself to me and get ahead in business. And halfway across the country, Sierra ripped me a new one, and rightly so, for potentially jeopardizing her career path, which she has diligently worked to forge.

Who would I want representing my company, championing the brand into which I've invested my blood, sweat and tears for years? Six months ago, I probably would have looked at Robyn and seen just bottom line numbers. No doubt this woman's attributes could close a lot of deals.

And I would have fucked her. On my desk. In front of the floor to ceiling windows. Against the wall. My hand would have been up her dress, fingering her under the table in meetings and business lunches. Just because I could.

What an ass I was. On the road to being a full-fledged Bob Mannon, just easier for me because I'm younger, better looking and I am the CEO. I'm ashamed. How did I get so far off track of what is right and wrong? It was so cut and dry when I was in the service. And when did I become so damn entitled?

After they leave, I call my personal assistant into my office.

"Blair, have a seat."

She looks nervous. "Is everything okay, Hale?"

"Yeah, yeah. Everything's fine. I need to ask you something and I need you to be really honest with me. There's a lot of people around me who will tell me what they think I want to hear, instead of the truth. I want the truth. Can you do that for me?"

"I'll try. Promise you won't fire me?"

Laughing, "It will probably get you promoted. My inner circle are my eyes and ears, Blair. How do you think I treat people? Be honest. Do not blow smoke up my ass and don't tell me what you think I want to hear."

"I think you are very professional. You drive people hard, but not unfairly and I think for that they respect you."

"How about women? How do I treat women?"

I can see the wheels spinning in her head as she's trying to formulate an answer.

"You don't have to be politically correct. Just tell it to me from the gut."

"Okay," she nods. "You're a guy's guy, Hale. Former military, CEO. Men respond to you. And you seem a lot more comfortable with guys. But it's not that you treat women badly. You're just more aloof with women. I don't think the women here feel close to you."

"Okay, I can see that," I take in her words. "Do you think women are given the same opportunity here at SpaceCloud as men?"

Hesitating, she has silently given me my answer. "Hale, I'm your only female direct report and I'm your personal assistant."

"Pretty lopsided, huh?"

"Yes, I think so," she agrees. "If we're going to be honest, it's a boys' club." She's mirroring my board's assessment. "But I do think people genuinely like working here. It's a great work environment, the culture is good."

"What could make it better?"

"I know you like to keep yourself somewhat detached, you are the CEO. But I think you need to reach out a little more. Let loose, have some fun with everyone once in a while. Bond with your staff in a non-work environment."

"I can do that."

"I think the staff would love that. There's a huge group going out tonight to Mexican Radio for Margarita's and Mexican food. You should join us."

"I've got a conference call at 5 P.M., maybe I can meet up with everyone afterwards."

"Hale, the whole staff will really love it."

"Okay, I'll try and make it."

Margaritas and Mexican food. That seems like an Austin, Texas thing, not a New York City thing. But it will be fun to shock the staff with an appearance.

It's a little after 6:30 P.M. when I enter the restaurant, Mexican Radio, in NoLita, the neighborhood just north of Little Italy. Entering the venue's warm, inviting atmosphere, my eye is first caught by the colorful Mexican folk art throughout the restaurant, the neon pinks, greens and yellows, then my eye roves to the crowd of patrons in the bar area. At least twenty of them are on my staff. And it appears that Susan and Robyn have joined them.

Tipping a Margarita glass at me, Blair uses her other hand to pull up the corners of her mouth, reminding me to smile. I laugh. Am I really that much of an ogre?

"Boss, the rumors were true, we didn't believe them," Annette from accounting ribs me. "I said, 'I'm not getting on a ferry back to Staten Island until he shows up'."

I laugh with her, "I bet these folks thought you were going to have a long night here."

I see Blair is watching me talk to three women from accounting and she gives me an approving nod.

"You're so handsome. Why aren't you married?" Carmela from accounting asks. "My daughter is a real looker. She's twenty-six and is a paralegal at a very good firm."

This is why I don't do this, I think. *I would kill to be running the SkyTrack over at Level 9 right now.*

"Carmela, she sounds way too good for me," I say with a laugh.

Out of the corner of my eye I see red, so I know Robyn is approaching.

"What are you drinking?" Susan asks, as she pulls up right beside her colleague.

"You know what, let me talk to the bartender to open a tab for everyone. What are you two drinking?" They join me over at the bar where the bottles are on recessed shelves under cobalt blue lights, adding to the restaurant's warm and festive mood.

"We'll have two Margaritas rocks, one with salt, one without and I'll take a bourbon Manhattan up. And I'd like to open a tab for everyone in this group over here." Blair joins us, along with some of the programmers and Annette and her accounting crowd.

"Isn't he handsome," Carmela starts in again. "Hale, do you have a girlfriend?"

I'm looking at Blair as she makes a comical face at me. I never talk about my personal life with staff and today she called me aloof and detached. Scanning the faces as they wait for my answer, it occurs to me that these people give me the better part of their days and while I compensate them handsomely, provide good benefits and a pleasant work environment, I really do owe them more than that.

"There is someone very special in my life." It feels good to admit that truth.

"Call her. Have her come join us," someone suggests.

"She doesn't live here in New York. I split my time between here and Austin and she's out there."

"You have no pictures of the two of you in your office," Susan notes.

Playing dumb, "You know you're right. I need to change that."

"You need pictures of all of us. We need selfies with you," Carmela suggests as she and Annette flank me, holding a cell phone high. "My daughter is going to be so jealous." Carmela elbows me and I actually laugh. These women are hysterical.

"What about your husband," I tease, taking a sip of my Manhattan. The cherry is only partially submerged and just the thought of feeding it to Sierra makes my cock twitch.

"Twist my arm, I need one of the two of us to share with my husband. He can't get mad, you're the boss and you pay for our medical insurance," she laughs and holds the camera high, putting her cheek next to mine.

I look over and Blair is shaking her head at me approvingly. Apparently I'm doing a good job of shedding the reputation of Mr. Aloof.

"C'mon Annette, let's get one for your husband." I put an arm around her. "Tell him he needs to take you out for a night on the town or you're going to be forced to run away with the boss."

"Who knew you were so funny, Mr. Lundström." Annette clinks her beer stein to my Martini glass.

"Mr. Lundström is my father." I wink at her. "You need to call me Hale."

"Would you take our picture?" Robyn asks Annette. Handing over her cell phone, she changes places with the older woman and struts between my legs, taking a seat on my left thigh, where she crosses her legs with great flourish.

I'm in shock. Literally in shock. We both know she's commando and her bare, hairless everything is on my pants leg. Turning to look at me with a smile, she grabs the cherry from my Manhattan and holds it before her lips as Annette shouts, "Perfect" and then she pops it into her mouth with a self-satisfied look.

Practically pushing the woman from my lap, I catch Blair's face in time to note her shocked look. With a deep exhale of breath to keep my cool, I place my molested drink on the bar, excuse myself and head toward the men's room. With a glance over my shoulder, I motion for Blair to follow me.

"Hale, Robyn is not wearing underwear." Blair seems not quite sure how to react.

"I know." My face mirrors her reaction. "Do me a favor and run interference for me tonight. If you see her hanging on me, get in between. Or send Carmela and Annette over."

"Will do. Oh my God, you need to get those pants to the dry cleaner ASAP," she laughs.

"What are you kidding, I'm going to burn them. So, you really wanted me to go out tonight?"

"You're doing great, boss." She pats my arm. "With the exception of having some nasty hoochie rubbed on your leg, you're doing great."

"You can't make this shit up," I laugh, as we walk back to the bar and I insert myself into a group of techie boys.

"Do you want me to grab your drink off the bar?" Blair points to my half full Manhattan still sitting on the blonde-wood bar.

"That's not going anywhere near my lips." The thought of Robyn's fingers in my drink pisses me off.

"Why don't I get you a fresh one," Blair offers. "One that's, ummm, *untouched*," she laughs.

Laughing, "Remind me to give you a raise."

"You really are a nice guy." She smiles and heads to the bar to order me a new drink.

CHAPTER
Seventeen

ouring over my reps sales reports, trying to decipher if the deals are real and will come to fruition before the end of the calendar year, or if they are fairy dust, just figments of the reps imaginations, is not my favorite activity. Several times a year, senior management tasks us with putting together the quarterly stack rankings, where I have to rank my sales team from top to bottom. This is an exercise everyone in management hates. Your bottom players are always vulnerable and usually this activity takes place prior to a layoff.

I always have terrible guilt about the people I have to rank at the bottom. Especially if they have families. Delivering bad news never, ever gets easier. Sitting at my dining room table, I recheck all the numbers I've calculated. This is not something you want to get wrong. It's actually not something I want to do at all.

Stretching out my arms and shoulders, I think maybe I'll take a break and shoot my daily photo for Hale. It's become quite the joke between us as I place the mermaid in a different position every night. Just as I reach for my phone, it rings. Perfect timing for a break.

"Hey Monica," I answer the phone, "what's up?"

"Do you fucking believe the photo that skank had the nerve to send us?" I hear the indignation and anger in her voice.

"What photo?" I have no clue what she's talking about.

"You haven't seen it?" Her voice rises an octave.

"No, sorry. I've been working on something for Kemp."

"Check your texts. Now." The now is emphasized.

"Okay, hold on." Pulling the phone from my face, I go into my texts. There is only one unread one. It's from Robyn Stiles. *That's odd,* I think. *Robyn's never texted me before. Why would she be texting me?*

It's a group text to me, Monica and Beverly. **Hands off, girls. He's right where he belongs. #Mine** Below the text is a photo.

"Hold on," Dropping my phone to the table, I dash to the bathroom, sinking to my knees. My dinner quickly makes its way back up, as I sob. I'm not sure if I'm sobbing from the photo I've just seen or because I'm throwing up and that always makes me cry.

Robyn? Seriously Hale? Seriously? You big fucking player. Robyn? Oh God, my heart hurts. I let you in, thinking we could be something. Share something. What a fucking mistake that was.

"Oh crap," I realize I've left Monica on the phone. I don't even want to touch my phone. I don't want to see that picture again.

"Are you okay?" she asks.

"No. I'm really not okay. Fuck. I really was falling for this guy, Monica, in a way I haven't fallen for anyone in a long, long time. And he's just a big fucking pig. It's one thing after another with him. Then he comes back with the trust me stuff, so I do and then it's another thing. It's just too much."

"Why would she send this to the three of us? That is what I don't understand."

"I don't know." A fresh round of tears begins.

"I know this is probably not the best time to bring this up, but can you see her vijayjay?"

"What?" I screech and look at the photo on my phone. "Hold on, I'm going to mail this to myself and look at it on my PC."

Opening the photo, I gasp. "Someone needs to tell her that pink and red clash." There it is, on display, right under the hem of her red slut dress, a very pink body part.

"Ewww," Monica starts laughing, "she's got a really nasty looking one. That is the ugliest vagina I've ever seen."

Laughing through my tears, "It really is. It's as nasty as she is." Looking at the picture I notice she has the cherry from his Manhattan and that hurts more than anything.

I thought that was our thing.

"What a dick, Monica. I am really glad I didn't sleep with him. He's just a big playboy. Love the one you're with must be his motto. I would love to pull myself off his project. Wait, didn't I just say that like, umm, yeah, recently. He is just trouble."

"I just don't understand why she sent it to us and with that message. It's just weird."

"Hold on, Monica, Beverly's calling." I click over to the other call. "Yes. I saw it," is how I answer.

"She is a disgusting tramp."

"So is he." I choke on my words.

"Why did she send this to us? I don't understand why she sent this to us."

"I don't know. Maybe it's the modern version of an engagement announcement." The sarcasm more than drips from my words, it gushes.

All I know is that for me it's the end of something that was clearly never meant to be. If I needed a sign to say, stay focused on your dream, stay focused on that promotion, this was certainly it, delivered in flashing red and pink neon lights.

⋆⋆⋆⋆⋆⋆⋆⋆⋆⋆⋆⋆⋆⋆⋆⋆⋆⋆⋆⋆⋆⋆⋆⋆

Hey, where's my mermaid pic?

I'm jostled from my wine-induced sleep by the text tone on my phone. I fell asleep after a full blown meeting of The Swale Club and three glasses of a salmon-colored, iced cold rosé from the south of France.

Is he joking? What a douche.

Looking for your mermaid? I don't know. Is she sleeping next to you?

Huh?

Who's next to you tonight, Hale?

Same as every night, Sierra. No one.

Mmm-hmm. Yeah, right.

What are you talking about?

This

And I send the picture Robyn shared.

There's no response from him.

And then my phone rings. Decline call is one of the options. I gladly choose it, stabbing the touchscreen.

He follows it with a text. **C'mon Sierra, answer your phone. We need to talk.**

Do you really think I want to talk to you? Seriously? Goodnight Hale. I turn my phone off and crawl back under the covers, wiping the tears away as I unsuccessfully attempt to fall back to sleep.

For one brief, shining moment I'd actually let myself dream a new dream. The man *and* the career. But that dream was merely a fantasy.

CHAPTER
Eighteen

I drove past her house a few times over the weekend. No lights on. No car in the driveway. Wherever she was, she wasn't home. I even checked late Sunday night, thinking she'd be back from wherever she'd gone and getting ready for the work week and her trip to Chicago. But she never returned.

The woman seriously does not want to see me.

Talk about feeling like a whacked out stalker. Between that and looking at pictures of that heavenly neck that is just begging to be between my hands, my mouth finally claiming what needs to be mine.

I hate this silence. I'd forgotten that pain grew in the emptiness, thriving on the hollow echoes that replaced the connection and laughter. The hurt is distracting and permeating. It's taking over and I can't let that happen. Especially not now.

We are only a little over a month out from TFV1 and it's a bit late to replace Sierra and get someone new up to speed. With the sensitivity of the event, logistics and discretion needed, she and I need to get our shit together so that we can work side-by-side as professionals. I've just spent the last ten days hoping she wouldn't bail on the project, but she hasn't and that just reaffirms to me her professionalism, and if I'm really honest, corroborates her reason for not wanting to mix business and pleasure.

I can understand why she doesn't want to talk to me. I really can. Just days after the intimacy we shared in her doorway, I'm photographed in that picture. That damning picture. I literally groaned out loud when I saw it. It was bad. Nightmare, bad press bad. Robyn's legs were loosely crossed and you could see everything. Every fucking thing. And that bit with the cherry. Sierra probably thinks the cherry is a move I pull on all women.

And it's not. It's *our* thing. Hers and mine. No one else's.

Why Robyn would send that to Sierra is beyond me. I don't think I've given off any vibe about how into Sierra I am. I've been discreet. I keep my personal life compartmentalized; that's a well-known fact. Now I'm questioning, do I get some love-sick look or a giddy tone to my voice when her name is mentioned? Do I have some kind of 'tell' that Robyn picked up on? I am falling hard for Sierra, that's obvious, but I think I've done a good job of keeping that to myself. So good, in fact, that even Sierra doesn't know how obsessively crazy I am about her. She is never far from my conscious thoughts. Ever. Even in business, I find myself wondering what she would think of things, how she would react, would she like it, dislike it, what would her strategy be?

My thoughts of Sierra Stone are permeating both my business and personal world and that never happens. There's girlfriends and there's business and they are distinctly compartmentalized. I keep them very, very separate. The closest they will ever become is a woman accompanying me to an event or to a dinner. But with Sierra, she can talk to me about my business, strategize with me, she "gets" it. There are no boundaries as we easily skip back and forth, encompassing the different facets of my entire world. And those no boundaries keep getting me into trouble.

I want her back. She needs to know what happened at Mexican Radio. And she needs to know that I would never betray her. I need her back.

Strategically walking into the boardroom a few minutes late, I know that everyone will already be there, seated and waiting. I haven't talked to her in nearly two weeks. Our correspondence have all been through email and very cut and dry, totally professional.

"Good to see everyone." I make eye contact with everyone around the table as I sit down. "So, we are in the home stretch and there are a lot of logistics to work out. Let's get to it."

In front of me sits a handwritten list. No copy of my notes exists on a computer anywhere. When I'm done with this, it will be destroyed. It's amazing how Special Services training remains some of the most useful skills I possess, no matter what turn my career has taken. It's best that certain things don't exist, just as I partook in certain missions that I was never on, for they never existed and our government would unequivocally and vehemently deny them. As would I.

"Anthony," I address my Security Chief, "were you able to get hold of Garber?" I notice Sierra look up at the mention of Jeff's name. Her eyes wide at the ramification.

Nodding, "Yeah, he hooked me up with their division chief and they'll be able to provide an additional seven in personnel for the entire length of the event."

Committing to memory what I can't commit to paper, I make my way around the table and receive updates from the staff. With several of the participants, there will be additional one-on-one conversations on topics that can't be discussed in a group forum.

When I reach Sierra, she reports succinctly on her outstanding agenda items, directly holding my eye contact and not backing down.

"Will we have representatives from the tech incubators presenting Saturday afternoon?"

"Yes, two have committed, one of those being UT."

"Excellent. Thanks, Sierra."

And I move onto the next person at the table, but my attention is fixated on Sierra's neck. Her bare neck. She's not wearing the mermaid and I know that was a conscious choice. Her message to me is, the chain has been broken, I am not yours, Hale.

Yeah, Sierra. I hear you loud and clear. Message received.

As the meeting ends, I catch her eye. "Stop by my office." I stride out of the conference room not looking back.

I'm at my desk going through email when she knocks on my door. "Come in, close the door behind you." When she does, I direct her to have a seat. We just look at one another. It is so good to see her, but I need to destroy this wall between us and I will do so if I have to rip it down brick by brick by brick with my bare hands.

"I'd like to talk to you about that night."

"You don't owe me any explanations, Hale." Sierra is shaking her head.

"Will you give me the courtesy of listening to me?" my voice comes across a little sharper than intended.

"Sure." She seems resigned.

"My PA in New York, Blair Cummings, you've spoken to her, right?" Sierra nods. "Blair and I had a conversation earlier that day about the corporate culture at SpaceCloud. Basically, she told me that I'm not a very accessible person."

"Well, you made up for that." Her attitude is purely defensive.

I ignore the barb and continue, "She told me that I'm aloof and disconnected from the staff. I wasn't totally surprised to hear this because I'm a person who likes to keep things separate. It's how I best cope."

"Really, I see you as just the opposite. You certainly haven't respected work and personal boundaries with me. And it doesn't look like you did with Robyn, either."

"That's not true. With you it is, I'll give you that. My situation with you is very out of character for me. Anyway, Blair said they were going out for drinks to some Mexican place and asked me to join them. I got there a little late and was having a drink and talking to two of the women from the accounting department, Annette and Carmela. They are both probably close in age to my mother and they're from Staten Island and very funny. They were taking selfies with me to get their husbands jealous or something, when Robyn handed Annette her phone and asked her to take a picture. The whole thing happened so fast and I practically threw her off my lap and that's it, Sierra. That is the whole story."

"She took your cherry."

"I know. It really pissed me off." Amazing that the cherry was the first thing she responded to in that story. But I'm really not surprised. That cherry in Robyn's hand was a smashing invasion of what Sierra and I had been sharing. One little Maraschino cherry represented so much more.

"Why did she send it to us, Hale?"

"Us?"

"Yes. She sent it to me, Monica and Beverly."

"Seriously? That's really weird. She was trying to send you guys a message." I pause and think, "What did it say? Do you remember?"

Digging her phone out of her purse, Sierra scrolls and passes it across the desk to me.

Hands off, girls. He's right where he belongs. #Mine

Reading it over a few times, I try and recreate that day in my mind. And then it hits me and I start to laugh. Son of a bitch. I did cause this. All this heartache. Hers. Mine. This horrible silence.

"What's so funny?" She doesn't look amused.

"It is my fault. Holy shit, I totally caused this. It really is my fault."

Sierra looks confused at my confession.

119

"Earlier that day, Susan and Robyn stopped by my office. They were asking me all about the Universal event and I was telling them how fantastic it was." I stop. "It was, Sierra, it was fantastic and because I'm ex-military, I can tell you just how meaningful and perfect it really was. Anyway," I continue, "I mention that I met Monica and Beverly and how much I liked them and then said that I was considering moving all my business to your Los Angeles office." Again I stop, this time to smile at Sierra, "I did it just to fuck with them because I know how competitive those two are with your team and I wanted to get a reaction."

For the first time all day, Sierra's face breaks into a smile and I feel it, I actually feel the movement of her cheeks in my heart.

"I even went so far as to tell Robyn not to spend her commission check yet," I can't help but chuckle. "I know that was pretty evil, but it was fun. Sierra, that is what this message and picture are about. She was insecure about what I said about pulling the business from her. Who knew she'd turn around and pull a stunt like this?"

"Hale, that picture." I can see in Sierra's eyes how haunted she is by that.

"Trust me, I didn't appreciate her commando bottom on my leg. That picture personally hurt you, it hurt us and if that were ever to show up on the internet, well, it's not a good representation of who I am." Smiling at her, "And I had to burn a perfectly good pair of pants."

Reaching across the desk, I put my hands out, palms up for her to take them. Looking at them for a moment, she gently lays her hands in mine. "Do you believe me?"

Nodding, "I do. The whole thing fits. It makes sense."

Squeezing her hands, "What do I have to do to get you to trust me?"

"I don't know. I want to, but look at you."

"What does that mean?" I'm perplexed by her statement.

SLAVE TO LOVE

"You're you. You're kind of this international figure. Magazines write about you. You have some kind of clandestine military background where Presidents know who you are. They follow you and your business. You might just be a little too, what's that saying, rich for my blood."

I'm shocked. Clearly we've spent too much time apart and she's had way too much time to think.

Giving her hands a last squeeze before I let them go, I come around to her side of the desk and sit down in the chair next to her. Taking her hands again, gently I rub my thumbs over her soft skin. Her eyes don't look as open as I've seen them in the past. I need that door to reopen. *Let me in, Sierra.*

"You started out by saying 'You're you' and out of everything you said, that was where you nailed it. Everything that followed that is just stuff, details to sort through. I want you to trust me, Sierra. How do I get you to trust me?"

As she looks at me I realize there is a story there, a story she is not yet ready to share. That will only come with time. I want to know everything now. That's the only way to save her, but she has to choose to share with me of her own volition.

"I miss your nightly pictures, mermaid."

"Hale..."

"Shhh." Bringing her hands to my face, I kiss the center of each palm. "I know what we have to be for the next few weeks until the event is over. I respect that. Universal was an eye-opener for me, but I watched and learned. You handled yourself with so much finesse and grace. You've worked hard and with integrity and it makes me look at things differently. You've set the benchmark and you've set it high."

"Thank you." And with a small smile, "So, would you think less of me if I kissed you?"

Sitting forward in the chair, I laugh. "Expect the unexpected from you."

As she leans in with a smile, I cup her small face with my right hand. "You're safe with me, Sierra. Don't run. Please don't run."

"I just don't want to ruin everything."

Kissing the edge of her mouth, "I need you to have faith that this will all work out. Can you do that?"

"I can try."

"That's my girl."

Her look is priceless. *My girl.* I place a small kiss on her lips, "Want to hear something else?"

"Only if it's good."

"It's very good."

"Okay, then."

"That same night, with Susan and Robyn right there, one of the ladies in accounting asked me if I had a girlfriend."

"What did you tell her?"

"I told her the truth."

"And what is that?"

"I told her that there's someone very special in my life. And they said, 'Call her. Have her come meet us.' And I told them I can't, she lives in Austin."

"Anyone I know?" Sierra looks most amused.

"I don't know, you might know her. She's a really pretty, intelligent blonde. Very driven. I'm working with her on an event and she's got amazing, kissable lips." Putting my lips close to her ear, "And nipples that like to torment me."

CHAPTER Nineteen

"Where have you been, Bev and I have been trying to reach you?"

Putting my cell phone onto speaker, I bring Monica into the bathroom with me so that we can talk as I wash my face and brush my teeth.

"I was having dinner with Hale."

"Dinner with Hale? Oh my God, we have so much to talk about."

"What's going on?" Looking in the mirror I can see how much happier I look. One conversation that set everything straight was like lifting a hundred pound blanket of gray gloom. Being out of sorts with Hale causes this odd, empty pain. Everything feels out of sync and I'm too distracted to function properly. I hate the feeling.

"The rumor mill is spinning wildly. Have you spoken to Kemp?"

"What's the rumor and no. He was flying back to New York today. He's been at that seminar in Seattle all week."

"Rumor is Mannon is going to announce his so-called retirement soon and will be out the door December 31st."

"Where did you hear it? I mean, we've been hearing this same shit for eighteen months now, when is he just going to fucking leave already?" Toweling off my face I leave it a little wet and grab my Vitamin C serum. With a squeeze to the rubber tip of the little medicine dropper, I release some onto my fingers and start to massage the slightly viscous liquid into my cheeks. "Just think, Robyn will need to find a new mentor," I laugh. "So, where did you hear this tidbit?"

"From my little buddy in HR."

"Ohhh, he's usually a good source. So maybe this is going to happen."

"Oh my God, you are going to be promoted," she practically sings the words.

Pulling my tank top over my shoulders, I take a seat in the middle of my bed. "We don't know that. It really could go either way with me and Cuntessa or they could totally fuck both of us and bring someone in from the outside. And if they did, you know it would be a man."

"Ugh, I know. They always find places for the boys, even if they are incompetent. Seriously though, what will you do if you don't get it?"

"Start looking immediately for a new job. Someplace where there is room for advancement and opportunities for women." Opening the drawer of my nightstand, I pull out a small white box and lift the mermaid from her bed of satiny, cloudlike billows and fasten it around my neck, patting her down in place at the apex of my cleavage.

"You are so driven."

Smiling, "Hale used that word today to describe me, too. But you know I have to be, Monica. My dad left us high and dry after making the commitment to support his family so that my mom could stay home and raise us. He just unfortunately made that commitment to more than one family. I will always be able to take care of myself and my family. That can never be left to anyone else to make good on that promise."

"Speaking of Hale, what happened with him?"

I recount the story for her of Robyn and the selfie, "You know, I actually believe him. It all fits. Do you believe him? Was he believable when he was telling you?" Monica usually has a really good bullshit meter.

"I do. The whole thing makes perfect sense and he seemed really sincere."

"Sierra, you know I'd tell you if you were chasing your tail, but I think this guy is crazy about you and I think that you two make a really good pair. You're both so serious about business and so smart. And you look good together."

"I don't know about that. After Googling him and seeing pictures of him with model-types at all these events, it's intimidating. I try not to let it get in my head, but it's hard. He keeps telling me to trust him." I realize I'm holding onto the mermaid when I say that.

"Well, you'll see if he earns it. What he doesn't know about you is that your trust issues with men go back to when you were just six. That's a lot of fucked up to fight, Sierra."

Sighing, "I know. I wish he'd just leave me to my career." I get under the covers and turn off the light.

"Is that what you really wish?" Monica is not buying my story.

"No, I really wish I wasn't so fucked up. I wish he wasn't a colleague. I wish I trusted him. I wish all these stupid things to make me not trust him, like sluts rubbing their hoochie on his legs, would stop happening. And I wish he were falling in love with me."

"Really on the last one?"

"Yeah. I feel like I'm a train barreling down these tracks on a mountainside. Totally out of control. I'm falling so in love with him and I can't stop it. I'm so far out of my comfort zone and I'm really afraid I'm going to end up there alone." Tears are springing from my eyes but I'm trying to keep them out of my voice.

"You are beautiful, smart and successful, so don't sell yourself short. I don't think he knows what to do with you, Sierra. I don't think he's used to women who can challenge him in the way that you do. And face it, girlfriend, you are a bit of a challenging personality. So now the only question that remains is this, is Hale Lundström up for the challenge?"

"You are so good for my ego."

"You know me, I only speak truth."

"I hope you're up for it," I later whisper to no one as I approach the edge of sleep and it welcomes me into its fold.

* *

"If you invite me over sometime, then I can stop showing up unannounced." Hale is smiling down at me, the sun low in the sky behind him making me squint up at him.

It's Sunday morning. 8:30 A.M. My hair is a tangled rat's nest. No make-up. White tank top (No bra. Nipples plotting devilishly) and a pair of UT sweat-shorts that says TEXAS across my ass.

Lifting up two bags to show me, he thrusts one at me and I take it to the dining room table.

"You're not a morning person, are you?" his smile tells me he is most amused.

Unloading the bag, there are two large coffees, I pop the lid of the first one, then the other and hand Hale the black coffee. Two croissants, four breakfast tacos, a bag of beignets and a large container of fresh-squeezed orange juice. Grabbing plates, glasses and utensils from the kitchen, I bring them out to the dining room table and sit down across from Hale.

After the first sip of coffee has permeated my bloodstream and the caffeine has done what it's paid to do, I am finally able to speak. With a smile, "What a nice surprise. Thank you for bringing over breakfast."

SLAVE TO LOVE

How can a man make sipping coffee from a cardboard cup look so damn sexy? I wonder how many days it's been since he last shaved, his stubble beard is so thick and dark. So masculine. I want to run my fingertips over it to feel the sharp sting and even more than that, I wonder how it would feel scratching the skin of my neck following his lips and teeth. My thighs twitch at the thought and I'm too afraid to look down and see what my nipples are doing. I can hear them screaming, *"Bite me through the shirt." "Yeah, bite her, but suck me."* I silently tell them, "Shut up, sluts."

"I hope you like the assortment." He's looking for validation.

"Perfect. Coffee and tacos make me very happy."

"You were so cute that you couldn't speak before you drank coffee.

Laughing, "I'm glad you find that cute."

"Your mussed up morning look is very cute, too."

The Google images flood my mind, "Yeah, not quite what you're used to. I don't quite have that model in the morning thing going."

His coffee cup comes down with a thud and he's looking at me like I'm crazy. "Sierra, they don't hold a candle to you."

"Yeah, right," I scoff.

Shaking his head, like he's disgusted with me. "Starting this week we are going to be sleeping, eating and breathing TFV1, so I was hoping we could take some time before the craziness kicks in to get to know each other better. We've known one another for several months now and I hardly know a thing about you. And I want to. I know that after today you're going to be seeing a very different person in me at the office. As we go into the homestretch, there are matters that are going to require my complete focus. So, I might seem more than a bit distant to you."

I want to tell him everything about me. I want him to know and understand who I am. It's just not as easy as he makes it out to be. But I fear this window of opportunity he's describing. Like the Hale I know is about to disappear. And I don't want him to go.

"I have an idea," I smile at him. "Give me a few minutes to get dressed."

"You look fine to me." He's staring at my nipples.

I look down at my high-beams. "They like you, too. But I really need them to behave in public."

He laughs, totally surprised by my admission. *I'm talking about my nipples to the man.*

A few minutes later I emerge in jeans and sneakers, wearing a hoodie over a black tank top that is much less revealing, and hand Hale a long clear plastic pack filled with bright rainbow colors.

He looks at it for a moment, "A kite?"

"A dual control kite," I clarify. "I got it as a gift and I've never used it. And today is cool and breezy, so I thought maybe we could go over to Zilker Park and fly it."

"Do you know how to fly a kite?"

I shake my head no. "Hold onto a handle and run?" My ventured guess is bringing out his sexy smile.

"This should be good," he laughs. "Let's go."

Maneuvering both my body and the kite into the Lotus is a feat.

"That just might be harder than getting in here in a short skirt." There was no way he was going to miss that opportunity to tease me.

Looking over at his beautiful profile and stubble-covered jaw, I realize that I can't deny how much I really enjoy being in his company.

"I like being with you," I blurt out as we head down Riverside Drive toward Barton Springs Road.

Taking his hand off the shift, he slides it to my leg, giving my thigh a quick squeeze, before returning it to downshift.

SLAVE TO LOVE

"I'll one-up you," he says as we pass a food truck court on the edge of the park, "I don't like being without you."

CHAPTER
Twenty

We've finally got this damn thing airborne, soaring into the clear azure sky, the growing Austin skyline providing the perfect backdrop for our wayward rainbow bird. We're running with it, pulling on the cords to follow the wind and remain aloft. It dips right and I pull hard, catching an incoming gust. Sierra lets out a delighted screech and then pulls her cord before it dips too far and comes hurtling downward... again. She catches it right as the wind kicks up and off we go running as it pulls us across the great lawn. And we run until a shift in the wind has me backing up, trying to rein it in and slow it down. I turn to my left and run right into Sierra, a tangle of arms, legs and cords. Instinct puts me into protect mode and I grab Sierra before I hit the ground, letting her drop on top of me so that her fall will be cushioned.

Splat! We're down on the hard ground and my right shoulder is taking the heat for this fall, but my grip around her remains steadfast.

"Are you okay?" She's my first worry.

Sierra's face is down by my shoulder and I can't see her eyes.

"Yeah. I'm fine, but I smushed you. Are you okay?" She lifts her head to look at me.

"My shoulder hurts like a bitch, but nothing a hot shower won't fix." I smile at the girl on top of me and don't loosen my hold. Not even a little bit.

Inching up me, I feel her whole body along the length of mine, pressing in all the right places and the pain in my shoulder evaporates as if I'd never landed on it. I feel her breasts against my chest, and my cock, pressing her thigh, instantly hardens.

Moving an arm up to my face, she stares intently into my eyes, her look very serious, as she pushes back hair from my forehead, raking it with her fingers, before running her palm back and forth on the sharp stubble covering my jaw. Looking up into her eyes, I'd kill to know the thoughts running through her head right now. I'm surprised by the way she is touching me. Tender is the only word I can come up with. Tender. This world isn't tender. My world has never been tender, and I briefly curse her because after this moment, I know I will always crave tenderness. Damn you, Sierra Stone. Tenderness is not part of the bargain.

Her head dips to mine, softly she kisses the side of my chin. This is all so unexpected. Continuing, her lips softly graze my jaw farther back, close to my ear, and then she plants a third soft kiss on the crest of my cheekbone, before pulling back to regard me.

"Three more weeks and we will no longer be working together. Surely I should be able to control myself for three more weeks, right?"

She doesn't wait for my answer.

"But you know what I really fear. I fear that you are a thrill seeker. Actually I know you are a thrill seeker. Look at your life. Who leaves MIT to go and do what you did? A man who needs to be so far out on the edge that one precarious shift in the wind and it's all over. But there's a thrill in that for you, isn't there, Hale? And so I fear that after the conquest, you move on. And after this event is all over and we have fucked on every surface, vertical and horizontal, you will just be a memory of a guy that wanted to nail me because I said no."

"Is that what you think?" My anger is rising and my hold on her tightens even more.

She nods.

"I love the edge, Sierra. I've faced dangers that would make most men shit their pants and I'd do it all again in a heartbeat, without thinking twice. That's as natural to me as breathing. I thrive on it and I excel at it. It's why I'm here. So, you got that absolutely right. Where you are wrong, dead wrong, is about us. When I told you that I don't like being without you, that was a huge admission for me to tell you that. That is really going far out on the edge for me. I have never told a woman that before. But it's the truth. When you're not with me, you're always with me. And that's why I want you always with me. So if you think I'm in it for the chase and then next, that's not what's going on."

"What *is* going on, Hale?"

"You tell me, Sierra."

She just shakes her head. I see the emotion building and I know she's not able to speak.

"You're seeing three weeks as the end, mermaid. I'm seeing it as the beginning. I'll be able to touch you without you worrying if you are throwing away your life's dream, everything you've worked so hard for. I'll be able to be open that you are a special part of my life." I laugh, "I'll be able to put out a picture in my office in New York of the two of us together. That's going to really freak some people out."

She almost smiles at that, but not quite.

"What happened to you, Sierra?" I'm hoping that lying here, flat on my back in the grass, with her molded on top of me, that she helps me to understand why she thinks I'm such a douche.

Watching her facial muscles twitch in sequence as she licks and bites her lips, I have to wonder what is causing this turmoil. This is not about me, I know that. I just have to convince her of it.

"Talk to me, mermaid," I implore. "I want to know."

With a deep breath, her eyes wander and pinpoint some spot across Lady Bird Lake that she fixates on. "I've been so focused on my career and relationships have been a distant second because I learned very, very young that you can only depend on yourself."

I wish she'd look at me, but I understand that telling me her story and looking at me is more vulnerable than she's ready to be. This is step one.

"I was six when my father left us. My sister was eight. My mom was a stay at home mom. My father didn't want her working, he wanted her home raising us. So, she did. She really didn't have any workplace skills, so when he left, we were in a world of hurt."

"Did he pay alimony and child support?"

Sierra finally looks down at me, a small smile on her face does not paint a happy picture.

"Well, that's kind of where the problem came in. What my mom found out when she went to divorce him was that my father was married. Just not to her."

"Son of a bitch." I feel her pain sear my solar plexus. This event shaped her and this man tainted her.

"You're being too kind. Turns out that mom was quasi-wife number two. There was his legal wife, quasi-wife number one and then my mom. He had kids with all of them and he was very good at figuring out how to go off the grid and not be found. So my mom never collected a cent."

"Wow. That's harsh." I think of my own cushy childhood. Two parents, a beautiful home in Marblehead and a summer house on Nantucket. Growing up certainly wasn't without pain, but security and deceit were never issues.

"I can't fuck things up, Hale. And if I do, it can't be over a man. Do you understand that?"

Removing one of my hands from her back, I cup her small face. "I'm not him."

"I want to believe that. I do. But you grabbed my ass after a business meeting."

Closing my eyes, I take a deep breath. "We have come a long way since then, Sierra, and you know that. I've kind of told you, but let me finally tell you the full embarrassing truth behind the ass-grab. And it is embarrassing. That was not my lame attempt to pick you up." I stop, here comes the whole truth, the God-awful, embarrassing truth. "I had been fantasizing about you. Throughout that whole meeting I was daydreaming, if you will, about me and you. And before that meeting you had been on my mind non-stop. So, when I touched you, at first appropriately, then inappropriately, it was because my mind was elsewhere, in fantasyland. And in fantasyland, you were mine and touching you was natural, because there, in fantasyland, I always touch you."

I stop for a moment, then continue. "Yeah, process that. While I lie here drowning in utter embarrassment."

Throwing her head back in laughter, "That is hysterical. You are so lame."

"I agree with you there. I am seriously lame." And what I don't say is, you scare me more than having a gun pointed at my head, close range, although you both hold the power to stop my heart.

Rolling off me to my side, Sierra stays within my arms, burrowing her head into my shoulder. Absentmindedly, I comb my fingers through her loose waves.

"So what are we going to do, mermaid? Tell me what you want. Do you want me to take you home and I'll see you in the office tomorrow? Do you want me to ask you out in three weeks? Do you want me to totally back off?"

She's shaking her head against my chest.

"What are you saying no to?"

"All three."

"So, you don't want me to take you home. You don't want me to ask you out in three weeks and you don't want me to back off."

Now, she's nodding, yes.

Rolling over, I cover her with my body, balancing my weight on my forearms. The rush is physical as I feel her under me, but it's the emotional onslaught that feels like a blow to the back of my head. "I'm a guy. You need you to spell this out for me or I will get it wrong and you'll be pissed. Tell me what you want." I know what I want. The bottom halves of our bodies are molded and it's taking every bit of willpower not to start grinding into where her thighs meet, especially when she moves her legs apart slightly and my body falls into hers, perfectly aligned for pleasure. My nose is just inches from hers as I await her answer.

"I don't want to lose you."

"Waiting three weeks is not going to make you lose me, Sierra. These next three weeks are going to be insane. I'll start sharing some of the particulars with you tomorrow and you'll have a better understanding of what we're tackling and how focused we'll be until the event is over."

Snaking her arms around my back, her hands end up in the back pockets of my jeans. She's pressing me into her. Laying my head face down between her breasts, I warn, "That's going to get you in trouble, little girl."

"You're so not safe."

Laughing, "No, Sierra, I am not safe. But I will keep you safe. So, what is it you want?" I ask again.

"You said after today things change."

I nod.

"You said that you're going to change."

Again, I nod, "I don't want you to think it's anything between us gone wrong, if I go into a very different mode than you've seen me. I'm coming back to you. I promise."

"Then I don't want to lose one minute of now, Hale, while I still have you." She presses her hands into my ass.

"Sierra…" The word is part warning, part question.

"Either I have to trust you, Hale, or walk away. You're going to be my leap of faith."

"Are you sure?" My hips press down into her as I ask that.

"I'm sure."

Pressing my face into her cleavage, "Girls, I hope you're ready to meet me," I address the luscious nipples that have intrigued me since the King Cole Salon.

Sierra laughs, "Be careful doing that or you'll poke your eye out."

CHAPTER
Twenty-One

$\mathcal{H}$ ale groans as he dips his body into the seat of the Lotus. "Oh man, my shoulder is really feeling that fall."

"That's because you're old," I tease.

"I'm only thirty-seven, Miss Spring Chicken." He gives my thigh a squeeze.

"You're only four years older than me and I think you've probably experienced twenty more years of stuff than I have."

Looking straight forward, he nods. "You're probably right."

And I wonder what would make a guy on the path that he was on, as MIT is one of the top technological schools in the United States, exclusive to the brightest minds, veer so far off that course.

"How long were you in the military?" I need to unravel the mystery that is Hale Lundström.

"A little under eleven years."

"Wow, I didn't realize you were in for that long. Did you just enlist or did they recruit you?"

I can tell he's thinking about how to answer this. I love watching him; he gets very still, and I would kill to see the thought process that goes on within his mind. So dark and masculine, with those loose curls and stubble, I try and think if I've ever been so attracted to another man as I am to him. Yes, he's exceedingly handsome, no doubt about that, but it's the intelligence, the wry humor and the portions of his world that render him an enigma, that make him so damn attractive.

"Umm, a little of both." Is finally his response.

"You can't tell me, can you?" While these secrets make him even more attractive, I am frustrated and wonder will I ever scale his walls. Will I ever be allowed to?

He looks over and smiles at me with a closed mouth smile. He can't tell me and I wonder in what kind of badass shit he's been involved. Sexy just climbed another notch. And my freaking nipples are clawing at my tank top.

"Want to go out for an early dinner?" We're approaching the light on Barton Springs and South Lamar.

"No." I shake my head, "Get over into the left lane. Let's just go over to Whole Foods, pick up some wine and cheese and stuff that's just easy to munch on, and take it back to my place."

The suggestion evokes a full-blown smile and he maneuvers the Lotus over two lanes with just a flick of the steering wheel. Why am I feeling every single thing between my legs? His smile, the turn of the car. I'm on fire.

"Let's go, mermaid," He helps me out of the Lotus, his arm immediately going around my shoulder with an ease, as if he's done it a thousand times before. His hand gently rubs my upper arm as we walk through the underground garage and take the moving ramp up into the chain's headquarters store.

I wonder if this feels as good to him as it does to me.

Entering this building that takes up a square city block of very prime Sixth Street real estate, I grab a small cart and we head toward long buffets of prepared hot and cold foods.

"Finger food?" I look up at Hale with the question and know I'm in trouble the minute it is out of my mouth.

"I hope so," and there is that wicked, sexy smile.

I can't even imagine how red I am. "I walked right into that one, huh?"

SLAVE TO LOVE

"With your legs wide open, babe," he replies, looking at the food choices. "Yum, cold Chinese noodles in peanut sauce?"

I nod voraciously and Hale starts filling a container. After putting together an odd assortment of ethnic foods, we head to the cheese shop and then to the bakery section for baguettes.

I stop the cart to gawk. "Yum, look at these desserts." The shelves are filled with delicate pastries and a lavish mélange of cakes, cookies and chocolates. "Should we grab two cupcakes?"

Standing very close behind me, Hale extends his left arm and puts his hand on our shopping cart's handle, just to the left of where my hand rests. With his right hand, he moves my hair away from my neck and kisses it. A shiver lights up my body and he laughs, then scratches his stubble across my neck.

"I think tarts might be more apropos for you," he whispers.

Without thinking I ram my elbow back into him.

"Oww," he laughs.

"You called me a tart," I act highly insulted, but all I can think about is how much he is making me smile and how yummy his lips felt grazing my neck. Silently, I'm begging, do it again, and as if reading my mind, I feel his lips back for round two. This time my shiver is almost a quake as that neck kiss is felt everywhere throughout my body.

"Mmm, a salted caramel tart," he says. "You're so sweet and more than a little salty."

Laughing, I lean back into him. Three weeks, schmee weeks. How can I resist this? "Let's get some wine." I get the cart moving before he has my legs turning into jello and I swoon amongst the bread puddings and pot de crèmes.

Grabbing some plates and utensils from the kitchen, I set out the spread on the coffee table in front of my couch. I'm excited, I'm nervous. The intellectual part of me says, wait the three weeks, you know what the stigma is like for women in management, but my emotional side is telling me to straddle him and unzip his pants, show him how you feel about him. What's a girl to do?

"Do the honors?" I pass the corkscrew and a bottle to Hale. "So, I have this idea."

"I'm listening."

"What if we turned the air conditioning down low, so that it gets really cold in here." He reflexively looks at my chest and I continue, "And we start a fire in the fireplace."

"Sounds cozy. How many nights a year do you actually use it?"

Thinking for a second, I laugh. "Maybe six."

"Well, it is fall. In most places, anyway. Let's get the chill on in here."

As I knock down the thermostat to start our little seasonal adventure, Hale looks at me and smiles, his handsome face making me melt. "I have a request though."

"What is that?" I have no clue what he's going to ask for.

"Change into your white tank top and Texas shorts."

He has issued a challenge knowing my nipples are going to go insane in the cold air and that I'm going to be freezing.

Without saying a word, I turn and disappear into my bedroom. I pull out the tank top and sweat shorts. I know what he wants. No bra under that shirt. I laugh, there is nothing in the world a woman loves more that taking off her bra the minute she gets home, so I'm going to be very accommodating. And I'm actually going to take it a step further because underneath those very short sweat cut-offs, I won't be wearing any underwear. Whether or not he's going to find that out is yet to be seen.

Before I head back to the living room, I grab a few seasonal items from the closet in my guest bedroom to help create an autumnal ambience.

SLAVE TO LOVE

Hale is positioning the wood on the grate when I return. I love seeing him down on one knee in front of the fireplace. On the mantle above him I place fall colored hurricane vases with candles inside. Grabbing a torchière lighter, I light three candles and immediately the light begins to flicker off the glass, projecting dancing shadows on the ceiling. When I'm done, I hand the lighter to Hale who lights some kindling under the grate. Immediately the dry wood begins to catch, illuminating Hale's face as he sits back on his heels quietly lost in the flames sensual movement.

Pulling some pillows off the couch, I join him on the floor and pour both of us a glass of wine. Looking at one another in the fire's light, we don't immediately make a toast. Today has been an emotional one.

"To an incredibly successful TFV1," I toast.

Hale smiles and nods. "Thank you for all your help on this. You've been a pleasure to work with." He clinks my glass.

"Why does that sound like goodbye?" I'm taken aback by the formality of his words.

"Only for three weeks, mermaid."

"I forgot something." Popping up, I head to the kitchen. I actually need to collect myself. Is he already starting to separate? Is that what is going on?

Returning with two sets of chopsticks, "Excellent," he comments and grabs a set as he opens the container with the noodles.

Sitting on the floor next to him, I start to unwrap the cheeses. Hale sidles a little closer to me and leans forward, noodles hanging from his chopsticks as they approach my lips.

With a smile, I open my mouth for the unexpected feeding of this treat. Slurping in the noodles, I can see the movement in his muscles to my sucking motion as the strands slowly disappear into my mouth. Everything seems enhanced, the flavors, the texture, the pulsing shadows of candle and firelight. A cold spray of sauce drips to my chin. Reaching forward with his free hand, Hale's index finger gently swipes the peanut sauce and then he paints my lips with it before sucking his finger into his own mouth.

Picking up some noodles with my chopsticks, I lift a few long strands to his mouth, he sucks in the ends and then I run the chopsticks down the length of the noodles, bringing the far ends to my mouth. Smiling, I start to chomp toward the center of the strands, as does he, ready to stop only when our lips touch and I start to giggle.

I can feel his smile against my lips as he swallows the noodles. "I can't kiss you with a mouthful of noodles."

"Oh, are you going to kiss me?"

"I have you on the floor, in front of a roaring fire, we're drinking wine. I'd lose all respect for myself if I didn't kiss you." His eyes are dancing with delight.

"The question is, would you lose all respect for me?" Leaning forward I slide my fingers into his shiny curls and pull him in for a kiss. Right before our lips meet, I can see how amused he is that I am the aggressor. Kissing him softly, I swipe my tongue over his lips and taste the peanut sauce.

"Mermaid, I respect that you go for what you want in both business and pleasure. You are truly a force to reckon with and you are like no other woman I have ever met."

"Is that a good thing or a bad thing?"

"You know the answer to that."

"Tell me, Hale. I want to hear it."

"You drive a hard bargain."

"Oh, I'm sure nowhere nearly as hard as you do. But tell me why I am like no other woman."

"Look at that look on your face. So smug and amused, like let's watch this guy just totally try and bullshit me."

"Well…"

"Sierra, Sierra, Sierra… here's the thing about you, you challenge me. Constantly. I've got to be on my "A" game because you are always on yours. Whether it's in a business meeting or just hanging out, you really keep me on my toes. And yet, you are so easy to hang out with. I see you as my equal in every way. I never have to think, what am I going to talk to this woman about? You're engaging and you engage me. That in itself puts you into a totally different league."

"I hope you mean that. Because I really, really like you. I like you more than I have liked anyone in a very long time."

"I know the feeling. I want to be in Austin all the time because you are here. I'd move headquarters here, but then we'd be working together again and we'd be right back to you not shitting where you eat. And I don't want that."

We both laugh.

"So, let me ask you a question." I pick at the crust of the bread.

"Go for it," he offers.

"You just said you don't want that. What is it you do want?"

"Well, besides ripping that tank top off and having my way with your gorgeous nipples, which I hope you realize is imminent, I want this to be something real between us. We're not twenty-one year olds. I want to wake up here in the mornings. I want you to feel totally comfortable in my place. We'll give you a drawer to keep a stack of white tank tops over there," he smiles a smile so sexy, I'm on the verge of tackling him. "I want to make you one of my famous salads."

"You make famous salads?"

"In the Lundström world, I am known as 'Salad Guy'."

I love that he is telling me this. It's personal and unguarded, which is so not Hale Lundström and that, in itself, makes it extremely intimate.

Sitting in front of the fire, fully clothed, it feels as if we are slowly disrobing and soon both the ripped muscles and scars will be on display. I want to see how they merge and the story that they write.

"And I want you to meet my nephew, Oliver," Hale's face lights up at the mention, "and watch him kick my ass at Hedgehog's Adventure."

Slathering a piece of French bread with Delice de Bourgogne cheese, I hand it to him with what I know is a silly smile on my face.

"I'm shocking you, aren't I?" he laughs.

Nodding, "Totally."

"That night at the Beverly Hills Hotel when Bob was thrusting his key at you…"

"That's not all he wanted to be thrusting." I sneer as I eat a piece of bread.

"Well, exactly and you handled him so beautifully. But I just felt such a myriad of intense emotions that night. It was really overwhelming and that was very unexpected. I was jealous, I felt protective, I was angry that he was putting you in such an awkward position, I was incensed at myself over how I'd made you feel. And I would have been really upset and disillusioned had you gone to his bungalow."

I hand him another slice of bread. This time covered in Cambozola cheese and refill his wine glass.

"You really did not think I would go, did you?" Sitting back, I grab my wine glass, holding the stem tight and forgetting to inhale while I await his response.

"No, intellectually I knew you wouldn't go. But emotionally, from that deep, base place where our caveman instincts still live and thrive, there was this jealousy and fear creeping in. What if you went with the other guy?"

"Is that why you checked on me that night?"

146

Laughing, Hale throws his head back, "Busted. Totally busted, huh?"

"Kemp checked on me too that night."

Hale is very amused by that little piece of info. "Of course he did. You're our girl."

Our girl. A warm feeling glides through me and I love the protective nature in him. Our girl. Those two words are making me tingle.

"I loved that you stayed true to your convictions that night. So many people would not have. They would have gone off with him for a vague promise." He smiles at me and I can see a memory has taken hold, "And then you wolfed down that burger. That sealed the deal for me."

"How attractive," I add, sarcastically.

"You have no clue. It totally was, Sierra. Very hot. You were clearly starving and you did not care about anything but what was in that bag. And I loved that. Do you know how cool it is to find a woman who will chow down at 2 A.M. versus these carb shunning, stick figures?"

"You're just saying that."

He's shaking his head, "I had to leave that night or I was going to go all Bob Mannon on you."

Laughing, "He's now a verb. I love that. So…"

"So, let's get through TFV1 and then no holds barred. Okay? Let's do this."

"Let's do this," I whisper back.

Taking my hand, he stands and pulls me to my feet. "We have a really long day tomorrow and I've got to get out of here before I don't get out of here, and I keep you up all night. Walk me to the door."

At the door he faces me. He still hasn't let go of my hand.

"Sierra, Sierra, Sierra."

"What?" I'm smiling up at him.

"This is what." He bends down to kiss me, pulling my body into his.

Part of me wants to whisper the word "stay" in his ear. But I also know by letting him walk out the door tonight means that when we finally come together in three weeks, it will be with the freedom to share the depth of what I ache to express.

Taking my face in both hands, Hale deepens the kiss and my entire body reacts. Waiting to make love to this man is going to make it a very long three weeks. I want to see his chest bare and know what his arm muscles look like when he cups my face.

Finally pulling away, Hale just looks at me with a smile. And then he rubs the back of his fingers over my tank top, the pressure and warmth from his touch coaxes my irreverent nipples to strain against the uneven fabric in their quest for more of his attention.

"Something to remember me by, mermaid."

Taking the hand that just stroked me through my shirt, I return the surprise, guiding his fingers into the hemline of my shorts and placing them directly into the warm, wetness for which he is directly responsible. The look on his face is pure shock, followed by enjoyment and self-satisfaction when he realizes just how my body has responded to his kisses and his touch.

"Something to remember me by." I smile and press his fingers deeper into my wetness.

"Bob Mannon can kiss my ass and stay the fuck away from my girl." His breath in my ear is hot as he pulls my head in with one hand for a rough, demanding kiss. The other hand stays inside my shorts, slowly exploring uncharted territory for a future claim. I want to urge both his kiss and his touch further, deeper.

As our lips part, our foreheads come together. "I will definitely remember you by that, mermaid. Every single night for the next three weeks." He withdraws his fingers, finally, and places a soft kiss on my lips.

SLAVE TO LOVE

His strides take him to the Lotus and away from me far too quickly. I don't want this day, this amazing, out of the blue Sunday, to end. He's warned me multiple times that he will somehow be changed for the next few weeks and I want the man who spent the day with me to stay. Maybe forever.

As he reaches the Lotus, I can tell by the look on his face that he has just thought of something. Something he wants to share with me. Smiling, "My bungalow was bigger than his," he informs me, testosterone barely in check.

"I'm betting it was a lot bigger," and I love the smile that brings to his face.

Standing in the doorway long after he's gone, I put off the inevitable entrance into my home, where there are still remnants of him scattered throughout my living room. I just want to delay the oddly painful feeling that his soul still permeates the premises, although he's physically gone. Parting is beginning to feel like a little death.

And as I breathe in the crisp fall air, a thought makes me smile. *My girl.* He can call me that any time. Or all the time.

⁕⁕⁕⁕⁕⁕⁕⁕⁕⁕⁕⁕⁕⁕⁕⁕⁕⁕⁕⁕⁕⁕⁕⁕⁕⁕⁕⁕

It's with a smile and an extra latté that I enter his office the next morning still riding the crest of Sunday's high and floating on the promise of what three weeks' time will finally bring. Merely two feet through the door's threshold, the bottom drops out and I plummet without warning, a surfer whose board has been hijacked by a shark at the wave's apex.

I barely recognize the man on the far side of the desk. He resembles Hale Lundström, and if I look hard enough, I might find a remnant of the man whose kiss made me believe that I could actually have it all. That it was really going to happen for me. But with every moment I stand there, coffee cup in each hand, those

149

remnants dissipate rapidly, evaporating into the ether and I'm left with this sinking feeling that it was all a fantasy, from the night in the King Cole Salon right through to last night in front of my fireplace.

Well, I can't say he didn't warn me. He did, he tried to warn me, multiple times. I just had no idea it would be like this.

CHAPTER
Twenty-Two

I can see it in her eyes. She sees it. She feels it. And every fiber in my being is screaming "Wait for me, Sierra. Wait for me." Three weeks really isn't a very long time, but when things are so new, as they are with us, there is no security in the realness of it all. And three weeks is an eternity that just might be interminable.

"Come on in."

"I figured extra caffeine couldn't hurt." She places the coffee cups on the desk.

"Before you take a seat, please shut the door."

We're alone, behind closed doors and it's time to tell her what is going on. Up until now I've been very stringent about only giving partial information. Everyone knew their part and nothing more. I never handed out the key to successfully build the puzzle. Classic military strategy.

"I trust you, Sierra. You're a professional who can be relegated sensitive materials and information without worry that you will betray a confidence."

"Well, thank you." She squints as her head slightly cocks to the right.

I can tell that she's perplexed by that statement.

Grabbing a yellow legal pad, I begin to create a list, adding to each line. When I'm done, I look through it, mentally counting the entries. After I am sure it is correct, and that I've forgotten nothing, I put the pen down and wordlessly slide the pad across the desk to Sierra.

Watching her face as she reads through the list, it is easy to see the shock register and increase as she works her way down the page. Silently, she looks up at me. There are so many questions swirling for her as our eyes meet. Extending my hand across the desk, I gesture for her to return the paper. From my left drawer, I extract a silver lighter. Flipping back the smooth top with my thumb, in one fluid motion, my finger is across the spark wheel and the yellow paper is in flames. Dropping it to my desk, I let it burn out. The expression on Sierra's face is priceless. Our eyes meet again.

"Hale, what are you doing? What was that?" Her eyes are the size of saucers.

"The confirmed attendee list for TFV1." I feel a huge weight lift as soon as it's out of my mouth. The first of the secrets has been exposed.

"They are all going to be there?"

I nod.

"How is that…" she can't finish the sentence as her brain is outrunning her mouth. "Hale, some of these people can't be on the same continent together, much less in the same room. And some of them, are they even allowed in the United States? How is this happening?"

"When I told you that I needed people that I could trust to be discreet…"

"Does the government know you're doing this?" she cuts me off before I can even finish my sentence.

"I am doing this as a private citizen and a U.S. businessman. I've reached out to government connections who are providing assistance in security, logistics and facilities. The President, Secretary of State and Director of Homeland Security are all aware of who will be on U.S. soil that weekend, what the meeting's agenda entails and what I hope is the outcome result of the weekend."

"And what is that?"

"A pact among the participating nations to help ensure that war is not fought on the technological front as well as how to build safeguards and back-ups to our systems together to stave off technological terrorism."

"By countries or rogue groups?"

"It could be either, so we're looking to accomplish two things: this group of countries represented entering into a pact as well as working collaboratively to develop shields against factions outside of government who can launch cyberattacks that have global implications."

I watch as Sierra sifts through the ramifications and how all-encompassing they are.

"And you are doing this as a private businessman?"

I shrug and smile, "As the head of a tech company, I often interface in a much more positive way than governments do."

"These are some very high level players."

"Yes they are, and while a few are just figureheads, some of the other players, such as the other ministers of technology are much more involved in their countries technical infrastructure and development."

"Do some of these people know who their fellow participants are?"

Nodding, "They know the scope of what's happening and the need for it. A well, planned world cyber-attack could literally bring countries to their knees. Actually it could decimate the planet and change the world as we know it."

"You're right, people would die without Amazon and Facebook," her voices drips sarcasm.

"Energy grids, water supplies, mass transportation systems, banking and commerce, gas pumps, water treatment facilities, nuclear facilities, warheads, satellites, and so much more. We all know the possibilities. Organized governments generally are not the issue, they are the safety net, if you will, because if they initiate an attack, the retaliation would be on their end and they know that. Every so often a crazy despot ends up at the helm and we worry he'll push the wrong button, but for the most part, it is lone wolf hackers, religious extremists and underground anarchists who can wreak havoc on the world as we know it because we are so dependent on technology for every facet of our daily existence."

"How are we getting them in and out of here? How are we keeping them safe? What safeguards do we have in place each step of the way? What are the contingency plans? What am I supposed to be doing?" Her mind is spinning. "Hale, what am I supposed to be doing?"

Moving a manila file across the desk that says, Sierra, I tell her, "Review this, commit it to memory and burn it. If there is anything you forget or have any questions about, just ask me. This outlines the next three weeks as well as your involvement that weekend."

"Burn it? Are you serious?"

"Sierra, in thirty minutes I expect the contents of that folder to no longer exist. Is that understood?"

Her head snaps up from the folder to look at me, eyes narrowed. Ms. Stone does not like to be given orders and as far as I am concerned, we are executing a highly sensitive mission and it is imperative she understands the chain of command, her position in it and how things will unfold.

She doesn't answer and I repeat the question. "Is that understood?"

"I'm not an idiot," she begins and stops herself. My eye contact with her is very direct and in that split second, I can see that the entire picture has come into very clear focus. Including who I am. "It will be done," she acquiesces.

As she stands to leave, the intercom on my phone buzzes, our receptionist, Ashley, announces, "Mr. Lundström, Colonel Hoffmann is here to see you."

"Please show him in."

Walter Hoffman is coming through the door just as Sierra is leaving. Cutting a sharp figure in uniform, Walt has always had an eye for the women.

"Ma'am," he greets Sierra with a smile and a nod. With his pale blue eyes and gray hair, there is something very Paul Newman-like about his looks.

"Colonel," I'm on my feet and across the office to meet him with my hand outstretched.

Extending his hand to me, "Lieutenant Colonel, it's good to see you again." He addresses me by my last rank.

"Sir, this is Sierra Stone, she is a member of my logistics team."

"Ms. Stone, it's a pleasure." He extends his hand for a long, warm shake. Too long. "I look forward to working with you." He's devouring her with his eyes and she is savoring it, her shoulders doing a little dance.

"And I you." She smiles warmly at him. "Shall I close the door on my way out?" she addresses me.

"Please," is my terse single word response.

We have both totally pissed one another off this morning.

CHAPTER
Twenty-Three

I feel lost. That man before me was a total stranger. In my office, I stare at the spires of the Frost Bank building, so familiar, and yet so different from this vantage point. Kind of like Hale Lundström. Today a military strategic ops guy sat before me, well-groomed in an expensive suit, not the man nuzzled into my neck on my living room floor.

With a sigh, I open the folder and start to peruse the week by week activities leading to the event. As I read through the details, I'm fighting tears and I really don't know why. I think it's because I really want to know this man, and this morning has been an eye opener, and the only thing I've learned is how little I really know about him.

Refocusing myself on the material before me, which is about to be incinerated, I review the logistics and agenda. The event is taking place in a facility that I had no clue even existed. It was one of Lyndon Baines Johnson's secret cold-war facilities here in central Texas, equipped with an enormous bunker, which will be fully outfitted for the event. That seems so odd to me, like the clips I've seen on PBS of schoolchildren lining up in the school hallways, heads down, during Cold War air raid drills.

Forty-five minutes later I text Hale. **I don't have a lighter. Come to my office.**

As I approach Hale's office, the door opens and he extends a hand for the file. Handing it over to him, I search his face, his eyes, for something, anything. Forcing a small smile I just want to let him know I'm still in this with him. He doesn't return my smile.

"Thanks, Sierra." And with that, he closes the door.

Walking back to my office, I'm fighting tears again, still not understanding why. I just need to get myself as focused as he is on what lies before us. Based on what he has shared with me this morning, this event is more than a high-level tech think tank conference, this is something no government or the United Nations has ever pulled together, and here is Hale Lundström at the helm of this, brokering and constructing an international alliance that could shape global technology's security for the foreseeable future.

And it hits me like a brick just how big this is, how important. I'm proud of him, I'm in awe of him and I'm honored he saw something in me to choose me to be part of this team. And with this newfound clarity finally crystallized in my mind, the picture becomes so much larger and I feel almost giddy, I can't wait to experience this with him. His prodigious focus is not a slight on me, and I need to check my ego at the door. This is not about me at all, this is about something so much bigger than any one single person or individual relationship. And I wonder if this is a crusade for Hale, and he the charismatic commander, leading the charge.

One of the toughest things about this is not being able to share it with anyone. It's exciting and I want to brag about this man. But I can't share it with anyone. And in the meantime, I can't even share with him.

Sitting in my chair, I stare out the window ticking through a daily calendar in my head of what I need to accomplish for the next few days. I cannot wait to see this happen and to be part of this historic event. Now that I understand what is behind Hale's aloof behavior, I can let go of my own insecurities. This is a mission, one that needs to be pulled off with exact precision and he knows the level of focus that entails. He doesn't need that focus to waver because of me. I'm not going to become a burden.

I get it.

Three weeks. I can handle three weeks. Reaching toward my neck, I let the mermaid's delicate chain run through my thumb and forefinger. Laughing aloud, I think I called this one correctly. I knew accepting a chain from Hale Lundström would be just the beginning of the chains that would bind me to him and I was right. The events of this morning have now bound me to him even tighter, as we share both a secret and a quest.

Three more weeks. And I will no longer be wrapped in just his chains, I'll also be wrapped in his arms.

CHAPTER
Twenty-Four

I get the all clear from Garber on his sweep of the property as the sun sets over the hills in the west. This beautiful remote section of Hill Country is an area of the Texas landscape with which I had previously not been familiar. As the guests are served their dinner in the expansive formal dining room, the fall sky is providing a pink and orange Impressionist's canvas that reminds me of Italian ices in summer.

Surveying from the perimeter of the facility's rustic Texas themed ballroom, I feel a deep satisfaction as I scan the room, dotted with antler chandeliers hanging from rough-hewn wooden beams, and marvel that these participants have come together with a common goal. I'll need to send a thank you to the commanding officers at Lackland Air Force Base for making the transportation of many of these guests possible. The news media has no clue that the occupants of this room are even on U.S. soil this weekend, and won't, until they have safely arrived home. In attendance is only one tech blogger, whom I trust implicitly, but even with the history we have, I've made him sign his life away via a myriad of legal documents that nothing from this weekend is leaked and no reports appear until all occupants are safe on their home soil.

Quickly pushing the momentary satisfaction back where it belongs, I focus on making sure I am honed in on everything that is occurring and that nothing seems or feels out of place. I see Sierra approaching from the left. She has been invaluable performing the tasks needed to make this weekend possible, exceeding my every expectation, and it is impossible not to notice that tonight she looks even more beautiful and radiant than I've ever seen her. She too is caught up in the magic of this weekend and all it represents.

"Your opening speech was so compelling. You had everyone eating out of the palm of your hand. I really believe you'll accomplish everything you've set out to do this weekend. I don't think there is a person in this room that is not onboard with the mission." She ribs me with her elbow.

Just the physical contact, the first we've had in days, feels so good. I let myself realize, for the first time in weeks, how much I've missed her, even though she has been by my side the entire time.

"I hope you're right." I never like to be too confident until everything is completed.

"Hale, it will do you good to realize I'm always right." She smiles at me and walks away, making her way through the room to ensure all the guests have everything they need. Talk about having people eat out of your hand, as she moves from table-to-table, the male dominated crowd is entranced by her.

I had totally underestimated her and how she would react to the three weeks of my aloofness and my super focus on the event. I was afraid she'd be insecure and clingy and needy. But not Sierra. Sierra Stone took this in stride. Understanding the importance of the event and its outcome, she made it her own, taking ownership of what she was assigned and more. I didn't have to babysit her. I didn't have to worry about her. In fact, she made my life a whole lot easier. So much more than I could've ever imagined.

I don't even want to let myself begin to think about the weekend being over and where our relationship will take us. For the moment, I need to be focused on the here and now, and I shoo that thought away with a grin as I watch her royal blue skirt between the starched white linen table clothes.

Standing by the bar, also surveying the room is an old friend and colleague, Daniel Mizrahi. Now the owner of a very successful tech firm specializing in missile sensors, Daniel and I share more than probably any two people in this room. The man was my counterpart multiple times, on missions neither of our governments worked on, or so they would claim.

Making my way over to the bar, the wiry Israeli regards me as I approach. "I'm really glad you decided to attend. I hope you'll lead up some of the discussions over the next few days."

"I'm just here for the booze and girls," quips the former intelligence officer.

"We've got plenty of booze. Not so much on the girls, though." I shrug.

"I'll take that one." He gestures toward Sierra.

"Spoken for," I let him know.

"Good for you. Get her pregnant, keep her pregnant. Make beautiful babies together. Keep them safe and far away from where we've been."

I nod, thinking we have to have sex first and then I sweep away the thought quickly.

"Tomorrow morning everyone will be breaking into teams to work on defining the mission. It sounds easy, but will probably be the toughest thing we do all weekend. Everything else we work on, strategically and tactically, will come off of that."

"What do you need me to do?"

I can't help but smile at Daniel. We fall into step immediately, anticipating one another, the brilliance of our past just a breath away, ready to carry us into the future, our sole, or maybe soul, mission never wavering.

"I've got you on a team tomorrow morning with Jiro Masahiro and Alborz Ahadi," my tone is quiet.

The Israeli smiles, "You're really going to shake it up, aren't you." The former Aman, Israeli military intelligence officer, has been teamed up with a formidable Japanese tech giant and an Iranian technology minister. "There's a lot of ego at that table. Does Ahadi know we're teamed?"

Shaking my head, no, I add, "I somehow think in this closed environment, he will be a lot more open and reasonable. But maybe it's just what I'm hoping. The same with Masahiro. Let me know by tomorrow night if they're really here to work. If not, I'll do some team shuffling and ameliorate the situation."

"I'll let you know." Daniel moves back to his table, understanding too long a conversation might draw interest.

As I make my rounds at all of the tables, my excitement builds. TFV1 has been a dream of mine, a way to make a lasting impact on the world, a chance to be able to take my training and my position and weave in and out, where governments can't, to create a global fabric that safeguards against terrorism.

After dinner, I pull together a meeting of my directs in what was once a "Situation Room" for the Johnson administration. The whole facility has amazing history, walking through the ranch-like structure, it's hard not to imagine LBJ's angst and stress as he dealt with civil rights movement issues and the pressures of Vietnam as it incurred the country's growing resistance.

I take a seat in a large worn leather chair at the helm of the long table, a chair I wonder if President Johnson himself may have sat in, as we run through Saturday's agenda. The day begins early with breakfast, then onto the opening address and goal setting for the weekend, and general questions and concerns. It is at this point where everyone will sign a formal document of participation. For the next several hours, small groups will tackle the mission. Lunch will be a working lunch within the groups and mid-afternoon we reconvene as a larger group to hammer out a unified mission. A late afternoon break, prior to dinner, with multiple on-site leisure events is planned and some presentations by companies in incubation. Dinner again will be served in the dining room, located high on a bluff with wonderful views of sunset, and then after dinner, another three hour block of work time to define strategy.

Garber is seated next to Sierra, "Ariel, how do you walk in those things?" He's checking out her legs and feet.

"Gracefully," she responds with a smile.

"Well, if you need a foot massage later," he offers.

"Are you my man?"

"I definitely would be if the slave driver here didn't have me working all night."

There is a small army's worth of munitions here with the staff guarding the attendees. Enough firepower to make even a diehard Texan proud. With the exception of Sierra, my entire staff is packing, as am I, as well as many of the attendees, including Daniel Mizrahi.

After the meeting, we join a small group in the bar. I'm amazed at the diversity of the crowd. No one would ever believe these people were in the same room, drinking together. Scions of industry from throughout the globe alongside political icons.

"A drink?" I ask Sierra.

She just shakes her head. "I'm working. I need to stay sharp." She's taking in the room, chairs covered in calf hide and soft-lit antler chandeliers. An American West of yesteryear. "This is an amazing place."

Garber joins us. "Everyone is in place for the evening. Shift change in four hours and then four hours after that."

"Do you need me for anything else this evening?" Sierra asks.

Yes. To crawl into bed beside me, so that I can snuggle up next to you. Fall asleep with one of your gorgeous nipples in my mouth. Wake you in the middle of the night as I slowly enter you pushing all the way in and rolling onto my back with you on top of me while I thrust you up and down on my dick.

"No. Get some rest. Tomorrow is going to be a very long day."

"I know. That's why I'm thinking it's best just to go to my room and relax a little bit, then get a good night's sleep."

"Aww, you leaving us, Ariel? Now I've got to look at all these ugly dudes tonight." Garber has taken a liking to her.

"Yeah, I'm beat." She smiles at him.

"I'm still available for that foot massage," he offers.

"I'm beginning to think you have a foot fetish, Jeff." Sierra looks at him seriously.

"You don't even want to know," he laughs.

Turning to me, "If you need anything, text me."

"I just need you to get some rest." I smile down at her.

"That, I can do, Boss. Good night, gentleman," she bids us with a smile.

Garber and I watch in silence as she leaves.

"She's something else." Jeff is shaking his head approvingly.

"That, she is," I agree.

"So, when did you first fall in love with her?" He's very matter-of-fact.

"In love with her?" I question as if he's nuts.

"Yeah, in love with her, Lundström."

I think about it. In love. Am I in love with Sierra? That might not be a good thing. I like her a lot. There's no doubt about that. I want to be in a relationship with her and although our intimacy has been limited, I want to be involved with her. Be her lover. But in love with her?

Crazy in love with her.

Laughing, "When she scarfed down a cheeseburger at 2 A.M. standing in the hallway at the Beverly Hills Hotel. How can you not love a woman who's not afraid to totally chow down a greasy burger in the middle of the night."

"She's really special, Hale."

"I know," I admit.

SLAVE TO LOVE

"Don't fuck it up. That one is a keeper. And if you mess up, I will be waiting in the wings to snatch her away from right under your nose," he warns.

"Don't waste your time. I have no intention of losing her." Especially now, after I've admitted out loud that I am in love with Sierra Stone.

In seventy-two hours, I will be ravaging and claiming every inch of her body. Living out the fantasies that have been crowding my brain for months. No holds barred. I can already hear her breathless voice calling my name, begging me to go deeper, take her harder. I want to hear her screaming my name over and over and over again.

After this weekend, she will be totally mine. And we won't be keeping it a secret. From anyone.

CHAPTER
Twenty-Five

Crickets are a sign of colder weather on the horizon in central Texas. As I stroll along the covered walkway toward my room, I zig-zag across the pavement so as not to step on one of the noisy little creatures serenading the night. The sky is clear and filled with the famed "Deep in the Heart of Texas" stars and the air carries that crisp scent that appears when the summer humidity finally loses its grasp. A garden area is lit by an almost full moon missing the top right of its curve. When I come upon a wood and wrought iron bench with a Star of Texas welded onto the back, I decide to take a moment to just breathe.

Inhaling deeply, the oxygen rushing through my veins is like an instant shot of caffeine, awakening both my tired body and mind. Sitting quietly, I continue to breathe in deeply as I observe my surroundings. One of Jeff's guys is at the end of the walkway in a dark suit and white shirt. I've seen some of the perimeter guys, decked out in fatigues and semi-automatics, but the detail closest to participants are low-key and professionally dressed.

"Got sidetracked, Ariel?"

Jeff sits down next to me.

"Yes, the stars and moon were just too beautiful to not take a few minutes to sit and enjoy them."

As he surveys the night sky, I take a moment to study his handsome profile and wonder, *what is his story?* Can men with these lifestyles, like he and Hale have lived, have successful relationships?

As if he knows what I'm thinking, "You're really good for him, Sierra."

"You think?" I smile as I look up at the moon. I love hearing this.

"Yes. I do."

These military types, they make you work for it. I just want him to tell me.

"Why do you say that, Jeff?" Turning to face him, I need to know why.

"You bring light to him, Sierra."

"Do you think Hale is a dark person?" I know Garber has been with him in dark and dangerous places, but does he see Hale that way? As dark.

"No, not in the sense you are probably taking it. He's a very serious and driven man. Look at this weekend. Just the fact that this is happening is all Hale's vision and intensity. I think you bring along a facet that just lets him be. Gives him a break from needing to save the world. Gives him a healthy balance that he's been missing."

"Do you really think he feels he needs to save the world?" That is what I hone in on from the information Jeff has shared. I know he's a crusader, but is saving the world really his life's mission? And is there truly a place for anyone else in someone so expressly focused on something so extraordinary?

"Yeah, Sierra. I do. I think it's been his reason for being. His raison d'être, as the French say. Well, at least until now."

"Until now?" I ask, totally perplexed.

"Until you."

Looking away, I look up at the beautiful, robust moon, hanging there as if she were a gift to me, and nod my head. *Until me.*

SLAVE TO LOVE

"Do you really think I can make a difference?" *Can anyone?* I wonder.

"You already have, Ariel. You already have," he assures me.

I make a silent wish in the moon's glow. Please let Jeff be right.

How can grown men of this stature need so much hand holding? I am all over the place Saturday morning making sure everyone is where they need to be. We have a few constant wayward stragglers who require a lot of shepherding and our fair share of arrogant participants who feel they are at the center of everything.

As the day progresses and each team finalizes developing their mission statement, the energy in each of the rooms becomes palpable. Men and women who entered the facility as individuals representing a company or a country are quickly shedding those personas as they become the architects of an unprecedented global mission. By late afternoon, all the separate teams have come back together to create and solidify their work into that of a unified mission, agreed upon by all participants.

Watching it come together has been surprisingly like a ballet performance teeming with exquisite skill and requiring precise timing. The stage began in the morning with the separate teams swirling, each performing a beautiful and unique dance, and as the day went on, commonalities emerged amongst the teams, and there was an engulfing that formed a new, larger and more inclusive unit. When it appeared they had all come together in this brilliant dance, dancers would break from the pack, pirouetting away and crashing into others, until they finally all reformed with the ultimate synchronization and no breaks in the formation.

And, at that point, the group's mission was born.

Moderating and prodding, pushing and poking holes the entire time, Hale Lundström, has been stalking the floor with the lithe dexterity of a large and deadly cat. It is easy to visualize who he was as a commander of highly trained soldiers. He has effortlessly led this divergent group and I can only imagine that every participant will feel as if they have become part of a brotherhood. I can't shed the vision of our nation's forefathers drafting the Declaration of Independence and the fraternity that must have ensued amongst the men whose names grace that document. All of these people will leave here with a different relationship with each and every one of the other participants than they had before attending. And in some cases, dialogue between nations may just begin with two people and a common goal upon which they agree. I can't help but think of the long-reaching effect this weekend will have in places no one can fathom at this very moment.

The hours set aside for the evening's strategy session are not nearly enough. After working two hours longer than the schedule has called for, everyone has voted to start earlier in the morning, beginning the final day ninety minutes ahead of schedule to ensure they will be able to work through the tactics portion.

Watching the participants retreat to their rooms, it is evident all are filled with a mixture of energy, exhaustion and exhilaration. Although I merely stood on the sidelines watching and cheering, I am as wrung out as the most vocal of the participants, bleary eyed, and yet both my blood and my mind are still racing.

Back in my room, I immediately change out of my suit. Bra off. Yes. Shoes off. Yes. And with a loud exhale, I flop flat on my back onto the bed with a giggle. Today has been the most exciting thing I've ever witnessed in my life. Gestation and birth are the two words swirling in my head. Watching an idea grow throughout the day, develop, morph, and grow some more, is not something I can just shut off.

What room are you in? I text Hale. I need to talk. Share. Celebrate. My energy is whirling.

312

Changing into a white tank, shorts and flip flops, I quickly brush my teeth and throw on a hoodie so the twins don't decide to flirt with anyone we might pass in the hall.

Five minutes later, Hale is opening his door. He's wearing sweatpants and glasses. That's it. Sweatpants and glasses. And my mouth goes absolutely dry as I am slammed with the visual I knew would be good, just not quite this good. The valleys between his abdominal muscles need my tongue. It would be like tracing my way through a maze. With my tongue.

Behind him, spread out on the desk are papers. He's still working.

"I'm interrupting." And suddenly I feel bad about disturbing him.

"You're a welcome break." His eyes are warm and tired.

He smiles. Something I've missed, but didn't know how much until now when I finally see it again. And I want to make him smile again, because I'm being greedy. I need it.

"I just have to talk. About today." I start rambling. "Hale, this was so crazy amazing watching it all come together. Are you happy with these results?" I make my way over to his mini-bar and grab a water to ease my Sahara mouth, then sit down cross-legged on his bed to open it.

"Yes, though I see we probably could've added another day to the schedule to really work through things. I didn't anticipate that time would become as much of a factor as it has."

I'm nodding, "Yes, because it is so interactive and everyone is so engaged and invested, things are running over. But the dialogue is so good, you don't want to shut it down. I really think these people have forged a kinship with one another through this process that could have far reaching ramifications and result in alliances even beyond this group's accomplishments."

Hale just smiles at me.

"But that was your plan all along, Mr. Lundström, wasn't it?" It's finally dawning on me that Hale Lundström is both an architect and a statesman. This is so much bigger than I even realized when he shared all the pieces with me three weeks back. "Wow," shaking my head as each realization hits.

Putting the water bottle between my legs, I unzip my hoodie, my mind spinning wildly as the pieces come together.

"Whoa, now that's not fair." He looks serious.

"What?" He's lost me now.

"That." He points to me.

Looking down at myself I realize to what he is referring. The white ribbed tank top.

Laughing. "Why not fair?"

"Because you are testing me, Sierra."

Gesturing with my hand at his bare chest, "And you're not?"

"I just got comfortable to work," he defends his attire, or lack thereof.

"And I just got comfortable to talk about today because I was so excited."

"And is that what you want to do? Talk?" He is standing halfway across the room, arms crossed over his delectable chest.

"Yes. And…"

"And what?" he cuts me off.

"And, well this time tomorrow night we will no longer be working together."

"But we still are." He reminds me.

"Do you want me to leave?" I'm confused.

"Hell no." And there's that smile again.

"I want to share this with you, Hale. I want to be here with you celebrating the success of your vision." I don't want to be doing this alone anymore.

"Fair enough." He's just looking at me, as if he's weighing data. "I have about another hour's worth of work."

Putting my water bottle on one of the nightstands, I stand up and toss my hoodie on a chair. "Okay, I won't bug you." And I lift the duvet cover and slip under it. Punching the pillow a few times, I get it just right to lay my head down. The minute my eyes are closed, I start drifting off.

"What are you doing in my bed, mermaid?"

I feel Hale's long body spoon around mine. I can tell from his legs that he's still in his sweats and I smile. Our first time in bed together and we're both clothed. It's really kind of cute. I've been imagining for months what it would feel like to be in his arms in bed.

"I was sleeping." I snuggle back into him.

"Do you really expect me to sleep with you here?"

"Mmm-hmm, I do. And I expect you to tell me how great you sleep with me in your arms."

"That's a given."

His lips on my neck cause an instant shudder and he throws a leg over mine, inserting his calf between my legs and pulling me tighter against his frame.

Reaching for his right hand, I cover it with mine and move it up my belly and under my tank top, raising it to my right breast where I leave it, still covered by my hand as if I'm giving him a personal introduction to the twins.

Giving my breast a hard squeeze, his thumb and forefinger encircle my already hard as a rock nipple and softly begin to twist it. I moan as the motion shoots an electric current directly between my legs. "Hale."

"Mmm," he moans into the skin of my neck, "do you know how long I've waited for you to call out my name like that?" He increases the pinch, twisting my nipple tighter.

"Oh God, Hale," my voice is a whimper.

"Yeah, babe. Just like that." And he twists tighter. With his leg, he pulls me up against him closer so that I can feel how hard he is, even through his sweat pants. "Do you feel that?" he whispers, pressing his hardness into my back. "Tomorrow night it is not coming out of you and that's a promise."

Just his words make me moan. The thought of him filling me all night makes me clench every muscle between my legs. "Hold me tighter." I turn my head around, needing to find his lips in the darkness. His kiss is soft at first, then increasingly demanding. When our lips part, I tell him, "I've needed you to kiss me for three weeks."

"You've been amazing," he nuzzles my neck. "I can't thank you enough for everything you've done and for understanding that all my attention needed to be focused on this."

"I understand. It doesn't mean I didn't miss you," I admit in the dark.

"It doesn't mean I didn't miss you either, mermaid."

I needed to hear those words. I squish back into him, a smile on my face. "Hale…"

"Yes, Sierra…"

"I'm falling in love with you." I didn't plan for those words to tumble out of me and hang on the night air. Fear would like me to grab them back and reel them in, but they are gone, out of reach.

SLAVE TO LOVE

Tightening his arms around me, he rubs his stubble across my neck, a delicious scratch of pain, "That's a good thing. A very good thing, mermaid, because I've fallen in love with you."

And with those words, in the warm protection of his arms, I release fear, rejoicing that there will be a next phase of our journey. Letting sleep claim me, I know that by this time tomorrow, I'll be free to openly love him.

CHAPTER
Twenty-Six

*T*he final day of TFV1 and we are down to the nitty-gritty of how to implement the strategies we agreed upon last night. Today is tactics; hardcore plans on getting the ball rolling to safeguard technology throughout the world from attacks and meltdown.

In a room right off the dining room are nine Ministers of Technology representing countries from every continent. They are drafting an accord that will be presented to all United Nations countries for adoption. Sitting a few feet away from the table, I let them hammer out the details, and only step in when mediation is needed, or I see a glaring hole. The pride I feel is overwhelming and very paternal as I watch this group of, in some cases, warring nations, come together for the greater good of everyone on the planet. I am astounded, my expectations so far exceeded as they have bolstered my faith in people to do the right thing.

An hour later, I make my way to another room, this time filled with tech CEOs. Again, I sit on the outskirts of the action knowing that they will take ownership of what they craft. If it is theirs, they will implement it. What strikes me about this group is its diversity, from the young Turks of the fastest growing tech start-ups to the old guard at the helm of the institutions that have brought us the technology that has become inextricably woven into the fabric of our lives, since the first personal computers and automated teller machines changed our world.

Sierra enters the room and stands by the door, observing. Today I'm not even trying to hide my smile. In another two hours this will all be over and the participants will start departing. Their limos have already begun to arrive and are lining up in the great driveway outside the main building.

Our eyes meet and I don't think I've ever seen her look so happy, so content. Waking up wrapped around her early this morning felt like a gift. A gift I didn't know I had been longing for. And now seeing her standing against the wall, looking very professional in a deep blue and black silk dress, I can't help but think that she is wearing the mermaid and the high black Louboutins for me. Just me. With a hard push, I shove away the vision of her legs wrapped around my neck, still wearing the Louboutins. That is a vision I know will definitely become reality and I will be requesting those sparkly pumps she wore on the first night we met.

Turning back to the group to help mediate a sticking point on priority protocol, I find when I look back, Sierra has slipped out, just as she did this morning shortly after we woke.*Not happening tomorrow morning, mermaid. You're staying in my bed as long as I want you there. And by then, you won't be able to walk.*

There's a camaraderie and respect amongst this group and it is the diversity of the participants that is ensuring their product is so well rounded. It appears that there is mentoring occurring in both directions and the lack of ego among these profoundly successful men is the reason they have reached the pinnacle of their fields.

With a jolt, I am catapulted out of my seat, every fiber in my being poised to defend and attack. It's Garber's voice in my ear repeating the words, "Code Red. Man down at the main gate. I repeat Code Red. Move all participants to the bunker immediately. I repeat. Code Red. Man down. Participants to the bunker."

Immediately I am ushering the group down a set of fire stairs on the south end of the building to the subterranean chamber.

"Before anyone enters that bunker I want them searched for handheld weapons and explosive vests. Have two people stationed at the door so that we can do that fast and get them all in there immediately and get that room sealed," I issue the immediate order, for now everyone is a suspect, including all of this weekend's participants. Whoever leaked this location could very well be one of the people we are protecting in the bunker.

"CEOs delivered." I report, leaving the group with the personnel assigned to search them before providing safe harbor.

Bounding up the stairs two at a time, I am greeted at the top by one of our guards who quickly supplies me with a M4A1 carbine automatic rifle and three magazines.

"This is Lundström, give me an update on participants' locations." I speak into my wrist mic.

"Diplomats delivered," a voice informs.

"Just dropped off nine from the green room."

"Six heading to west stairwell. That will give us a complete headcount of all guests and staff."

"Heading there now," I inform him. My first priority is ensuring the safety of guests and non-security/non-military staff.

I reach the door to the bunker at the same time the last six occupants arrive. Sierra is amongst this final group; I can see the fear in her eyes.

Grabbing my arm, I hear the pleading in her voice, "Aren't you coming in with us?"

"No," I shake my head. "My job's out here. Stay calm you're going to be fine."

"And you?" Tears are filling her eyes, threatening a quick run down her cheeks.

She's worried about me. "I'll be fine. We have a date tonight." Then with an order to one of the men, "Seal it," and the door to the bunker seals closed.

"Bunker sealed," I message Garber and hear gunfire the minute I exit the stairwell. "Give me a clear route."

"Through the kitchen to the main dining room. I'll meet you there." As I make my way through the facility, "Palmer, update," I make contact with my chief of security.

"One down, one wounded. Two down of theirs. Appears to be eleven total standing and they've breached a second point on the perimeter. Northeast corner."

"Have we called for help?"

"Yes, Texas National Guard is in route out of Camp Mabry. Both Lackland and Fort Hood have been alerted," he apprises me.

Reaching Garber, I take a look at the bank of surveillance cameras being monitored by one of the men. "Assault rifles." I comment on the well-outfitted interlopers. "If we go to the roof on the north side of the main building, we can take out these three." I'm out the door as soon as it's out of my mouth.

"No Hale, stay here. You're a private citizen. I'll handle this." He pushes by me before I can protest.

I know he's right. I can't be in this fray unless defending myself face-to-face. I want to be solving this issue, not sitting on the sidelines. Leaning down with my hands on the edge of the surveillance console, I begin to bark out orders. "Two more dissidents approaching from the main drive, both are armed, 500 meters out, will be a clear shot from the west in approximately nine seconds. Four seconds." The interval passes, "*Now,*" I command and two go down in a hail of gunfire.

Looking back to where Garber is, "Jeff, clear shot in approximately six seconds."

"I've got it silenced," he informs me, in what is slightly more than a whisper. He wants all three down before they have time to react.

"Now," I yell in his ear and we watch the third guy in the group go down, followed by the second. The lead guy takes off in a run, and lobs something toward the building with the arm of a quarterback, before Jeff's bullet neutralizes him.

The blast is deafening as the walls and floor take on a jello-like motion and secondary crashes ensue. We no longer have video coverage of the north side of the building.

Grabbing the assault rifle, I turn for the door.

"Mr. Lundström, you should stay here," the guy monitoring video warns.

Shaking my head no, I don't miss a step. "He's my guy," I call out, heading toward the north side of the facility. The smoke still smells far off, but I can hear the shushing sound of the emergency sprinklers.

I've got to get to Jeff. Find him and get him out of there. He's here because of me. Because I asked him. And just as I would never have left him or any of my guys behind in Afghanistan or Syria, I'm not leaving him behind and vulnerable here.

To my left is a fire stairs that will give me roof access and I can try and make my way north from there. Wind was out of the south this morning, so that should bode well for me to make it as far as I can in a smoky situation.

"Garber," I yell, as soon as I'm out of the staircase. "Gaaaarberrrr."

Smoke and flames are obscuring a portion of the north roof. Calculating Jeff's angle, I cut a sharp left and see him partially obscured by rubble.

"What took you so long? Get this shit off my leg."

My boy is still with us and a hundred pound weight lifts from my heart.

"Give me a second, dude, and I'll get you freed." I start lifting the concrete from his leg. "You're not going to be dancing anytime soon. Your tibia and fibula have seen better days." With the third slab removed, I can see his leg. "Let's get you out of here." And with his arm slung around my neck, we start making our way to the stairs.

"It had to be an inside job, Hale. Someone in that bunker? Are they targeting someone else?"

"I don't know. I thought we had this thing airtight. What didn't I see? Lean all your weight on me," I direct as we hit the steps.

"We are clear of all dissident threat," the message plays in my ear.

"We've got them all," I advise Garber.

"What's that sound?" he asks.

"Emergency sprinkler system."

"Shit," he growls, "Hale, get to the bunker now. That was the target. This was just the diversion. They're all going to drown in there. This place is equipped with a high-flow military grade sprinkler system."

And in one stunningly painful moment, it's all clear as day. The bunker was always the primary target and trapped inside to drown are all the TFV1 participants, my staff and Sierra Stone.

Leaving Jeff in the stairwell with a handgun and my shirtsleeve tied tightly around his thigh, I'm at full speed across the facility to the south end where the entrance to the bunker is located. Calling into my microphone, "I need all available men to the bunker, they're flooding out in there."

By the time I reach mid-building, I'm wading through knee deep water rushing down the hall. It's impossible to move fast in the current.

"Palmer, can you hear me?"

"Yes, boss."

"Cut all sprinkler systems immediately. This place is on its own well system, figure out a way to take that down for now."

"I'm deploying two men immediately."

"Do we have an alternate way to access the bunker?" We've got to stop the flooding and we've got to get them out.

"I need your fingerprint, Hale, to override. How quickly can you get here?" Palmer's voice is stressed.

"The water is slowing me up," I'm quickly losing breath. "Probably still three to four minutes out."

"Hurry."

The halls seem interminable as I fight the deepening tide of water. I've got to get to them before they all drown. I need to save every single person in that room. I cannot let them drown. Not one single one of them. Including my mermaid.

My lungs are burning, my muscles fatigued. The hallway where I need to turn is finally in sight. I visualize basic training and I am twenty years old and indestructible. Wading through water. Nothing, totally easy. Save a roomful of people. I'm your man. Lead everyone out of here. Hell, that's why you recruited me. This is what I do.

"Palmer, I'm within visual." I pant.

One of the guys breaks away and wades to meet me. Grabbing my arm he helps to get me through the last of it.

"Here's the keypad, Hale. Your right thumb followed by your code." As I input the numbers, I say a silent prayer for what we will find behind the door.

The reinforced steel door starts to slowly move open, hampered by the pressure of the water on the outside, but after the seal lock is broken and the first few inches of movement, the pressure built up by the significant amount of water taken on in the smaller chamber forces the door open with a rush, sweeping the occupants from within the bunker as if they were toddlers riding in a wave pool.

"Station men down the hall to grab everyone and get them to their feet. And I need someone taking headcount." I yell.

Sputtering people float out in the initial wave and then it begins to slow off.

"How many are we missing," I yell.

"We have all but three."

"Come on," I say to two of the guys. And we make our way into the bunker.

Immediately I see her hair floating around her, like a mermaid, gently swaying in the tide. *Mermaids are supposed to breathe underwater,* is the thought going through my head. So this is all wrong, because Sierra is definitely not breathing.

Scooping her into my arms, "I need a place to perform CPR," I yell and two men are there to help, to take her from me. But I can't let go. I will not let go. Not until she is breathing again.

"Right here, Hale." Palmer yells out, pointing to a table that is well above water level.

I lay her down gently and simultaneously put my cheek near her mouth and nose and grab her wrist to feel for a pulse.

Quickly, I turn her head and water streams from her mouth and nose. Moving the mermaid necklace to the side, I direct one of the men, "Start chest compressions now," as I begin mouth-to-mouth.

Tilting back her neck to make sure her airway is clear, I cover her mouth with mine, exhaling into her. Her chest rises and I fill it again. My counterpart has his rhythm down and I send more air down into her lungs.

SLAVE TO LOVE

C'mon, mermaid, breathe for me. We've got a date tonight, you and I. Now's our time. I need you to breathe, baby. You're my mermaid, you can breathe underwater. You don't understand, I can't lose you this way. Not this way. Breathe, baby. I need you to breathe, Sierra.

More breaths sent into her. *I will breathe for you as long as I need to.*

"How far away is help?" I scream between breaths and then clamp my mouth down on Sierra's again.

A gurgle erupts from deep in her chest and I pull my mouth away and quickly turn her head to the side as a mixture of water and vomit erupts in spurts, followed by coughing and gasping and then more vomiting. I've turned her on her side and have her propped against me.

"You're going to be okay, baby. You're going to be okay." I brush her wet hair back from her face. "Everything's going to be all right."

"Texas Guard has arrived." I'm informed by someone.

"Let's AirEvac her out of here and we've got a wounded man in the north stairwell. His right leg is in bad shape. He's going to need fluid resuscitation."

"Sir, will you be going with them?" Someone asks.

"Yes. I'll be there in a moment." There's a part of me that feels responsible for everyone here and making sure that they leave here securely. That is typically what I would do.

But this time, I realize there is only one place I need to be and that is with the people I love.

Grabbing Palmer and two other guys, we head upstairs and quickly find our logistics guy and the site commander with the Texas Guard.

"We're moving everyone to Camp Mabry for individual debriefing, Mr. Lundström."

"You realize how sensitive this is?" I need to make sure my guys let them know with what they are dealing.

187

"We do, sir, and Homeland is going to be coordinating everything."

"Okay, great." Turning to Palmer, "Make sure Colonel Hoffman is brought into this immediately. I'm going with Ms. Stone and Mr. Garber to Brackenridge Hospital. You can get hold of me there."

And with that, I begin sprinting across the lawn so that I don't hold up their flights to the hospital any longer.

CHAPTER
Twenty-Seven

My lungs are burning. I want to cry out, but I can't. It hurts too much. And then I feel a sharp pain in my finger. *Where did that come from?* I wonder.

Opening my eyes, a nurse is squeezing my finger, trying to get blood into a little tube.

"Welcome back," she whispers with a smile.

"Where am I?" my voice isn't more than a weak croak.

"Shh, don't strain yourself. You're at Brackenridge Hospital and you are going to be just fine."

"How did I get here?" The effort to speak is enormous. My lungs and windpipe are searing.

"Shh, don't talk. You were AirEvac'ed in early yesterday afternoon. Your boyfriend can give you all the details." She looks at me kindly.

"My boyfriend?" I have no idea what she's talking about. *Early yesterday afternoon?*

She motions over to a sleeping figure in a chair, "He must've just fallen asleep. He's been by your bedside since you arrived."

In the dim light, Hale rests in a chair wearing hospital scrubs. The scruff on his jaw is heavy.

"Get some more rest. Your body needs it. I'm going to give you something to make you comfortable and it will also help the burning feeling in your lungs." She empties a syringe directly into my IV line.

I want to protest, I want to talk to Hale, find out what happened, but by the time she finishes injecting the medication, I can no longer keep my eyes open.

I feel his hands in my hair. His voice is gruff with emotion even though he's speaking at little more than a whisper. "That was a scary few minutes there, mermaid. I couldn't let myself think the worst. That just wasn't an option. If you think I'm going to let you go that easily, well, you don't know me." He continues to caress my hair. "We really need to get away. Maybe the mountains, go up to Wyoming. I would say the beach," he chuckles, "but I think the only water I'm going to let you near is the shower and that's only if I'm in there with you."

I wonder if this is a dream. My mouth is beyond dry. Opening my eyes, it's not a dream. Hale is sitting close to the bed, up near my head.

"I need water." He gives me an odd look at the request. "Thirsty." It hurts to talk. My throat and chest are in agony. I feel bruised and broken.

"I think you are allowed these." He puts a spoon of ice chips to my lips. They cool my parched lips and throat for a moment. Only a moment.

"More." He feeds me another spoonful. Looking around, I spy a small Styrofoam water pitcher and point to it with the arm not bound by an IV.

"Okay, I'll ask the nurse." He walks out of the room and I notice he's in blue scrubs and remember a memory from waking last night. A few moments later he's carrying a large cup with a lid and a straw. "She said to sip it slowly. They don't want you getting sick."

I can feel the ice cold water travel the entire journey down to my stomach, cooling the flames as it moves along. "What happened? Is everyone okay?" I have no voice and Hale has to put his ear close to my mouth to hear me.

"All the participants are okay. Jeff is down the hall with his right leg a bit messed up, and we lost two perimeter men." The pain in his eyes feels like a stab to my chest as he shares the update with me. I know him, he is beating himself up for all of it. Taking on full responsibility.

"Do they know anything yet?"

Shaking his head, "Homeland and the FBI are handling it."

"Up until that it was such a success."

"Yeah, it was." Taking my hand, he leans down and presses his lips to the inside of my wrist. "You scared me, Sierra." He's lost in his own thoughts for a moment. "Do you know how to swim?"

I nod and feel the tears coming to my eyes just recollecting the fear of not making it out of there.

"Do you remember what happened?" He's rubbing my hand softly on his scruff and it feels so good.

Trying so hard to pluck the memories and soon they begin to pop up in different parts of my head like Whack-a-Mole. "When the door just inched open, the water started to pull, like a tide. I got dragged under and then got my head up." Thinking for a second, "I couldn't move forward and I realized the heel of my shoe was caught in a grate in the floor and I couldn't unwedge it. So I bent down to try and pull it out and something must've hit into me because I felt pain. And that's all I remember."

The smile that makes me feel amazing is on Hale's face for the first time and the effect is like the nurse added some good drugs to my IV. "You went down for a shoe?" I'm not sure if his look is one of astonishment or amusement or a combination of the two.

"It was a Louboutin." I am dead serious and he loses it laughing.

"Mermaid, I will buy you one hundred pairs of Louboutins. Just please don't risk your life like that again."

"When can I leave here?"

"When a neurologist says you're okay. There's a lot of testing they're going to be putting you through before they release you." He weaves his fingers with mine. "I called your mom and Kemp. They're both up to speed and know you are out of danger."

"You spoke to my mom?"

"Yes. She was very nice. Kemp got the number for me. She wanted to fly out to take care of you when you get out, but I told her that it wasn't necessary because you would be staying with me and I promised I would take a lot better care of you than I did this weekend."

"Staying with you?" I feel like I can only repeat sections of what he is telling me.

"Yes. I told her that maybe we could all spend Thanksgiving together." His smile is huge as he drops bombshell after bombshell.

"Who does she think you are?"

"I think I might've used the phrase 'Sugar Daddy'."

I try to laugh but the burn turns it into a hacking spasm. Holding the cup and straw as I drink, Hale smiles, "Last night wasn't exactly what we'd planned. You owe me, Sierra."

"Start coughing up those Louboutins, Sugar Daddy."

"I think I'm going to keep you barefoot for a while. Shove over a little."

Scooching over to make room, he crawls in to the bed, lying on his side facing me. "You look exhausted, Hale." I press my lips to his forehead.

"Mmm-hmm," he takes my hand again, threading our fingers as he brings it up to his lips. A second doesn't pass before his lids close and his breathing tells me that exhaustion has claimed its next victim.

•••••••••••••••••••••••••••••

"I didn't expect to feel this weak." Leaning against Hale, we enter his apartment, and I'm immediately struck by the grand scale of everything. The curved glass walls make the space feel more loft-like than I had envisioned.

"This way," he steers me to the left and down to the end of the hall to the master bedroom. His headboard is a lush dark brown padded leather and the bed is topped with a down blanket in a white duvet.

"Let me get you something to change into," and he disappears into the closet. When he emerges he's holding a white button down shirt. "Get in bed, woman," he demands and gently pushes me down by the shoulders into a seated position.

Sensing my discomfort and slight confusion, "Let me go get you some extra pillows and something to drink."

Leaving me on my own, I start to disrobe from the hospital scrubs I was sent home in and slip his shirt over my head without unbuttoning it. It's longer than some of my dresses, I observe. Getting under the covers, I'm attempting to roll up the sleeves, when Hale reenters.

"Let me help you with that." He sits down next to me and expertly rolls the cuffs. When he's finished, "Sit forward, so I can get these behind you," and he places two king-sized pillows against the headboard.

"You need rest, mermaid." He takes a strand of my hair and lets it run through his fingers. "What can I bring you? Can I get you anything?"

I pat the bed next to me, he smiles, gets up and walks around to the other side, kicking of his shoes. Getting in, he remains above the covers.

Rolling over, I put my head on his chest and wrap my right arm around him. "Thank you for taking care of me."

Laughing, "Thank you for letting me. I didn't know if you would. I finally got you in my bed." He gently strokes my hair.

"So, are you ever going to kiss me?" I'm tired, I feel like crap, but I want to feel this man all over me and he's treating me like a porcelain doll.

"Baby, your body has been through a lot of trauma this week, you need rest. And you really need it for what I plan on doing to you." He gently pushes the hair from my face.

"You can kiss me." I am not letting this man leave the bed.

"Yeah, but I won't be able to stop."

"Are you going to make me beg you to kiss me? It's what I need more than anything."

Turning toward me, he gets under the blanket and pulls me into the length of his body. "How can I deny that?"

"Hale," looking up into his handsome face, "hold me tighter."

As his arms pull me closer, I can feel the tears surfacing, before they break into sobs, erupting out of nowhere and I realize how shaken and scared I am. Within Hale's embrace, I no longer have to call upon strength that's depleting my energy.

"Shhhh, it's okay, Sierra. I've got you," his voice is soothing as he starts a gentle rocking motion. "You're safe, baby. You'll stay here with me for as long as you'd like."

Reaching back to the nightstand, he grabs a tissue and dabs under my eyes.

"They were trying to kill somebody," I finally manage. "Who?" I search his dark blue eyes for an answer.

"The best intelligence resources, from multiple countries, are on it. They will figure out who leaked the location, who the shooters were, what group or person they are affiliated with, who the target was. We'll have all the answers," his voice is calm, intensely calm.

"Hale, do you think they were after you?" I'm so worried for his safety. If anything happened to him…

Shaking his head, "I really don't, Sierra. There were definitely higher value targets in there. I'm kind of low on that totem pole."

"Would you get a bodyguard for a little while?" I need him to be safe.

Smiling, he kisses my forehead. "You want me to get a bodyguard?"

Nodding, the tears begin anew. "I don't want anything to happen to you."

"I honestly don't think I need personal security, baby, but if you'll sleep better at night, I'll hire someone until we have answers from last weekend."

"Thank you," I manage.

"I love that you are worried about me." His smile is brilliant.

"I don't want to lose you."

Pulling me tighter, I bury my face in his neck. If there was ever a moment I needed to feel connected, have him joined to me, buried deep inside me so that I don't know where he ends and I begin, now is that moment.

"You need rest," he whispers in my ear.

Shaking my head, "I'll rest after you make love to me. I need to be yours."

"In my head you were mine from the night in the St. Regis. I just didn't know how wonderful you really were."

"You were so mean to me."

"I couldn't speak. I couldn't even look at you."

"Why?"

"I didn't want you to think I was a jerk," he admits, candidly.

"Why would I think that?"

"Because I was tongue-tied, Sierra. I wanted to impress you and you were all like, we need to leave, we need to go downtown. Susan clearly wanted to stay and you didn't give a shit. You could not wait to get out of there."

"I thought you hated me."

"And then I made that dumbassed comment about your legs and you just zinged me."

I laugh at the memory.

Running his fingers through my hair, "I wanted to go all cave man on you, drag you upstairs to a room and fuck your brains out."

"And now you've got me in your bed and you still haven't made love to me." I'm going to taunt him until I get my way.

"See, that's the big difference."

"What is?" I'm not quite sure what is so evident to him.

"I wanted to fuck you then. Which I still do. Over and over again. But right now, I want to make love to you. I want to make a memory with you that wherever we are in our lives, this will always be the standard for making love."

"You want me having sex with other men?"

The look on his face is classic. "No. Me, only me, Sierra. The other night I said, I love you. I meant that."

"So what does that mean, Hale? What does 'I love you' mean to you?"

"It means you have my heart. I will always put you first. You are the most important thing to me. You can trust me with anything and everything, but especially with your heart."

I remain silent.

"Trust me, Sierra."

Silently, I begin to unbutton the shirt of his that I am wearing. Watching me, I hear his breath catch. After the last button is opened, I shrug the shirt from my shoulders and kick the blanket away.

I watch as he takes me in, his eyes sweeping up and down my body that I have just offered up for his enjoyment. Reaching out, I take his hand and place his thumb and forefinger around my left nipple.

"Hard," is all I say and he complies with a rough twist. My smile tells him to go harder and he complies, twisting until I moan. Rolling to my back, both nipples are now open to him and both his hands are on them.

"Do you like it a little rough, Sierra?" His eyes are smoldering and I know there is no way he is going to stop now.

"I like it more than a little rough, Hale. But I think you already surmised that."

"Well today we're not going to get too rough, but I can't promise anything about tomorrow or the next day."

"Suck them," I direct and reach for his head to press it to my breasts.

"You're telling me what to do?" He's amused, but the look in his eyes is dangerous and I crave him even more.

"I am." I don't back down.

Taking my hands from his head, he holds them out to the side as he covers my body with his.

"You are really telling me what to do? You are so amusing. That's actually pretty hot."

He's got my body pinned.

"Women don't tell you what to do?"

"I do what I want." Right under the surface is the guy who plays Russian roulette with danger, who takes chances with his life because of some deep-seated need I've yet to uncover.

"Well, maybe that isn't satisfying to your partner. Or don't you care?" I hold his eye contact. We're in a don't blink situation.

"Do you think I'll leave you unsatisfied?"

His smirk makes me want to struggle with him, but I remain very calm and in control.

"Not if you care."

"You said before that you wanted to be mine." He uses my words as a weapon.

"Yes, but that doesn't mean I don't get to be an active participant." I realize that right now we are laying ground rules for the future and defining our relationship.

"Sierra, I wouldn't want it any other way with you. That's what makes you so damn hot and sexy."

"But you don't want me to tell you what to do." I'm confused.

"Nope. I want you to spread your legs and touch yourself. Show me how you touch yourself when you're thinking about me." He gets up and sits back on his knees between my spread legs. "Touch yourself, Sierra," he orders.

Suddenly I feel shy. No man has ever seen me masturbate before and now Hale wants to watch it from this very close up and personal vantage point. Pulling the blue scrubs top over his head, he flings it to the floor. Now sitting bare-chested between my legs, he pushes my thighs farther apart.

"Come on, Sierra. Show me how you get off when you think about my cock in you." And he spreads me even wider. I am totally open to him and the thought that he could be thrusting into me at any time is getting me very wet. With my forefinger, I slowly circle my clit. Very gently Hale runs a single finger up my slit, just slightly dipping inside of me and then moves his finger to where mine is to moisten the area. His eyes never leave mine.

"You are so damn sexy, mermaid. The night I met you, I went home and jerked off in the shower thinking about you. About your gorgeous hair, and those nipples, which yes, I will suck and your pretty smile and that you knew about the history of that bar and because you weren't even wearing make-up and you didn't care."

As my finger works in circles, my breathing gets ragged. He pushes his hair back and I notice he's practically panting, watching my finger.

"Look at me, Hale." I demand of him. "What do you want to do to me? Tell me."

"It's what I want to do to you first, that is the issue," and he laughs.

"I just want you to kiss me."

"I will after you come."

He's going to make me work for it.

"Well, how about this," Removing my finger from touching myself, I extend my arm to him. "How about if you finish me."

Taking my finger, he sucks it into his mouth. Smiling, he lies down alongside of me. Not missing a beat, his finger takes over. His free hand goes around the back of my head, bringing my lips to his.

"The things I do for you, woman."

I can feel the smile on his lips against mine, but I'm greedy, my tongue searching for his with a longing, although it has only been a few days since they last met. So much has happened and the minute our lips engage, I feel this overwhelming urgency. This almost didn't happen. Sunday's outcome could have been very different. So, this is a gift and the feeling in my heart surges.

His kisses are making me extremely wet, I need him to know so I press down onto his hand to show him just what he is doing to me. As if knowing exactly what my body is saying it needs next, I feel his fingers slide into me as the heel of his palm continues to apply sublime pressure to my clit. The exploration of his fingers have me out of control, attempting to feverishly ride his hand. When he dips his head and sucks my left nipple into his mouth, I totally fall apart against his palm, shattering into a million pieces. Pressing harder against my orgasm, the rumble continues until I'm wracked with aftershocks, trying to pull away because I can't take any more.

"Do you really think I won't satisfy you?" His grin is smug. And covering my body with his, he moves to sucking my right nipple, while pinching and twisting the left. "I have dreamed of these two little witches."

"They are sluts," I agree.

"My little sluts. They like me," he laughs.

"It's true," I'm laughing now, "they see you and start showing off."

Getting off the bed, Hale peels off the scrub pants, revealing a very hard cock under his black boxer briefs. "Are you on anything?"

I nod. And with that the briefs come down and I know that girth is going to feel good, so damn good.

Going back to kneeling between my legs, Hale takes the tip of his cock and rubs it the length of my slit.

Gasping when he applies slight pressure, but doesn't actually push into me, he looks down on me with a teasing grin, "You just got me nice and wet," he claims. "I think I'll do that again." Slowly he runs the length of his cock along me for another run, this time pressing a little harder as he reaches my opening and just hovering there. Taunting me.

With my feet behind him, I press them into his ass, trying to push him into me, but he presses back.

"So you want me inside you, huh?"

"You are a mean, mean man, Hale Lundström."

Laughing, "I'm going to have so much fun torturing you. But you've had a rough week, so I'll be nice, this time." And with a plunge, he is buried deep inside me.

"Yes," I exclaim, "I have waited way too long for that," and with my feet, I press him in deeper. "Stay for as long as you'd like."

"They're going to have to send a search party," he laughs.

He hasn't moved. He's just inside me, very, very still, holding my hands out to the side and looking down at me, smiling.

"I think you should kiss me."

"Great minds think alike, because I was just thinking that exact same thing."

Lowering his head down to mine, he nips at my bottom lip, playfully, then pulls back while I try and lunge for his mouth. With my body pinned under his and my arms restrained out, I don't make it very far.

"Yup, mean, mean man," I mutter.

"What did you just say?" And he stabs himself deep into me, a look of satisfaction on his face and a smile in his eyes.

"I said, you should kiss me."

"Mmm-hmm, yeah, that's what I thought I heard." Again his mouth comes down and the minute his tongue is in my mouth, I tighten my muscles around his cock that he's kept remarkably still. The man has some serious self-control.

"Now that feels good," he scrapes his teeth along my jaw before claiming my mouth again.

Continuing to squeeze him, I change the tempo up with short fast muscle bursts.

Ending our kiss, Hale looks at me, smiling, "It's got a good beat and I think I could dance to it. I give it an A."

I burst out laughing and squeeze him as hard as I can, "Well, then dance."

"You asked for it." He starts to pull out of me and I want to scream *no, please stay*. He looks amused at the shock on my face and rams back into me hard, causing a gasp. "Didn't think you'd get rid of me that easily, did you?"

I shake my head, no. "More." Is my single request.

Pulling my left leg up to his shoulder, his tongue draws a line from the back of my calf to my ankle, where he scrapes his front teeth lightly on the bone.

"Oh my God." The sensation is exquisite.

Pulling my other leg up, he repeats the process and I think I'm ready for it, but I'm not. With my legs closer together, it feels like electro-shock in all the right places. Slowly, Hale begins to move in and out of me, plowing down. The look in his eyes is tender and now serious after the fun and teasing of foreplay, but there is nothing tender in his driving motion as he gets lost to his own rhythm and sensations. His eyes close and watching his face as he builds toward release is incredibly sexy. I wait for the right moment, when he is truly lost, and bear down upon him, tightening my muscles. His eyes fly open, surprised and I mouth, 'now' and nod my head.

And with a groan and a final few thrusts, he is done.

"Wow." He kisses my left foot.

"Pretty damn good for a first time together."

"Very damn good," he concludes, lying down next to me and dragging my head to his chest. "I like the reality."

"Me too."

"That was definitely worth the wait, Sierra."

And I agree. The rapport we built over the months made making love both hotter and more comfortable.

"Have you ever waited for someone before?"

Shaking his head, no. "But there's never been another you before."

"You are trouble, Hale Lundström."

"More than you can imagine, mermaid."

There's a note on the nightstand when I wake, I'm on the other side of the floor in the office. Call or text if you need ANYTHING. I'll bring in dinner.

The great room in the apartment is expansive. On the dining room table are a bunch of floral arrangements. On the outside of a small white envelope I see my name and realize that the flowers are for me.

The first arrangement is a wicker basket filled with purple and pink flowers, it's from my mom and my sister. Next is an arrangement of Star Lilies and I know who they are from without even opening the card. Sure enough, Monica and Beverly. Moving down the table is what looks like a harvest centerpiece with a note from Kemp telling me this was the most unique way to get out of work. The last arrangement looks like it's about three dozen long-stemmed crimson red roses. The message makes me tear up.

> Mermaid,
> Now that you're mine.
> ~ Hale

I'm back in bed napping when he arrives with dinner.

"You hungry?" He pushes the hair gently from my face.

"Starved. And thank you for the beautiful flowers."

He kisses my forehead and takes me by the hand to the kitchen where he's got soup set up at two places on the breakfast bar.

"I hope you like Pho."

"Love it."

He's really adept in the kitchen and I'm enjoying watching him take care of me. It's an odd feeling, mostly because it is so unfamiliar.

"Any news on catching who attacked on Sunday?"

"Not the direct link, but oddly enough several terrorist groups have made claim. People who never should have known anything about the meeting. Intelligence will find the leak."

"I'm sorry everything got ruined and devastated that people were killed."

"Me too, but I've spoken one-on-one with most of the participants and they all want to move to a next round and keep the work of the group going. I think what happened actually solidified the mission even more for the participants."

"That is seriously great news." I run my hand down his forearm. It feels both natural and unnatural touching him, and I immediately decide I need to touch him more so that the feeling won't seem strange.

"Hey, after we finish, I want you to get back in bed and rest and I'm going to go over to your place to pick up some stuff. We can Facetime so that you can direct me around and tell me what you need."

"I can go…" I begin to protest.

"Nope. You need to be in bed for the next day or so. Get your sleep. Your body has been through a big trauma, Sierra." He pauses, "Is there anything in your underwear drawer you don't want me to see?"

Sputtering soup back into the bowl, "Yes. I'm sure there are a few things."

His smile is gorgeous and I can see the wolfish light in his eyes.

"Excellent. Well, then I'll decide which ones should come stay with us." Reaching forward, he tweaks my nipple through my shirt. His shirt.

Dog.

* * *

"Did you bring me anything besides white tank tops and lace underwear?" Looking through this stack, there are no clothes for me to actually step outside the apartment.

"Yeah," he smiles and holds up my Texas shorts.

"Great," I'm shaking my head. He didn't actually bring me any seasonally appropriate clothes. "Hale, it's fall out there. It's cold."

"Who said anything about you going out?" His smile is absolutely predatory, dangerous and hot. "I brought you your laptop, a new cell phone, and I even brought those fall decorations. I would've brought your Christmas stuff, but this was all I could fit into the Lotus."

"No pants? No jeans? My cowboy boots?"

Shaking his head and acting innocent, "Sorry, they didn't fit into the Lotus."

"You dog," I laugh.

"So, it's been five hours." He's very serious again.

"Since what?" I have no idea what he is talking about.

"Since the last time I was inside you."

And with that, he scoops me up in his arms and starts toward the bedroom.

"I thought you wanted me to rest?"

"I do. That's why I'm keeping you on your back. I'll gladly do all the work."

Placing me on the bed, he works off my underwear, but leaves on the tank top I've just changed into.

"Girls, I'm coming for you," he laughs. "And you'll be coming soon, too." Dipping his head, he bites my left nipple through the ribbed material and pinches the right one. "This is just what you've wanted, isn't it," he's talking to them. And if they could speak, they would've told him that he was doing to them exactly what they'd dreamed about. For months.

Grabbing his free hand, I place it between my legs.

"You're a wet one." He smiles and goes back to ravaging my nipple.

"C'mon, touch me. Please." I beg.

"How close can you get to coming with me just sucking your nipples? I need to know." The man is dead serious.

"Hale…" I am now officially whining.

"All in good time, little mermaid. How long did you make me wait for?" He raises his brows. "Months. You tortured me for months."

"Was I worth the wait?" He's got to know how torn I was the whole time, not wanting to compromise my values, yet wanting to explore with him an intimacy I'd never craved with another.

"More than I could've ever imagined." Stripping off his pants and underwear. "I lied about keeping you on your back."

Pulling me into his lap, he lowers me onto his waiting cock, filling me as he pushes me down his length. We're face to face and I put a hand on each scruff-covered cheek and lean forward to kiss him. No games, no amusing answers. He returns my kiss with the fervor to make me moan as I start to slowly move up and down on him.

Without our lips breaking, the motion intensifies, his hands now on my hips driving the pace. He's not being gentle with me and I know this one is for him, a release of the past few months and probably even more so, the past few days. Leaning forward into him I find the spot that's going to get me off fast.

"Oh God, Hale," I repeat.

"That's right, baby, just let go."

"Oh God, oh God, oh God. Haaaaaale." Losing all control, I'm clinging to him, riding him, slamming my body onto his. It's not enough. It's too much. I don't want it to end as I melt into him, shattered and spent.

Taking my face in his hands. "You amaze me. And as far as being worth the wait. I've waited a lifetime for you, Sierra. A few months more was nothing."

"What are you doing working? I thought you'd take a few days off. At least take the week." Kemp's call is in response to my latest email.

"Ugh. You know me, I can't sit still. I've been taking it easy, reading and watching TV for the last four days. Relaxation is definitely overrated."

"I'm really glad you are okay, Sierra. What's with you Texans and these western-style shoot-outs?" he kids.

"Kemp, this was more like streets of Baghdad-style. It was crazy and truly horrifying." Sitting up in Hale's bed, I look out at the clear blue sky over the western hills, truly grateful to be here, enjoying another day in this world.

"I'm glad you're okay, Sierra. I put you on this project because Lundström asked and if anything had happened to you..."

"I'd be haunting your ass," I laugh.

"That is one of my big fears anyway." There's something in his voice when he says that.

"Why Kemp?" Fifteen hundred miles apart and I can feel the air between us get heavy.

"This really isn't a good time to tell you. With what you've been through and all."

My stomach knots. I obviously know what's coming before it's out of his mouth.

He starts, "It's been no secret that Bob Mannon is going to be moving into an advisory capacity. And I'm moving into his role."

I don't even let him finish. "What was the reason behind your decision?" I'm not letting the punchline come out of his mouth.

"You're both so qualified. It was very tough. Right now her numbers are better than yours."

"Seriously, Kemp," there's venom in my voice. "My team has outperformed hers for several years. Not months. Years. And, as we all know, her team's numbers are driven by SpaceCloud revenue, which that team did not sell. It was handed to them on a silver platter. Additional sales were not made by them either, that happened in the freaking Polo Lounge in LA." I'm physically shaking, I'm so angry. "So numbers are a bullshit reason. You need to do better than that."

"She also had a backfill, Sierra, ready to step into her role immediately." I can hear the defensive tone in his voice.

"Who?" I have no clue who the fuck he is talking about.

"Robyn." As if I should know.

"Robyn?" Pussy-baring selfie queen, Robyn, has been promoted to my counterpart? Am I seriously hearing this?

"So, I'm going to be reporting into Susan with her protégé, Robyn, as my counterpart?" I need clarification of the obvious because this is turning into the gateway to insanity.

This is how good performance is rewarded?

"I know there's the potential for you to leave under this scenario."

"You think?"

"Sierra…"

"Kemp, do not go into the valued employee shit with me right now. My team has led the way for years and represented this company with the highest integrity and what? What does it tell me? Bungalow fucking four was my only option for advancement? That is disgusting."

"That is not at all the message. I know this is very emotional for you."

"Don't you dare go down the emotional road with me." I am so angry that my muscles, head to toe, are literally spasming.

"You know I don't want to lose you. You are one of the best employees I've ever had," his voice is calmer now. Now that the bombshell has been dropped. "But if you do decide to leave, you'll be unemployed for under five minutes with probably more chance for growth than you'll ever get in this organization."

"What are you talking about?" He's already got me out the door.

"SpaceCloud. It's no secret that Hale's board and investors have been pressuring him to bring in women at the senior management level since he's got such a gender inequity on his staff. He's ready for you the minute you tell me to take a hike."

"What do you mean he's ready for me?"

"He's prepared to offer you a job," Kemp clarifies.

"Hale Lundström knows I didn't get the promotion?" All the air has been knocked out of me. Sucker punched.

Kemp is silent and I want to make sure I'm reading this one hundred percent correctly and not misinterpreting anything so that I don't go accusing someone of something that is not true.

"Kemp, Hale knew?"

"Yes. And I thought it was good that he had an option waiting for you," he defends.

"Oh you did, huh?" This is way too much for me to process. Hale fucking knew. He never said a word to me. He honored Kemp's confidentiality at my expense, while he was fucking me. Bros before Hos. Isn't that the saying?

"You didn't think it was inappropriate that a client knew I wasn't being promoted before the employee herself knew it?"

"Sierra, it just came up organically in a conversation about how competent you are in all facets of the business and Hale's need for someone like you to round out his organization."

That's all I ever was? Someone to round-out his organization? The employee who said, "No" to the almighty tech god, Hale Lundström, making him even more determined to bed me.

"How long ago did this conversation take place?"

"Several weeks ago," he admits.

"So, both you and Hale have known for several weeks that Susan was going to be offered your position and that Robyn would be my counterpart?"

"Yes, that's what I said." I can hear the annoyance in his voice. He's annoyed with me? He's testy because he has to have this conversation with me? Seriously?

And that's it. *That* is the end of my rope.

"Okay, great. Well you won't need to say it again. I'm done, Kemp. I've worked my ass off and done everything the right way, with integrity. I didn't stab people in the back or use their shoulders as rungs on my personal ascension ladder, I didn't blow anyone or spread my legs to secure my next role. I did everything honorably. But clearly this is not an organization that respects dignity. After nearly losing my life last week, for my job, I remind you, I am done giving. I am resigning, effective immediately. I'll ship my laptop, printer and files to you within the next forty-eight hours."

"Sierra, no one wants you to leave. I don't want you to leave."

"Yeah, Kemp, but you didn't want me to stay."

And with that, a very long chapter in my life is closed and a short segue grinds to an unforeseen halt.

CHAPTER
Twenty-Eight

*S*he walks into my office wearing my shirt, a tank top and her shorts, purple hospital socks on her feet. In her right hand is a Whole Foods reusable bag, filled with things.

Looking up, "Why didn't you text me?" I go to rise from my chair and she motions with her hand for me to stop. "Sierra, what's the matter?"

"What's the matter is that you've been using me. Your board wants you to have a woman exec and I was, what? Auditioning?"

"Baby, that's not…"

"Don't you *baby* me, Hale." The look on her face is terrifying.

"Sierra, calm down," the minute it is out of my mouth I know that was a supreme mistake.

Pointing a finger at me, "Say that again and those will be the last two words you ever speak to me."

And I know she's not bluffing.

"I have not been using you." I wonder what Kemp has said to her. They've obviously had a conversation.

"Bros before hos? Is that it? Keeping Kemp's secret was more important than being honest with me?"

"It was not my place to tell you."

"Wrong answer. You keep telling me that I need to trust you. You really think siding with him is going to build my trust?"

"I didn't side with him, Sierra."

"You kept it from me, Hale. Why, you didn't want me to lose focus and bail before TFV1? You needed me to complete my task so why tell me the truth?"

"I'm sorry I wasn't honest with you. It was a funky situation and I didn't want to risk anything for you."

"Bullshit, Hale. There was nothing left to risk. I didn't get the job. You knew that."

"So what are you going to do?"

"Change everything in my life, because none of it is working for me."

"Did you quit?"

"Yes."

"I couldn't see you working for Susan."

"It's insulting to have Robyn as my counterpart."

"She's really quite bright." Again, the minute that is out of my mouth I want to reach in the air and retrieve it.

"Don't even…" She points at me. "Well I'm glad you enjoy her intellect, she can now spend as much time humping your leg as she'd like."

"What does that mean?"

"It doesn't mean anything."

"You asked me what 'I love you' meant to me, well, what does it mean to you, Sierra?"

"I'll tell you what it doesn't mean, Hale. It doesn't mean being lied to, deceived, used. It doesn't mean putting your needs and other people's needs in front of mine. Everything about your *love* for me was calculated and manipulated to fulfill your corporate and personal agenda and have total power over me," she pauses. "I hate to break it to you, but that's not love, Hale."

"Sierra, yes I want you here at SpaceCloud, you are smart and competent and we work very well together. Having you on my team would be a huge asset. But that is not what this is about."

"You knew what that promotion meant to me. But you kept his confidence. We became lovers and you were keeping secrets and telling me, trust me, trust me. How do I trust you, Hale? Truths are based on your agenda, not my welfare."

She picks up the Whole Foods bag she'd set on the chair. "Please ship the rest of my stuff to me. Don't bring it by. Don't call. Don't text. Do not do drive-bys of my house. I want you to disappear as if I'd never laid eyes on you."

"You don't mean that."

"If you think I don't mean that, then you don't know me at all."

"You're making a mistake, Sierra. Walking out without a job. Without me."

"No mistake, Hale. I'm walking out with my dignity."

And with that, Sierra Stone walked out of my life.

We were just beginning so I'd never even thought about what my world would be without her. She had been in my thoughts constantly from the night she walked into the St. Regis bar and ridding my mind of her was not going to be an easy feat. The months we'd spent making memories were the most real thing I'd had in my life since my time overseas. It was lucid, colorful, painful, exhilarating and wonderful. And it was gone.

The things that fulfilled me before Sierra, felt empty now. But I knew the emptiness was just me and in time, the memories wouldn't be so painful. I needed time. I also knew that Austin was a small city and eventually our paths would cross. Or at least I hoped they would.

She was right. How do you trust a person who doesn't put you and your needs first? My fuck-up was colossal. And self-serving on so many levels. But what I think hurt the most was that she really believed the whole thing was a scam and that I didn't love her. Nothing could've been further from the truth.

Breathing life back into her after the flood jumpstarted my heart in a way she could never fathom. Had she died in my arms that day, I would not have been able to go on. Instead my breath became hers, as I breathed for her. I would have kept going for as long as I needed to had her body not responded. But it did. And in that moment, I exorcised a ghost.

Never, in a million years, would I have thought that within a week I would be so haunted again.

New York City and the SkyTrack at my health club, L9/NYC became my salvation. While running I would replay that last conversation over and over again. I should have pushed Kemp to tell her, not hold off to meet my needs. That was a douchebag move.

"Where's the picture of your girlfriend?" Annette from accounting has wandered into my office.

"She dumped me back in the fall," I confess.

"Now why would she do that, you're so rich and handsome?"

I motion for her to take a seat.

"Because I was an asshole. I wasn't looking out for what was best for her. I did what was best for me."

"It sounds like you've learned your lesson. The holidays are coming up soon. Maybe she's missing you as much as you are missing her."

Laughing, "I doubt that." I smile at Annette who is like a wonderful aunt, "What makes you think I miss her?"

"Not for nothing, Mr. L. but you've had a basset hound face for the last month or so whenever I've seen you. You get these sad, puppy dog eyes. And they are very sad right now. You're still handsome," she adds, "just sad."

Nodding, it feels good to be having this random conversation with this very unlikely woman. "I am very sad, Annette. I wish I could make this right."

"Don't give up hope. If you want to make it right, you will find a way."

I laugh, "She'll tell me to go fuck myself."

"I like her," Annette laughs. "As long as she's not married to someone else, all in love is fair. Remember that, Mr. L."

Later that week at a dinner with Kemp, Susan and Robyn, I feel like I'm cheating on Sierra. I know I'm their client. This is business, but it is difficult to pretend that I'm happy being there. That I'm happy being with them, like nothing's changed. Because everything has changed. The excitement of those months getting to know her, working side by side, sharing in each other's worlds with the Universal and Texas events. The time leading up to when we could be together. And those four days I cared for her. Four days in my bed. I'd saved her. And I'd saved myself.

The most painful moment was going back into my apartment that night. I'd walked in there so many nights and never had it feel that empty. I walked the rooms secretly hoping I'd find her curled up in a chair asleep somewhere. My bedroom felt like a portal to Hell with a big black hole at the center sucking the life out of any breathing matter. My heart hurt being in there. Literally it ached to the point where my breathing felt labored.

The pillows and sheets smelled of her. The scent of us remained long after she was gone. But the single most painful thing was glistening on the nightstand on her side of the bed. Puddled in a small mound was the gold chain I had given her for the mermaid. Sitting on the edge of the bed, I let it run through my fingers over and over again, like sand running through an hourglass, marking the inevitable. Sierra taking the necklace off and leaving it was a symbolic gesture. She'd removed my chains, but I was still bound tightly in hers. I wasn't ready to remove them.

"Where are you tonight, Hale?" Robyn squeezes my hand, bringing me back.

Laughing, "Thinking about things in Austin."

"I cannot wait to go there. I'm thinking about coming in for that music festival in the spring. What's it called again? It's a bunch of initials."

"South by Southwest."

"That's right." Her hand is now on my forearm. "SXSW."

Kemp cuts in, dragging it back to business and my comfort zone. "We're planning our annual sales kick-off meeting agenda. It takes place in January and we rollout all new products and services to the sales team at that time. We also do the annual awards dinner and our President's Club winners are announced. It's a fun time and we would really love to have you there to give a speech to the sales force on growing symbiotic relationships. It's going to be down in New Orleans, so it will be a blast."

"Have Blair check my calendar to see if it's viable." I don't want to commit either way while sitting here.

Moving to the bar after dinner, Kemp pulls me aside. "Have you spoken to Sierra?"

"No. Have you?" It was a question I was dying to ask all night long and obviously so was he.

"No. Not a word. I'm sure Monica and Beverly have been in touch, but I haven't talked with either of them directly. I didn't think she'd quit."

"There was no way it was going to work with Susan trying to micromanage her."

"I thought she'd end up with you."

I thought she'd end up with me, too. But I lost her. I can't tell him that.

Kemp orders a beer and I take a Sazerac. I can't stomach the thought of a Manhattan.

"Do you think she'll stay in Austin?" I ask, leaning on the bar's polished brass rail.

"Oh yeah, she loves it there. I can't imagine she'd leave. There's currently so much growth there and a lot of opportunity. I'm surprised you haven't run into her."

Laughing, "It's not that small a town, dude."

Taking a sip of his beer, "I really miss talking to her. Things just seem so out of balance without her."

You can say that again. "Do you think you made the right decision?"

"Time will tell. But I do wonder," Kemp admits.

CHAPTER
Twenty-Nine

Clicking through my inbox, I open the email for my Austin Business Journal and there he is, front and center. And he's not smiling. But he's staring at me. Intense. Serious. And so fucking hot I don't know whether I'm going to cry or melt.

Miserable doesn't even begin to describe my state of mind since my phone call with Kemp. Devastated that I trusted Hale and he had a freaking agenda the whole time. I was just something to be checked off a list.

I really fell hard for him. He was a man, not a boy. A man who stimulated me intellectually and emotionally. I wanted to know everything about him. Yet, in reality, I knew nothing except the expertly crafted image.

Forwarding the email to Monica and Beverly, I write, "As if Monday's didn't already suck."

"Too bad he's a dick," is Monica's response.

It's another forty minutes before I erase the email, just not ready to stop staring at those deep blue eyes.

"Do you guys want to go somewhere for New Year's?" I email later. It's kind of a rigged question because these two would prefer to be in a casino than anywhere else.

"If my darling husband doesn't throw a fit," is Beverly's response.

"Vegas?" I toss out the bait.

"I'm in."

"I'm in."

Two emails arrive in rapid suggestion.

Laughing, I feel the clouds part for the first time in forever, exposing a thin sliver of blue sky. A beautiful azure stripe reminding me that better days lie ahead.

* * *

Consulting for one of the incubators in town has turned into an amazing gig. I'm helping four start-up companies to get off the ground. One non-profit, two small tech companies and a farm-to-table distributor specializing in meat, dairy and produce from local, family-owned organic farms.

Being able to help them in all facets of company set-up and launch is pure fun. While I've developed and introduced many new products and services in my career, I've always had a big corporate budget behind me and never had to do it in the traditional way of start-ups, by bootstrapping.

Calling on creativity, moxie and contacts, bootstrappers will launch a company seemingly with sheer will and a good, viable idea. There is something so pure about it, versus big business, it becomes a mission, and failure is not an option.

It was scary giving up my golden handcuffs to experience entrepreneurism at its purest. No big salary, no stock options, no first class seats and upgraded hotel rooms, gone is the big expense account and the corporate card. Losing my golden handcuffs has been wildly liberating and I know now, I never, ever want to be bound by a pair of them again.

Working at the incubator has saved my soul, if not my heart. My daylight hours are spent building and growing and creating. It's just the night time that has become interminably long. I miss him. I miss him so much. He permeates my every thought and I want to be sharing everything I'm doing with him. I want his input. I want him to be proud of me. I want him to be excited about my successes. But I can't trust him. And I spend my nights waiting for the dawn when my soul is saved by the salve that daylight brings.

It's dark when I pull my car into the driveway and I can smell the wood burning in neighbors' fireplaces. It's one of those cold December nights that makes me forget I'm living in Texas and I look forward to my flannel pajama bottoms and UGG slippers. Sitting outside my front steps is a box. I scoop it up and unlock the door.

The house feels so toasty and I can smell the pine from my little four foot live tree. Tonight is a soup night, I decide. Opening the box, I realize there is no label on the outside, nothing saying *Harry & David's*, which would immediately clue me in that it was a package from my mother.

There's an inner box, which I slip out. The paper is adorable and I smile as I read it. Covering the box are recipes: Hot Apple Cider, Fruit Cake, Pumpkin Bread, Hot Mulled Wine. Carefully, I remove the paper, so that I can save the recipes. Gasping at the lid of the Kraft colored box emblazoned in white script *Christian Louboutin Paris*, my hands begin to shake.

Opening the box, any slight doubt I may have had as to the sender, dissipates. The box contains the same style black pumps I lost in the flood. Clearly not a coincidence. Searching the box, there is no note, anywhere.

I really don't want to contact him. If I reach out it could be misinterpreted that I want a dialogue. And I don't. I want to heal, rid myself of the unceasing thoughts I have trouble controlling. And they are OCD-like obsessive. I can't extricate him from my heart and he remains, steadfast, an unwanted criminal, who has stolen from me more than I ever thought I possibly possessed.

Do I send them back? Wear them around the house naked as a big fuck you? Throw them out (no, that's a stupid thought).

There was a box outside my front door when I got home. I text Monica.

What was in it?

Black Louboutins. Same ones I lost in the flood.

Hale?

It's got to be.

Have you called him?

No.

Are you going to call him?

No.

Are you going to thank him?

I don't know.

Are you going to keep them?

I don't know.

What size are your feet?

8

Those aren't feet, those are banana boats

Bitch

Hehe. Well wrong size for me or I would have taken the burden off your hands ... or feet ?

Why would he do this?

It's his Christmas present to you.

That's so weird.

No it's not. He's obviously thinking about you, Sierra. He wants to talk to you. Maybe you should talk to him.

If he wants to talk to me it's only because I was the one who said fuck you and he likes to be the one in power.

What he did was very fucked up – on a lot of levels, but I think he had feelings for you and obviously he still has.

Ugh. I can't wait to go to Vegas.

New Year's is going to be EPIC.

SLAVE TO LOVE

I need epic. I think I'll wear my new Louboutins out on New Year's Eve.

You're evil.

❋❋❋❋❋❋❋❋❋❋❋❋❋❋❋❋❋❋❋❋❋❋❋❋❋

Thank you for the replacement shoes. That was really unnecessary.

I didn't do it because it was necessary, Sierra.

Well, thank you anyway and Happy Holidays to you and your family.

Same to you and yours. Will you be home during the holidays?

No. I'll be traveling.

Stay safe, Sierra.

Thank you.

I stare at that conversation and cry. Part of me wants to get in my car and drive across the river to his building. But I don't even know if he is in town anymore. Showing up there would lead to one thing. Sex. And afterwards I'd feel shitty and weak. Totally pathetic that with a gift I go running back to a man that lied about loving me. Lord knows I should've learned about him and his gifts from the chain he gave me.

It isn't worth setting back my heart's healing any more than the shoes have already done. So I just stay home and cry and swear I am going to have a wild time in Vegas and come back with a new outlook and ready to start the new year living again.

CHAPTER Thirty

"Are you ever going to go after her?" Garber lifts the beer bottle to his lips. With just a soft cast on his leg, he is semi-mobile, but not ready to report back to work.

"I don't know that there's any point. She doesn't trust me. Not a great way to start a relationship."

"She does not know how much you love her, Hale. If she knew, I'll bet she'd feel different."

"Maybe." I finish my beer. "But I think it's time for me to just move on. I was fine before her. I'll be fine without her."

"Are you happy without her?"

"Do I look happy?"

"No, you look like a miserable sack of shit."

"Yeah, well I feel like a miserable sack of shit. I've been thinking about spending the holidays out on Nantucket."

"By yourself?"

"Yeah. You're welcome to stay here while I'm gone."

"Thanks. I appreciate that." Pausing, "Lundström, why aren't you going and getting the girl? Drive over there right now and pound on her door."

"Because she's done with me."

"You don't know that for sure."

"Yeah buddy, I do. I fucked this up on so many levels. It took her two damn days to even text me to thank me for those shoes."

"I thought that would at least start a conversation."

"Yeah. Me too. But no such luck. She made it very clear that she wanted that conversation to end. Quickly. She's not coming back to me, Jeff. I've got to move on."

"Can you do that?"

"It's not my choice to make."

CHAPTER
Thirty-One

"Bungalow Four? Seriously? We're in Bungalow Four? Well this is at least one key I won't throw away."

As we pass through the glitzy lobby and head to the west end of the Cosmopolitan Hotel, it becomes increasingly clear with every beat of the dance music that this is not going to be a relaxing little vacation.

"Holy crap, guys. The bungalows are smack in the middle of the Marquee club." I'm immediately overwhelmed by the sights, sounds and throng of people. Gorgeous people.

"We're not letting you pine away for some guy on New Year's Eve." Monica opens the door to the three-story structure and we all let out a collective "wow".

Our triplex bungalow is amazing: media room, theater, bathrooms bigger than my house, a private splash pool on the roof, Mother-of-Pearl walls, fabulous view of the Bellagio fountains and huge freestanding mirrors with TV's built into them.

"Not too shabby," Beverly is inspecting every inch of the place.

"We've got tickets for the New Year's Eve party and reservations for dinner at STK at 9 P.M." Monica smiles at me. "We thought a big slab of meat would be good for you."

Laughing, "It definitely might be. But remember what happens or is eaten in Vegas, stays in Vegas."

Settled in, I wander back through the casino and see a slot machine that immediately catches my eye. "That machine's calling to me," I tell the girls and head off to sit down. Laughing to myself, I feed a twenty dollar bill into the Double Mystical Mermaid and start a good run. Forty-five minutes later, I'm still working on the same twenty, which is now worth three hundred-forty dollars, which makes up for the rank taste of the absolutely terrible Manhattan the hostess has brought me.

"This machine likes you." The deep voice takes me by surprise.

Looking up at the man standing next to me, I'm surprised at how pleasant his face is. Completely bald, and a bit older than my taste, he's a handsome man and definitely Monica's type.

"Yes, it appears to. It's kept me occupied for quite a while now."

"Not going to cash it in?" he asks.

"No, I think this mermaid owes me a bit more."

Laughing, "She looks like you."

The stab to my heart is quick and clean. "Mermaid is my nickname," I confess.

"Are you a good swimmer?" he asks, I guess associating I must like swimming if my nickname is mermaid.

If he says anything about wanting to see me in a bathing suit, he's history.

"Average, I guess."

"Can you breathe underwater?" he jokes.

Looking away and back at the machine as I reach for the lever, "No. I wasn't a very good mermaid after all." Mermaids breathe underwater. I don't know why I hadn't put that together before. I was his mermaid. I was supposed to breathe underwater, not drown. I had totally failed as a mermaid.

Again, I yank the lever down hard. "Woo Hoo," the man yells. "Well, this mermaid was very good to you." The lights are spinning and the sirens and bells ringing as the fabricated sound of coins dropping continues. A red light flashes, 'Call Attendant'.

A man in a dark suit approaches, "Congratulations, Miss. It looks like you've just hit the jackpot. Let me just get in here and verify your machine."

I'm speechless as I rise from my chair and step back. Win? Me? Never. A crowd gathers and I scan for Monica and Beverly, who are finally approaching.

"It's me. It's me. I won a jackpot. They are just verifying it now." I'm shaking, I'm so excited.

"Figures you would win on a mermaid game." Monica ribs me.

"Mermaid was his nickname for me, so I had to play it."

"You're not supposed to think about him, but right now I'm glad you did. Now you can buy dinner and champagne tonight!"

"Definitely my treat." I notice the man who was talking to me is still there. "Monica meet," and I pause.

"Phil." He extends a hand to her.

"I'll be back," I tell the girls. "Tax form and check await me." As I follow the man back to the business office to collect my check for $4,745.25, it's impossible not to think of Hale and the mermaid. I still haven't gotten another chain for the necklace. I'm not ready to wear her yet.

Returning to the mermaid machine with my winnings carefully tucked away, "ready for drinks everyone?" Phil is still there with them. "Would you like to join us?" I offer, and we make our way through the casino to the Vesper Bar feeling as lit up as all the clanging machines.

A few hours later, I stand on the third floor terrace of our bungalow people watching at the Marquee Club below. Monica comes and joins me and we stand silently watching the mating game at its finest.

"Is Phil going to join us for dinner?" We seem to have picked up a fourth, but over drinks we discovered this was a spur of the moment trip for him when he decided to drive in from Sacramento. Recently divorced after twenty-plus years of marriage, he figured he could park himself at a poker table and feel less alone. He generally seemed like a nice man, but we all teased him about being a psycho-killer until we took a tour of his West End Penthouse at the hotel, which put our triplex bungalow to shame. And with that, Phil's stock shot up like a bull market.

"Yeah, he's going to meet us at STK."

"Great. He's really nice, Monica, and not too far of a commute for you. And clearly he can afford your evil ways and champagne taste."

"We'll see," her tone is coy, so I know there's a chance.

Again we lapse into silence as we watch the crowd below. Gorgeous women are dressed to the nines and the men either all work out like crazy or are on steroids. This is worse than Los Angeles for image and I long to be back in Austin where the vibe is always laid back and casual.

Monica is the one to break the silence, "So, Beverly and I have something to tell you."

Turning to her, "Do we need to get Beverly?"

"No, I'll just tell you myself."

"What's going on?"

She takes a deep breath, "We're going to see Hale in two weeks."

"What?" My heart skips a beat and that pain rushes in, spreading throughout every centimeter of my being.

"They have him speaking or doing a presentation or something at the January Sales Kick-Off.

I'm speechless, feeling adrift. He's still there in my world and I'm the one gone. The stranger to my own life. How could this be?

SLAVE TO LOVE

Kick-Off was always the best meeting of the year and a great way to start the new calendar year's sales right. It begins with the annual awards dinner for the year prior's top performers and the winners of President's Club are announced. This is *the* night of the sales year. You are either a winner. Or you don't want to be there. And if you are a winner, you proudly preen as you walked up on stage to receive your award. This year's President's Club, which I would have qualified for, having my team come in over quota, was an extravagant all-expense paid week for two in Monaco.

"Wow. So, you're going to see him." Staring out at the crowd I see nothing. My best friends are going to see him.

"Are you okay?"

"No. Not really. It just hit me how fucked up this all is. I did a really good job. I didn't screw anyone or stab anyone in the back to be successful, and I'm the one on the outs. Everyone will be there. But me. And now Hale is going to be there. With Cuntessa and the slut." I don't want to cry, but holding back the tears isn't going to happen. "I know I chose to leave the company and leave Hale. Those were my decisions, but it still all feels really shitty."

And later that evening, at the stroke of midnight on New Year's Eve, champagne flute in hand, I stand on our balcony in my new black Louboutins and watch packed bodies gyrate on the dance floor below, as Beverly enjoys a slot machine and Monica is lost in the crowd with Phil.

Looking up at the fireworks emblazoning the sky, I make a wish. A very simple wish. That in the new year, I know happiness and peace.

CHAPTER
Thirty-Two

$\mathcal{I}$ was told that the first night of the sales meeting was dress-up night. This was the annual awards ceremony that the entire staff looked forward to all year long. So, here I am, all dressed up. Standing in front of the mirror, I look like a CEO in my tailored charcoal suit and white shirt.

Tonight I'm going to be helping to hand out awards on stage and tomorrow morning I kick off three days of sessions with a keynote on symbiotic relationships in business.

This whole thing feels really odd to me. Everyone here knows Sierra. They worked alongside her for years, and yet she is not here tonight. But I am. There's something wrong with the symmetry and it's really bothering me.

Having had a lot of time to think over Christmas and New Year's, I've decided it is time to start doing for others, time to start giving back. I don't need to save the world anymore, just make a difference in people's lives. And stop thinking about myself so damn much.

Entering the ballroom, I look around and spot bars set up on either side of the room. The lines are fairly lengthy and I randomly pick the one on my right and get in line.

Standing there, a complete stranger to the people both in front and behind me, I listen to the chatter around me.

"So, how's your new boss?" the little redhead asks.

"He seems okay. Kind of a micromanager though." The tall brunette makes a face.

"Well I'll bet Susan is micromanaging him."

"Without a doubt." The brunette rolls her eyes and they both laugh.

"Have you talked to Sierra? It's so weird that she's not here." I want to tell the redhead, you can say that again.

"Almost our entire team is going to get an award tonight. It sucks that she is not going to be the one handing them to us. This guy doesn't even know us. She was in the field with us, earning it. It meant something that she was proud of me. With this guy, it doesn't mean anything, you know." The brunette is clearly emotional about this. "I know you work for Susan, but that job should have been Sierra's."

"You know our whole team was praying she'd get it and we didn't even work for her. It's so weird how this turned out. None of it makes sense."

The emotions coursing through me as I listen to this make it feel like yesterday that she walked out of my office for the last time. What surprises me most is that I have not moved on and as I listen to this conversation, my feelings are all over the place. I'm proud of Sierra and what she built and I'm angry that even the staff sees the injustice. Obviously I'm mad at myself for not being upfront with her and keeping the promotion news from her for my own gain. The overwhelming emotion though is anxiety. I am anxious. I want to see Monica and Beverly and talk to them. Yet, at the same time, I fear what their reaction to me will be.

"There you are." Robyn is touching my arm. "You look so handsome tonight." Wearing a short black dress with sequins that wraps around under her arms, the dress leaves her shoulders bare. She runs her hand down from my shoulder to the middle of my chest. "We have a table over there and I've got a seat saved for you."

"I'll be over once I get a drink."

"Such an exciting night," she says to the two in front of me.

They give each other a look when she departs.

Like a bad penny that keeps showing up, Bob Mannon is at our table. I thought the guy was gone, but it appears this is his last hurrah with a big send-off, a video chronicling his time with the company, gift presentations and speeches galore. His wife, Dorothy, is in attendance, making the most amusing sideshow of the night, watching the interaction between her and Robyn. Dorothy is the ultimate Southern Belle, well-schooled in the art of insulting others graciously while maintaining the most demure of demeanors. Robyn is outwitted, outmatched and outclassed.

"Aren't you a handsome one," Dorothy's eyes sparkle when she speaks.

"You beautiful women just make me look better," I assure her.

"Are you married, Hale?"

"No Dorothy, it seems no one will have me." I love talking to her. She is a lady. And what she's doing with this dog is beyond me.

"That, I cannot believe. Handsome, well-educated, an entrepreneur. There's really no one special in your life?" Her matchmaking wheels are turning.

"There was someone very special until recently," I confide.

"And she let you go?" Her eyes are wide as she waits for the story.

"The truth is, I lost her, Dorothy."

"You aren't over her yet, are you?" The woman is perceptive.

"Not by a long shot," I admit. "You get people to confess their darkest secrets, don't you?" I kid.

"Executive's wife. We have to be multi-skilled." Her eyes quickly shift to Robyn and then back to me.

Leaning over I whisper in her ear, "There isn't anyone here that holds a candle to you." And I'm dead serious.

A few minutes later she asks Bob, "Where is that adorable blonde? Is she sick?"

He looks at her with a blank face.

"Sierra."

"Oh, she's no longer with us," he informs her.

"Well, that's a loss to the organization," is Dorothy's assessment.

Yes it is. I couldn't have agreed with the woman more.

✺✺✺✺✺✺✺✺✺✺✺✺✺✺✺✺✺✺✺✺✺

How I got on stage for the awarding of plaques to the top performers, I'm not sure. But here I am, shaking hands and congratulating them on a fine performance. Since it is not my organization, it is odd for me, as I am not familiar with the employees or their accomplishments.

Seeing Monica climb the stairs to the stage, I feel my breath catch. In an odd way I am one step closer to Sierra. Kemp presents her award and holding up the plaque, she comments to the crowd, "Another trivet," sending laughter throughout the entire room. Posing for a picture with Kemp and her new boss, Jonathan, buys me a second to wipe my suddenly wet palms on the side of my suit.

Sticking out my hand as she approaches, Monica doesn't take it, as all the winners announced before her had. Smiling up at me with a bright beautiful smile, in a low voice she clearly says, "Douche" and walks on. I know there is a smile plastered to my face, but she has caught me off-guard.

A few minutes later when Beverly takes the stage, I'm prepared for her. Taking my hand, her eye contact is direct and intense. With a smile, she utters "Dick" and makes her way down the stage.

SLAVE TO LOVE

Frankly, I am shocked. As a huge client of their company that was unprofessional and rude. But they love Sierra and must know how deeply I have hurt their friend. I need to talk to them. Alone.

After the last award is given and all the President's Club winners have been announced, a video starts running announcing next year's President's Club and getting the team psyched up for a stellar year so that they qualify. The trip is a week in Maui and the room erupts. As the video ends, a light show begins and a DJ sets the room on fire with dance music. Still standing by the stage, Robyn grabs my arm and pulls me onto the dance floor. My eye catches both Beverly and Monica who are witnessing the hijacking.

"Help me," I mouth to them. "Please help me."

Captured in the middle of the floor, I'm searching for the nearest escape route. Certainly my military training can help me with that. It's under a minute before I feel Robyn start to rub on me. With Bob out of commission tonight, I'm her number two man. Like a SWAT team poised to go in, Beverly and Monica flank me before Robyn finishes her first full rub.

Each grabbing a hand, it looks like the three of us are dancing, as we slowly snake our way through the crowd. When we get to the edge of the dance floor, I motion for them to follow me.

Pulling out my keycard, we get into the elevator that serves the penthouse floors and I punch twenty-two. As soon as the door closes and it's only the three of us in there, I look at them, "I owe you."

"She's special, that one." Beverly's voice drips with sarcasm. Clearly Robyn is not her favorite person.

"Where are we going?" asks Monica.

"Someplace where we will not be disturbed by Robyn, Susan or anyone else. And the booze is unlimited and free."

Opening the door, I flip on the light to the Presidential Penthouse, and before us lays an impressive living room richly decorated with a baby grand piano, fireplace and expansive terraces overlooking both the Mississippi River and downtown New Orleans.

"Are we putting you up here?" Beverly asks.

Laughing, "No. I wanted this suite, so I'm putting myself up here."

"Is this the only one like this?" Monica has my number.

I nod, smiling.

"So, Bob doesn't have the biggest suite?" She's smiling back at me.

"That would be correct." Pausing, "I don't like the way he treated Sierra."

"We don't like the way you treated Sierra." Beverly turns from her inspection of the room.

"I'm not thrilled with myself either. I would do anything to go back and handle that whole situation differently." Stepping behind the marble-topped bar. "What can I get you two?"

"Vodka and orange juice." Beverly doesn't look up from examining books on the roll-top desk.

Monica takes a seat on the bar stool across from me, "I'll take a white wine."

"How is she?" I finally ask. I'm dying to know everything. I want even the smallest detail to help make me feel like she's real and was part of my life, that I didn't imagine her. My mermaid.

"She's good."

I know that I'm going to have to keep these liquor glasses full to get anything out of these two.

"Is she working?"

"She is." Monica sips her wine.

"Give me something here, I'm dying to know how she is and what is going on in her life."

"Why?" Beverly comes and sits on the other bar stool.

"Because I care about Sierra. I worry about her."

"She can take care of herself." Monica takes another sip.

"I know that. She's very self-sufficient. But that is not going to stop me from thinking about her and being concerned about her well-being."

"You think about her?" Beverly is looking at me through squinted eyes.

"All the time," I admit. I realize I need to be very candid with these two for them to share anything back. They are loyal to Sierra and very protective. "I think about her all the time."

"Why? Why do you think about her?" Monica takes another sip and I take the opportunity to refill her glass.

"Why do I think about her?" I repeat. "I didn't stop caring about her the day she walked out of my life. I never stopped caring about her." They don't say anything, so I continue. "I love her and I miss her and I'd do anything to make things right."

"So why haven't you?" Monica comes at me like a whip, stinging.

"She was very clear that she wanted me to stay away from her. Not contact her. So I've tried to respect her wishes."

"You sent her shoes."

Turning to Beverly to address that, "Yes I did. She lost the exact same pair in the flood. I know she loves her shoes, so I wanted to replace them."

"And you wanted to contact her." Monica takes another sip.

"Of course I wanted to contact her. I was hoping she'd be ready to talk to me. But that wasn't the case."

I refill Beverly's drink and place it before her. With her lips to the rim, she says, "She wore them New Year's Eve." Monica gives her a look for divulging the information.

My shoes on New Year's. I smile. There's something very Cinderella about that. "Was she wearing the mermaid?" That slips out of my mouth without my thinking.

They both shake their head. And we're silent for a moment. I pour scotch into a rocks glass and announce. "I want her back. And I need your help."

They are shocked at my admission and I know they are thinking why should we help this guy? He hurt her.

Cutting it off at the pass, I lay out my cards. "I love her and I'm not going to get over it, so I need her back. I want her as my girlfriend, I want her as my business partner and when we're ready I want her to be the mother of my children." Both their jaws have now dropped. "I handled a situation poorly and unfortunately it was at the beginning of our relationship where we really hadn't had the time to build up that foundation of trust. So tell me, what do I need to do to get her at least to listen? I'm miserable. Maybe she's fine and doesn't give a shit and I've gone down this dark road on my own, but make no mistake, I am miserable without her."

After way too many weeks of feeling a depression I haven't felt in years, experiencing loss and heartbreak, I have just opened myself fully to these two women. I have laid my heart in their hands and asked them to squeeze it just to keep me alive.

This time it's not their glasses I'm refilling. It's my own.

Beverly is the first to speak. "She's miserable too, Hale. She's not over you. Not by a long shot. She's hurt and she's heartbroken and feels how can she trust or give her heart to a man who will put her at the bottom of the list and manipulate situations to his advantage without thinking about how they affect her."

"I understand. But that is not who I am and I don't need to learn a lesson twice. When I make a mistake, I learn from it and change the behavior. That's where my success comes from. I've learned so much about myself in the past few months, well, actually since the day I met her. I think I'm a better man for it and I'd like her to meet that man." I look from Monica to Beverly, "Can you help me figure out how to make that happen?"

"Hale, we need to stay out of this," Monica informs me, so I fill her glass again.

"But I want her to have my babies." I am shitfaced and they have to be too with the way I am pouring.

"Are you drunk?" Beverly is peering at me through those slitted eyes again. She is intense. Very intense.

Nodding my head, "I am. But I still want Sierra to have my babies." Earnestly, I add, "Four of them."

"Four of them," Monica spits out her wine as we all descend into gut-wrenching laughter. "You want Sierra to have four kids, good luck with that." Tears are streaming down Monica's face.

"I can hire help. I can afford that."

"She's going to need it."

"I just have to knock her up. Four times." As if I've just delivered the funniest punchline on the planet, we are all in hysterics. "So Auntie Monica and Auntie Beverly, I need your help."

"Knocking her up?" Beverly looks confused and I pour her more vodka and orange juice from a carafe.

"No. I can do that myself. I can. I just need you guys to let her know I love her. Very, very much. But I'm going to tell her that myself, too." Pausing, I smile at them, "We need to start working on the babies. She's not getting any younger." Monica is pounding on the bar she is laughing so hard.

"We'll help if you promise to keep a picture of you and pregnant Sierra on your desk for Robyn to see."

"Done." I pound the bar with my fist like a gavel.

"So what kind of babies are you going to have?" Beverly is lost in a fog world.

"Humans and maybe a few animals, too."

"No, girl or boy?" she clarifies.

"Oh. I want three boys and the last one to be a girl." I am totally serious when I spell that out.

A minute later we are all howling like drunk hyenas.

I think this is the first time I've smiled since Sierra walked out of my office.

CHAPTER
Thirty-Three

They are seeing him tonight. Beverly and Monica are seeing Hale at the awards dinner and not being there makes me feel so disconnected from the last decade of my life. I'm adrift and tonight I feel like I'm drowning. Again. Only this time, I'm the only one who can save myself. And maybe a little red wine might double as a lifesaver.

Grabbing a basket, I browse the prepared food section of Central Market. Sliced steak in a Madeira mushroom sauce, twice baked potato and wilted spinach with olive oil and garlic. Moving on to the bakery, I grab a box of scones for the morning and a small container of Miles of Chocolate for tonight. I need a great red wine for this. Mmm, mmm, mmm, alternating bites of the chocolate with sips of wine is going to be orgasmic. And tonight, I really need orgasmic. It's cold enough for a fire, so I'm going to snuggle up in a cashmere throw with Vi Keeland and Penelope Ward's book, *Cocky Bastard,* and lose myself in their characters' world until Monica and Beverly call.

Reds, reds and more reds. The market has a sommelier named Andy with an amazing palate, so if the rack by the bottle has a sticker that says, *Andy's Pick,* I know it's going to be a great bottle of wine. Reading the back label of a Tempranillo from Spain, it touts undercurrents of cherry and plum, leather and oak. That feels about right for the cozy night I'm going to have trying not to think about the awards ceremony where some dude who doesn't even know my old staff at all will be presenting them with their plaques. And Monica and Beverly will be seeing Hale.

"Sierra?"

I look up and gasp. I've just gone from thoughts of Hale to Hale. But it's not Hale, though their resemblance is so strong.

"You're Noel, right?"

"Yes, it's nice to see you again." Extending his hand, I can't help but notice how similar it is to Hale's and for one brief second I want to thread my fingers with his.

"Yes. It is."

"Do you know where Hale is?" He looks concerned.

Odd that he's asking me about his brother and what's even stranger is, that after months of not knowing anything about Hale, this is the one night I actually do know where he is.

"Yes. He's in New Orleans."

Noel lets out a deep sigh and shakes his head. Something is not right. And then he starts talking and it feels like he expects me to know more of the story than I actually know.

"We are so worried about him. Being this down isn't something I've seen in years. I really thought that when he saved you that would be the tide-turning pivotal moment in his life, the thing that righted his ship, so to speak, and that there would be no more heroics to save the world to compensate for the past. I'd hoped that one act would negate the other and he'd feel some kind of redemption, you know."

I'm trying to catch up with what he said. So much of it is just gibberish to me. But the thing that catches my attention immediately, and retains my focus, is what he said about saving me.

"Noel, what do you mean he saved me?"

"When he pulled you out of the water, he saved you." His tone is very factual.

I'm shaking my head, not understanding specifically what he is talking about.

"Sierra, when Hale pulled you out, you weren't breathing."

Opening my mouth to speak, nothing comes out. No one told me that I had stopped breathing that day and once again, I can't get air into my lungs.

"You didn't know?" Noel looks as confused as I feel.

Shaking my head, I'm not sure how to respond. I'm not sure if I can respond.

"You weren't breathing, Sierra. Hale did mouth-to-mouth on you until you began to breathe on your own. I understand it was touch and go there for a while."

Tears spring to my eyes, burning a passage down the middle of my skull. I'm not quite sure why I'm reacting this way, but that is an overwhelming realization. I didn't start breathing on my own. Hale breathed for me.

"Hale saved me?" Speech finally returns.

Noel is nodding, "Yes, he did. And I thought that act in itself would right everything in his world, liberate him from his ghosts. Finally remove all the guilt and suffering he's carried with him almost his entire life. It was his second chance. And then to see him so depressed. He didn't even spend the holidays with us. It just doesn't make sense. This should have been his salvation." The pain in Noel's voice is making my heart constrict.

"Salvation? Salvation from what, Noel?"

"Maggie," the word is little more than a whisper.

The crack in my heart, the one that first appeared with Kemp's phone call, just widened. I swear I heard the crunching sound as it split a little more, new fissures emanating from the main artery.

"His girlfriend Maggie." My voice has a tone I didn't intend it to have, but it does. I think I'm going to be sick.

"Maggie wasn't Hale's girlfriend, Sierra." He pauses and I search his eyes for answers. His voice is choked, "She was mine."

I never felt the bottle of Tempranillo slip from my hands. The crash itself presents as a faraway sound, yet I'm vaguely aware that my legs are wet. Looking down, the red puddle spreads like blood from a gunshot wound, my feet at the epicenter. *How apropos*, is my thought, *it looks just like my heart.*

⁂

Sitting across from Noel in Central Market's Café, this time the red wine is in a glass and I take a healthy gulp before we start to talk.

"My grandparents owned a house on Nantucket that my parents now own and someday Hale and I will jointly own. Summers and all holidays were spent on the island and that is our family place."

I'm trying to envision these two boys, hair wild in the sea breeze as they run through the surf. Two very handsome little boys. The beaches and streets of Nantucket must've felt like their safe place. In my mind it's carefree summers and lobsters.

"Next door to us was the Myers. Their family had been there as long as ours and they were great friends of both my grandparents and my parents. Doors were never closed or locked and we just wandered from house to house. It was pretty idyllic." Noel is lost in a memory and the look on his face makes him look like Hale and I just want to reach out.

"Anyway, the Myers had a daughter, a granddaughter named Maggie. She was between me and Hale in age, a little closer in age to me. There wasn't a time we didn't know Maggie. We were all eating sand together in our diapers. It was hard to know where their family ended and ours began. As we grew older, Maggie and I became a couple, it was something we always knew would happen. So, by the time we hit our teens, Maggie and I were boyfriend and girlfriend.

246

We were each other's firsts. First kiss, first date, first time holding hands and eventually we lost our virginity to one another."

"What was her relationship with Hale?"

"Hale adored her and the feeling was mutual. He had a crush on her, it was impossible not to. The girl was like liquid sunshine. She could light up a room on even the darkest days. We were kind of like the Three Musketeers. Always together. But she was like a big sister to Hale. She babysat for him when he was younger and he loved her like she was family. She would spend hours playing with him on the beach, building sandcastles and walking the beach looking for starfish."

Swirling the wine in his glass, I wonder if Noel can almost see them in the amber liquid.

"The summer I was seventeen, Maggie was sixteen and we were sneaking off, as teenagers do, every chance we could get. We were out of control. Sex was this forbidden high and we thought we were so mature and sophisticated. It was the end of the summer and Maggie had been in a bitchy mood for a couple of days. I had no idea what it was about and I know I made asinine comments about being on the rag and what a brat she was if she didn't get her way. Well this one beautiful Thursday in late August she wanted to go sailing and for a picnic. There was this basketball game that day with some guys from Polpis, which is a town east of where we are on the island. We had a big fight about it and I took off with my friends to go play basketball.

"Hale saw her sail off that day by herself. She was in her Sunfish, so he just thought she'd be staying around the bay, just tooling around the harbor. It was a gorgeous day and he said he waved to her on her way out and she waved back. About an hour later, he was on the beach and a squall blew in from the west. Hale could see Maggie's sail out on the open water. It probably wasn't something she planned, but the winds were too strong for her to handle it alone. He stayed out there keeping track of it as best as he could see in the rain and then tried to swim out, but the current was crazy and she was too far out for him to get to. So he swam back to the beach, which was fairly close to the Coast Guard Station and ran there all wet and covered in sand to alert them. They got a rescue boat out immediately and recovered her craft, but she wasn't in it."

The tears rolling down my face are being shed for all three of the friends. One freak of nature thing and their lives would never be the same. Childhoods abruptly ended and guilt permeating everything that followed.

"Did they find her?" I manage through my tears, clenching my wine glass with both hands.

Nodding, Noel continues, "Her body washed up on the far end of the island later that day. Everyone was out searching all the beaches and coves. And it was Hale who found her. The last person to see her alive and the one to find her. He tried reviving her, doing CPR, but she was gone. And he didn't want to accept that. When the coroner's report came back, we learned that she was pregnant. Although he couldn't have done anything, Hale never forgave himself for not being able to save her and the baby. My baby. And I've carried the guilt of not going with her and losing both her and the baby because of it."

"What a terrible burden for two young boys to live with."

"So when Hale dropped out of MIT and joined the armed forces and started taking on very risky missions to save lives, we always thought this was his, probably not so healthy, way of paying penance for Maggie's death."

"I can see that. Even though he certainly was not responsible for her death and did what he could do under the circumstances to try and save her."

"So now you can see, when he was able to save you, and save you from drowning no less, I just thought this would be the act that would realign his universe. This time he saved someone he loved. He could stop risking his life trying to make up for it. But the last two times I saw him, he was so down. It was like he was after Maggie. I haven't seen him that way in years and I don't understand it."

Unfortunately, I do. And if I thought my heart had been hurting before, I'm beyond devastated now.

"Noel, I haven't talked to Hale since like four days after the incident. He wasn't truthful about something that was very important to me and I ended things."

I can tell by his blindsided reaction that Hale had not shared any of this with him before.

"So, he saved you. Then he lost you. What he thought he was able to recover ended up slipping away from him anyway. That was a two-times death for him."

I'm chilled by Noel's words.

And by the loss of Hale's second chance.

⋅⋅⋅⋅⋅⋅⋅⋅⋅⋅⋅⋅⋅⋅⋅⋅⋅⋅⋅⋅⋅⋅⋅⋅⋅⋅⋅⋅⋅⋅⋅

Halfway through the bottle of wine and three-quarters of the way through the Miles of Chocolate, I check my phone for the three hundredth time. Nothing. The dinner and awards have to be over by now. They usually do some kind of entertainment afterwards, but it's almost midnight. Beverly has to be dozing off in a chair somewhere, I know it, and Monica is getting some hot scoop. Maybe even from Hale. But no one has gotten back to me. Between what is going on in New Orleans and my conversation with Noel, I am bursting to talk to someone. I have to find out how Hale is.

Looking into the fire, I am haunted by Noel's story, and the insight into Hale and what drives him. I feel like tonight I learned the key to this man and I haven't even begun to process it yet.

Maggie. The woman I look like. Noel's love. Hale's, too. She drowns and Hale can't save her. I drown and he saves me. And I leave him. This is just too much to grasp.

At 12:45 A.M. I can't take it any longer. I'm stalking my living room, a cat ready to jump out of her own skin.

Where are you? I text Monica. **Why haven't I heard from you guys?**

Five minutes passes and I'm almost dozing on the couch when my phone buzzes.

We had to save him from the evil Robyn

Hale?

Yes Hale

Maybe he liked it and didn't want to be saved

No, he loves you

How do you know that?

He told us

He told you?

Yes. We escaped with him

Escaped to where?

His suite. He loves you. He wants you to have his babies.

Was he drunk?

Maybe. But he wants you to have his babies. Four of them.

Tell him to get a surrogate. LOL.

Ha-ha. No shit. He wants three boys and a girl.

Well you can't always get what you want. Call me.

I can't.

Why not?

I'll wake everyone.

Huh?

We all passed out in Hale's suite. Beverly and I are in the second bedroom.

Where is he?

Hold on, I'll go check.

Chuckling, I'm picturing Monica tiptoeing through some lavish suite to sneak up on Hale.

My phone dings and there is a picture of Hale, flat on his back, passed out, still wearing his suit.

That is hysterical. How much did you guys drink?

A lot. We came up here to escape everyone and talk and he played bartender. I think he thought getting us drunk he'd get more info out of us. But I think we got more from him.

That he wants someone to birth him four babies?

No. He only wants you to birth them. He feels bad about not making you his number one priority and he wants a chance to do better and take care of you.

I don't need taking care of.

He's well aware of that, but he loves you and said he's learned from his mistake. He wants you back.

When I don't answer, Monica texts again.

He can't get over you, Sierra. Sound like anybody we know?

I want to answer, but I can't. I'm too busy sitting there staring at the photo of him passed out in his suit.

Whether it's the effects of the wine, Noel's revelations to me, or hearing that Hale wants me to be the mother of his children, I suddenly need air. With the phone still in my hand showing his picture, I open the back door off my kitchen. Letting the cold air wash over me feels good at first, until the tears begin sending streams of salty water into my mouth and down the side of my neck.

What I had expected from this night, just to get some stories from the awards ceremony and gossip about Hale, was far from what the evening delivered to me. A story of two brothers having their lives destroyed as teens, a man trying to save the world to make up for one falsely perceived failure, my own brush with death and the heroic attempt to make sure history didn't repeat itself. And another person out there who just can't walk away from things, can't let it go.

My stupid heart knows that sentiment too well. My OCD brain has been in cahoots with my heart as I've obsessively carried him and the pain around with me.

But I don't want the pain anymore. I just want him.

Forgiveness sometimes doesn't come easy. At least not for me. But if he has learned from his mistakes and is willing to change, the compromise of a relationship means forgiving and trying to move forward together.

All the information that has bombarded me tonight has weaved an interesting and unexpected tale, one that in some cases ended in devastation claiming pieces of multiple victims. Yet, I was one of the lucky ones. My body may not have been responsive on its own, my heart may have felt bruised and battered at times these past few months, but I was truly a fortunate one.

I was given a second chance.

Hale Lundström gave me a second chance. And I took his away.

Shaking my head in the cold air I finally understand why things have happened the way they happened.

And now it is time for me to give a second chance.

⁕⁕⁕⁕⁕⁕⁕⁕⁕⁕⁕⁕⁕⁕⁕⁕⁕⁕⁕

Dear Mr. Lundström:

I am not certain as to what openings are currently available in your organization, but I am writing to you today to inquire if there is a job that potentially fits my skillset. It is my hope that should you not have anything currently available, that you will consider creating a position for me.

What I seek is a hybrid position of sorts:

From a corporate standpoint, I am interested in building a division that mirrors the spirit in which you originally conceived and built SpaceCloud. Although you have a robust new product development team, this new division I am proposing would be separate, established solely to incubate spin-off technology companies on the for-profit side, and to develop charitable organizations and foundations on the non-profit side that either utilize new technologies, fund entities in a pre-launch phase or help people and planet through the SpaceCloud umbrella.

As one of the foremost successful tech companies in the world, this would allow you, and your organization, to continue to enhance and give back via mentoring future technology leaders as you foster the entrepreneurial spirit and launch a diverse portfolio of organizations that will have greater success with the backing and expertise a SpaceCloud Incubator can offer.

The second aspect I seek of this hybrid post is for the position of love of your life. While I've only had limited experience in this role, I know that I possess all the attributes to achieve extraordinary success in making you happy. My passion, commitment and focus are second to none. Being responsible for putting a smile on your face brings me a happiness I never knew existed, and losing it, has made what I want and what I need a lot clearer. Actually, it turns out that what I want and what I need is the very same thing. You. I just want you. I only need you.

The reality is, without you, I feel as if half of me has been lost. And it is a half that was missing for a very, very long time. I just didn't know that, until I found you. I know I can search this world a million times over, and if I don't find my way back to you, Hale, I will never be whole again.

Clearly, this is not the most conventional cover letter you've ever received, but then there's been nothing conventional between us since the night we met. I'm totally serious about both parts of this position and I hope you'll consider creating a special role for me where I will be able to share in every aspect of your life.

Very sincerely and lovingly yours,

Sierra Stone

I know I could send this via email and he'd be reading it in moments, but there is something about an actual letter on your desk that takes it to another level and shows how serious you are. The outside of the envelope reads, Mr. Hale Lundström, Personal & Confidential.

Riding the elevator up to his Austin office is certainly a déjà vu experience, but when I enter the SpaceCloud reception area, I don't recognize the young woman behind the desk and she has no idea who I am.

"Hi. How are you today?" I give her a bright smile. "Mr. Lundström asked me to have you place this on his desk." It wasn't the truth, but I didn't want to get into a "who shall I tell him this is from" conversation.

Quickly, I thank her and leave the office. I have no idea when he will be returning to Austin and will actually get my letter. I try and tell myself what will be, will be. But I know I'll be on edge wondering. And hoping.

I haven't heard anything back I text Beverly and Monica.

It's been two days.

He could be in New York and hasn't even seen the letter. That was a dumb thing to do.

It was a stressful thing to do, but not dumb. I hope he loves it when he gets a letter from me.

He will. He's going to be so happy you reached out to him.

He'd better be or I'm going to be devastated.

Don't worry. The letter will make his day.

By day four I'm feeling like an idiot. Maybe he was just telling the girls that stuff just to fuck with me so I'd do something dumb like this. I push that thought from my mind. I haven't slept in four days because I check my email and text messages every hour throughout the night and that is seriously clouding my thoughts and making me think stupid things. I've decided to give it one more week and then shoot an email or a text asking if he's received it. But for now, I need to let it go and accept the possibility that I need to let him go. Cleanse my heart.

Late morning on day five and my phone rings.

"Sierra Stone," I answer.

"Hi Sierra, my name is Ellie Connor, I'm with SpaceCloud."

"Hi Ellie, how are you today?" Zero to sixty in 1.2 seconds. My heart sounds like the motor on Hale's Lotus.

"Mr. Lundström would like to set up a meeting with you."

"Okay."

"Are you available tomorrow afternoon at 3:30?"

"Yes. I can be available. Would he like to meet at the office?"

"I believe so. He didn't indicate differently."

"Great. I'll be there tomorrow at 3:30."

Looking at my calendar, my afternoon today is free, which is absolutely perfect. I want to feel good when I see him, and I want to look good, too.

"Ginny, I know it's last minute, but can you squeeze me in for highlights this afternoon?

My hairdresser informs me that she just had a cancellation, and I think, this is no coincidence, this is a sign. The universe is helping me, so that when he sees me, he'll realize just how much he's missed me.

Walking away from him, although I had my reasons, is something I've now learned I can't do. Not unless there are no other options and I've attempted all forms of communication.

Surprisingly, I sleep that night. Either exhaustion from the nights prior has finally won out or just knowing that either way, limbo ends tomorrow. We will either be together or not, but we will have decided it. Together.

As it is a business meeting and I've applied for a 'job', I look through my suits, which I have not worn in months. I finally settle on a black and white color block suit, a white silk tank, and a gifted pair of black Louboutins. Going to my jewelry box, I pick up the mermaid and realize I don't have a chain for her. Ugh. I really wanted to wear that to complete my outfit, to let him know just how I feel and in some odd way I kept thinking she would bring me good luck. Turning her over in my fingers, I slip her into the pocket of my suit jacket. She'll be nearby.

The man who I thought was a huge douche, who ignored me and acted inappropriately, *this* is the man my heart can't get over. Laughing out loud, "Lord, help me."

Walking into SpaceCloud's reception area, I wonder if I will see anyone who knows me, but it is only the girl behind the desk and I am a complete stranger to her.

"Hi, I'm Sierra Stone. I have a meeting with Hale Lundström." Just saying the man's name gives me butterflies. Will I ever get over the intense onslaught of emotions that permeates my body just knowing he is near?

"Have a seat. I'll let him know you've arrived.

I just want to tell her, oh I'll go wait in my office. Except I no longer have an office here.

Ten minutes later I'm still waiting, and now I'm starting to get pissed. Another ten and I'm out of here. Showing me who's in control here, huh Mr. Lundström?

"Mr. Lundström will see you now. I'll take you back." I so want to tell her I know the way. But I can't do that.

His door is open a crack and finally I say, "I've got it." I don't want anyone else around when we are face-to-face for the first time in months.

Giving the door a light rap to let him know I'm there, I slip in and close it behind me. Hale is standing at the window looking out. He too is dressed for business in a charcoal gray suit and sky blue tie.

Turning to me, I can finally see his face. And in his eyes I see what Noel described to me. Infinite sadness. And a vise tightens around my heart. Did I do this to him?

Cocking my head to the side, I just look at him.

He tries to smile, but it is not a smile.

"Mermaid," I see him say it versus actually hearing it and he opens his arms.

I cross the space as fast as my Louboutins will allow, but it feels like forever until I get to him. Wrapping my arms around him like a buoy in the tide, this man is going to have to pry me off his body, because I am not letting him go. Finally, pulling my head from his chest, I look up at him and get the Hale Lundström smile that makes my heart race.

Dipping his head down, he rubs his stubble along my jaw, scratching me in that delicious way, as he whispers in my ear, "You're hired."

Epilogue

Standing with my bare feet in the ocean, I'm glad my stomach has pulled up the length of my dress enough that the handkerchief hemline isn't getting wet. The sound of the crashing waves is soothing and today the ocean has taken over nature's radio station. Even the gulls are quiet this afternoon. I need quiet. Even for just a moment. It's enough to recharge my energy.

Letting out a very satisfied, "Mmmm," when he wraps his arms around me from behind, I lean my sizable weight back into him and am gifted with a rub of his scruff along my neck. "Did you finally get them down?"

"I did," he laughs, rubbing my stomach in gentle circles.

Turning my head so that I can see his handsome face, "You really are Superman. How can they still have so much energy after that many hours playing in the waves?"

"They're boys." He shrugs it off.

"If they weren't so stinking cute, I'd sell them," That's one of my standard teases.

His right hand flies off my stomach. "I'm taking that as a message not to sell her big brothers." His hand returns to the exact spot, gently massaging where she just kicked.

"Ugh, she's already a demanding little thing. And look what she's done to my body."

His hands move from my stomach up to my breasts. "You definitely are carrying very differently than you did with the boys."

"Can you say wide load?" We laugh.

"I like it." His lips are on my neck and his fingers are where they always are when we are alone. "It's very feminine. You really do look like a mermaid now." Planting kisses down my neck, he stops momentarily to pull at the gold chain with his teeth, before moving on to my shoulder. He's making it impossible for me to speak.

"Did your conference call go okay?" he asks without stopping the seduction of my neck. The call was the reason he was solo on nap duty.

"Yeah, fine. I walked them through what they need to do to file with the patent office and they can handle the rest on their own." I'm melting into him as his fingers twist my nipples harder. I am a second trimester, horny pregnant woman and I would do him right here in the sand if I were sure the neighbors weren't watching.

"Hale…"

"Yeah, baby." I can feel how hard he is against me.

"I think we're at the 'get a room stage' here. And we'd better do it quick before one of them wakes up and crawls into bed with us."

"What are you waiting for?" He pulls me by the hand and starts to run through the sand back to the house. Looking back he smiles, "Come on, faster. Move those gorgeous legs of yours, it's not like you're wearing Louboutins or anything."

<hr>

I am a slave. Seriously, I am. My shackles may not be what you're envisioning, for they are bright and shiny and sometimes dripping with pureed carrots. They can burp the alphabet in three-part harmony at the kitchen table, egged on by their father, have temper tantrums in the most embarrassing of places or curl up in my lap just to tell me they love me. Yes, to say my handcuffs are colorful would be an understatement. And I'm locked in them 24/7.

I hope I never find the key.

Acknowledgments

There's a lot of inspiration that came from those to whom this book was dedicated. The memories we share will always hold a very special place in my heart. I feel like we all grew up together, experiencing life's triumphs, joy, and losses and though we have all moved on, what we shared will always bind us. Right down to the hot fudge sundaes and foot rubbing freaks.

First and foremost, to my readers... from those who have been with me since, "Schooner Moore did not like turning forty-three. Not at all." to those who I am just meeting with SLAVE TO LOVE, thank you for buying and reading my books. You have allowed me to live a dream that is nearly as old as I am, and for that, I will be eternally grateful. I've gotten to know many of you through social media and I cherish our interactions. When you tell me that you've enjoyed what I have written or that it has touched you in some way, you make me feel like the luckiest person alive. So, thank you for honoring me by reading what I write.

To all the bloggers who have taken a chance and read my books. I appreciate the time and support you have given to me. I know you are pulled in a gazillion directions and I really am so thankful for everything you do to help share my work in the reading community.

To Kristen and Cleida, thank you for your friendship and support and for being there when I need a sounding board, help, a belly laugh, freak out partners over new Google images or a shot of Fireball. It means the world to me. You two mean the world to me.

To Vi and Penelope, I can't even imagine how I would keep sane without you two. In a landscape that is shifting like sand along the shoreline, you two are amazing co-pilots in helping to navigate and understand where we are and where we are going. I am so thankful to be on this journey with you two.

To Mindy, for being my first reader as soon as I write The End and the panic sets in. Someday I'll write our story... tramps like us ...

To Mom, for your time, and unwavering dedication, love, and grammatical expertise. Your enthusiasm and support of my work has been a guiding light.

As always... to MaxMan, you make me better every day.

And to every woman who has run through an airport in high heels... we have made the impossible look easy. Because that is what we do.

AUTHOR'S Note

To receive information on my new releases and giveaways, please sign up for my mailing list and as a thank you, I'll send you a sneak peek at what I'm currently working on. Here's the link: http://eepurl.com/RYac1

Till we meet again...

~Jan

ABOUT Julie

uthor Julie A. Richman is a native New Yorker living deep in the heart of Texas. A creative writing major in college, reading and writing fiction has always been a passion. Julie began her corporate career in publishing in NYC and writing played a major role throughout her career as she created and wrote marketing, advertising, direct mail and fundraising materials for Fortune 500 corporations, advertising agencies and non-profit organizations. She is an award winning nature photographer plagued with insatiable wanderlust. Julie and her husband have one son and a white German Shepherd named Juneau.

Contact Julie

Twitter @JulieARichman
or
Website www.juliearichman.com
or
Facebook www.facebook.com/AuthorJulieARichman
or
Instagram: AuthorJulieARichman

My website has my signing schedule, links for signed paperbacks,

character profiles and more.
www.juliearichman.com

Join the mailing list to find out about upcoming releases and
appearances.
http://eepurl.com/RYac1

Searching For Moore

I lost the love of my life when she disappeared without even a goodbye.

It was the 80's – there was no internet, no Google, no cell phones.

If you wanted to disappear, you could.

And she did.

She crushed my soul.

A friend just told me he saw her on Facebook.

And now I'm a keystroke away from asking her the question that's haunted me for two decades.

"Why did you leave me?"

Two decades after she broke his heart, sexy entrepreneur Schooner Moore uncovers the truth and betrayal his life has been built on when he Facebook friend requests college love, Mia Silver. Determined to win Mia's love once again, Schooner embarks on a life-altering journey that could cost him everything.

This is the first book of the Needing Moore Series trilogy and is not meant to be read as a stand-alone.

Julie A. Richman

Moore To Lose

Continuing the fight for their happily ever after that began in Searching for Moore, Schooner Moore and Mia Silver struggle to overcome the ghosts and baggage they accumulated during their time apart.

Exploring the missing 24 years when they were separated, Moore to Lose follows Mia's journey from heartbroken teen to kickass businesswoman to her emotional reunion with Schooner and the exploration of the love that was ripped from them.

But is their love really strong enough to overcome the damage of those missing 24 years or will they continue to be ripped apart by pasts that can't be changed?

Moore Than Forever

"You have no idea of what you do to me, Baby Girl."

"It's smoochal."

Is the love they always dreamed of enough?

Continuing the emotional journey of love and betrayal that began on a college campus in Searching for Moore and turned their worlds upside down in Moore to Lose, handsome, California entrepreneur Schooner Moore and sharp and sassy, New York advertising agency owner Mia Silver continue to be confronted with the harsh reality of the remnants from the lives they lived apart for 24 years.

Now, Schooner Moore and Mia Silver face the ultimate challenge — were they really meant to be together or will their pasts continue to tear them apart?

On the heels of the birth of their newborn son, Nathaniel, Schooner and Mia must decide if their love and loyalty to one

270

another is strong enough to learn to grow together as a couple or if the life they always dreamed of sharing was better left as a teenage fantasy.

This is the third and final book in the Needing Moore Series and is not meant to be read as a stand alone. Book 1 — Searching for Moore and Book 2 — Moore to Lose should be read prior to reading Moore than Forever.

Needing Moore Series Box Set

All three Bestselling, Top-Rated Books from The Needing Moore Series by USA Today Bestseller Julie A. Richman, **PLUS** never before seen **BONUS CHAPTERS** for each book.

"I have read well over 125 books since I received my kindle last February (2013). That being said, this first book in this series is the BEST book I have read. I am so sorry to say but it has to be said that E L James, Sylvia Day, etc. have nothing on Julie Richman."

"I loved this story. I could not put it down. Every girl wants a man like Schooner."

"Did I mention how insanely HOT these two are together? Scorching, fanning myself, hot!!"

"I think this is one of the best series out there, Hookers! It is an amazing story, it is full of emotion, and it is real. The relationships are complex and the characters are unpredictable. Julie will wring you out emotionally and leave you craving Moore!"

"I just finished this book and my heart is pounding! I too am a Facebook friend request away from a past love. This book has you hooked from the first pages! I cried, I laughed and I cheered! Such real characters and a love story that every girl dreams of having."

"OMG need "moore" Schooner now!!!!!! ... I cannot get enough of this story. Every once in a while a book or series comes out that has me salivating at every word and this fits that bill to the tee!"

"This is just writing at its best. It's so witty and the characters are so well written. I could not put this book down!"

"This series is awesome. It just sucks you in and doesn't let you go."

Bad Son Rising

People think I'm a douche.

And maybe I am.

I use most people.

It's what I know.

But if I love you,

I'd die for you.

I just don't know that I'm worth loving.

Handsome, privileged bad boy Zac Moore has always played by his own rules - at school, in business, with women. He's rewritten the rules to suit his own needs and his needs are all that matter.

Serious and focused family friend Liliana Castillo has one goal. Leave the pre-Med program at Yale to help people in developing nations.

As their paths cross and uncross, a tale of love, agony, betrayal and growth is woven, transforming two people who've hidden from relationships and love.

This is a stand-alone novel.

Henry's End

Dreams.

I used to have them—before the nightmares started.

I dreamed of nice guys, love…normalcy.

Things like reading the Sunday paper in bed with my lover.

But who needs dreams when your reality is filled with a string of faceless dominating men in uniform? Men that pack a thick bulge and are only too happy to satisfy my deviant sexual cravings.

Me. That's who.

And then HE walked through the door and shared with me, a total stranger, his intimate dream of love. Damn him for verbalizing every single detail of the dream I buried long ago.

And now I don't know how I'm going to live without that dream.

Or him.

54176938R00158

Made in the USA
Lexington, KY
04 August 2016